I thought contained good dialogue. For me, she successfully "showed" the romantic connection, and that's what I look for in a romance author.

-Lex Kent's Reviews, *goodreads*

I0891669

Praise for the works of Bette Hawkins

Running Deep

This is a very well written second-chances sports romance where the MCs are geographically placed across continents (Australia and USA) from each other. There is something about Bette Hawkins's writing that gets you thoroughly involved in the story. We love the hark-back in time when letters and short (and very rare) long-distance calls were the means of being in touch. Those days of pen pals. The chemistry between them is great which makes this a lovely read. Definitely recommended.

-*Best Lesfic Reviews*

The leads had great chemistry and I liked that they went for what they wanted without unnecessary angst thrown in for the sake of drama. The writing was very engaging and the flashbacks didn't take away from how well the story flowed. I really enjoyed the behind-the-scenes look at the swimming world. I'm glad I discovered this author.

-Melina B., *NetGalley*

In My Heart

Set in 1958 in small-town Southern US and focused on the early days of the country music circuit, this is a really sweet and gentle romance. The setting gives it a bit of a nostalgic feel, but Hawkins keeps things realistic and the setting comes alive. Hawkins provides enough detail to set the scene and give the reader a feeling of being in the moment without resorting to dumping information and context. Narrated by Alice, *In My Heart* follows her struggle to find her place in the world. There's a wonderful innocence and inner strength in Alice—smothered by her life in a small southern US town, she wants more than to follow in the footsteps of her mother and sister, she wants to make her own way in the world and make her own mark. I especially appreciated that Hawkins wrote Alice within the context of the time and place—in some novels, the main characters openly, and rather unrealistically, challenge the societal norms but Alice's resolution and rebellions are subtle and small. ...This isn't a long book but Hawkins uses the time she has with the reader to focus on the characters and creates a wonderfully sweet romance.

-C-Spot Reviews

In My Heart is a well-written romance with good pacing and dialogue. The interesting plot is about two strong talented women, country music, small-town mindset, being different... All in all, a really enjoyable story which I will read again. I recommend it, and am looking forward to the next book by the author.

-Pin's Reviews, *goodreads*

Like a Book

Like a Book is Bette Hawkins's second book and it has a lot of good things going for it (especially June!). If you enjoy contemporary romances, especially those set in Australia, you should check this one out. I look forward to seeing what's next from this author.

-The Lesbian Review

No More Pretending

I don't know what it is, but something about romances that involve a movie star falling in love with a girl-next-door type, are some of my favorites. I must be honest, this book was not on my radar at all. Therefore, it was such a pleasant surprise how much I really enjoyed this. Then to find out this is a debut novel, I'm even more impressed. The way she writes is believable and

LEADING LADY

Bette Hawkins

Other Bella Books by Bette Hawkins

In My Heart
Like a Book
No More Pretending
Running Deep

Bella Books, Inc.
P.O. Box 10543
Tallahassee, FL 32302

Printed in the United States of America on acid-free paper.

First Edition - 2023

Editor: Medora MacDougall
Cover Designer: Kayla Mancuso

ISBN: 978-1-64247-433-6

PUBLISHER'S NOTE

LEADING LADY

Bette Hawkins

BELLA BOOKS

2023

CHAPTER ONE

1992

Andie checked her watch, jogging her leg under the table. Her father had told her to bring her A-game to this meeting, yet she was waiting for him like when she was a kid ready to be picked up from her mom's.

She went to the bathroom to kill a few minutes, glancing around as she crossed the room. He always wanted to meet here. The restaurant was a converted dining car with crisp white tablecloths, and served the best steak in town. It was the kind of place where celebrities rubbed shoulders with bankers and lawyers, but she didn't recognize anyone in the lunchtime crowd.

Even after meeting so many famous people over the years, she wasn't above getting starstruck. When you loved cinema as much as she did, it was inevitable.

After washing her hands, she smoothed down her dark curly hair in front of the mirror. Her dad was going to hate this outfit. The black T-shirt, jeans, and boots were like a uniform for her, and he'd never been a fan of her punk-tinged style. At thirty-nine years old, she'd stopped trying to please him, at least when it came to her clothes.

When she pushed the door open, she left a sweaty handprint. It might have helped her nerves if he had told her what this meeting was about. He was bringing his producer, long-time friend and ally, Ben Haynes, which indicated something business-related, but she had no idea of the details.

A few years ago, she would have been more excited than anxious about a meeting like this. Back then, she had the luxury of picking and choosing her projects. She'd directed four features in a decade, and the first three were modest hits that the critics loved. She became one of the hottest directors of the '80s, and journalists had plenty of hooks on which to hang their stories.

She was Doug McKenzie's daughter, and a wunderkind.

Then, three years ago, her last movie tanked. It looked like the '90s wouldn't be so kind to her. The adoring critics turned, labelling the film a turkey. When the phone stopped ringing, it proved that in Hollywood you were only as good as your last hit.

She spotted her father and Ben settling into their chairs across the room. As she approached, she pulled her shoulders back.

"Hey, how are you doing?" her dad said.

Half the restaurant patrons were watching by now. They might not have clocked her, but they recognized one of the directors who spearheaded the New Hollywood movement of the '60s and '70s. Her father looked the part, handsome and tanned in a leisure suit with sneakers. His black hair and long sideburns were shot through with silver.

Andie had grown up on his movie sets, a precocious kid more at home around adults than people her own age. A famous shot showed her at seven years old sitting on his lap, each of them staring thoughtfully at storyboards. Following in his footsteps was as natural as breathing.

They pulled their chairs into the table, and the waiter returned. Ben and Doug exchanged a look as she ordered a club soda.

"No, I'm still not drinking. If that's what you're wondering."

"Are you in the program? I've wanted to ask you that for a while now. Nothing to be ashamed of. I have so many friends in the program. They swear by it. It's a great thing," Ben said, his brown eyes dancing under bushy white brows. He leaned forward excitedly like they were talking about something other than AA. He was in his late seventies, but her father's oldest friend was like an oversized kid.

"Nothing against it, but no, I didn't feel like I needed that kind of help. Once I made the decision, it was easy for me. I'm happier this way."

"Good to hear you're sticking with it," her dad said.

They all knew how Andie's early success had spoiled her. She'd never been a saint when it came to women or partying. Her mistake was letting her messy personal life spill onto the set. After her movie failed, she took a long look at herself and decided it was time to grow up.

"So, Ben, tell me about this Michael Spencer movie you're working on. Dad said it was shooting now."

"Oh, yes. It's going great. Michael is a great guy, the best."

Ben had produced almost all her father's films and none of Andie's, but he'd always been around to give filmmaking advice. In some ways, he'd influenced her style as much as her father. She loved hearing him talk about his work.

By the time their steaks arrived, Andie was dying for them to get to the point. She hoped they were offering her a script-doctoring job. Rewriting had always been a lucrative side gig for her. She'd never scripted original stories but had a talent for refining others' work. It was satisfying to put the finishing touches on scripts as they went into production—her directing experience had honed her instincts about what would work best on set. She knew which project they were working on together, and she wanted in, but was too proud to ask.

There weren't many roles that she'd turn down. The well of inspiration had gone dry, she had nothing in the pipeline, and the cure was work.

"I've withdrawn from *Creature Island*," Doug said.

Andie tried to cover her surprise. Nothing was ever a done deal in this town, and last-minute changes happened often. Still, she'd been so excited when her dad bought the rights to that book, because of its great female protagonist. That was years ago now, but she got her hands on a copy when the screenplay was done.

It captured the subversive, fun tone of the cult novel on which it was based. *Creature Island* was one of those books that its fans loved hard. It was science fiction packed with horror and action, a character study, and a deeply political work about mistrusting authority. There had been talk for years about a movie adaptation.

"What happened? I thought you were in preproduction?"

"We are. Everyone's been working double time to get the location ready. It's a little spot in Fiji. Mermaid Island," Ben said.

"Then why did you back out?"

"I fell out of love with it. I don't think this kind of high-concept movie is for me. I want to go back to my roots. We're developing a good script for a gangster film," he said, gesturing toward Ben with his fork.

"That's right. Doug wants to put a lot of energy into getting that together. A big production like *Creature* would tie him up for the next year."

She was trying to keep up. So, she might get to work on a serious gangster drama. It didn't excite her as much as the crazy premise underpinning *Creature Island*, but her father had made his name with mobster movies. Whatever he did in that genre would be an instant classic.

"That sounds great. People will be so excited you're doing that."

"So, we need someone to step in on *Creature*. We know how much you loved the script. We want you to do it, and I'll stay on as producer along with Ben. That way, we can still be involved, but we can fly back and forth when we need to work on the gangster flick."

It took a while for the words to land. But, as soon as they did, Andie's heart thumped madly. Never in her wildest fantasies could she have imagined this. "That's...I've never done anything on that scale, with that many big set pieces. The budget must be way beyond anything I've ever worked with. I don't know if I could do that."

The men looked at one another, her dad smirking. "That's what I said when I signed on for *War Stories*. Right?"

"And we won an Oscar for it. Close your mouth, kid. You look like a goldfish."

"I'm just a little shocked. You don't usually get handed a big movie like this when your last one bombed."

"You made one bomb, so what? Who hasn't? This will help you get back on your feet. And you can learn some new skills. You've always made great use of your budgets. This won't be any different."

"I can't tell you how much I appreciate you thinking of me for this, Dad, but I need a minute. This would be a lot to take on."

"We don't have a minute. We don't want to let it go, but we don't want to hire one of those music-video directors who'll make it look like every other action movie. We want someone with a vision," Ben said.

Andie's mind raced, the possibilities taking hold. The script was excellent and while reading it, she'd visualized whole sequences, clear as a bell. She never thought she'd have the opportunity to make those images a reality.

"We'll be there to help, and there would be a fantastic team around you. We've already cleared it with the studio. We rewatched all four of your features, and we know you can do it," Doug said, looking her dead in the eye.

That was all it took. If they believed that she could do it, then she had to. She couldn't afford to sit around and wait for her confidence to come back. She had to build it up again, brick by brick. She'd be crazy to turn this down, anyway. They must have lobbied the studio so hard to get the green light to hire her.

She took a deep breath, then stood and shook their hands, Ben slapping her on the back.

"This is going to be amazing. Doug would have done a stellar job, but this feels like destiny. And your sister has a part too."

"I know. It's hard to believe Cary and I have never worked together before. That'll be fun."

"You'll have a blast. A real family affair, this picture. Plus, it's going to be great to have a woman directing."

"You're good with actresses," Doug added.

Andie flushed with pride. From him, compliments were rare.

"Wait, who do you like for the lead?" she asked, sure that the role hadn't been cast. She would've heard about it, but they must be close. Her older sister was formally offered her role weeks ago.

A top part for a woman in an action film was unheard of. Actresses were starved for good roles, so it was heavily sought after. With their budget, they could have their pick.

"We're about to lock down our leading lady. They're calling her agent this afternoon to offer her the part," Ben said, reaching down to his briefcase then sliding a glossy headshot across the table.

She studied the face smiling back at her. Everyone knew who Skye Buckley was. There was no need to show her the picture, but Ben could be theatrical when he wanted to get his point across. He was encouraging Andie to look at that face and see Skye as her lead.

She ran a hand through her hair, trying to not react too strongly. But really, were they kidding with this? "It's such an interesting choice."

"When she came in to read, she blew us away. We weren't expecting it. We had her in a few times after that, and she knocked our socks off every single time. And that face? Tremendous."

Andie stared at the picture again. Blond hair, soulful blue eyes, and a quality that was hard to put your finger on. Skye Buckley glowed. Her eyes and lips stood out, her features unique and exciting.

It added up to breathtaking beauty, but she didn't fit the vision of the Dr. Jessica Foster that had already formed in her mind. It was too important to keep quiet about. She pushed the picture back across the table.

"I just don't see it. Can we consider other options?"

Another one of those private looks passed between the two men. It was starting to irritate her.

"If you'd been in the room when she came in, you'd be on board. We'll set up a meeting with the two of you, and you'll see," Ben said, waving a hand.

"You guys know what you're doing, and if you saw something special, I'm sure she is. I'd still like to look at some other actresses."

"Trust us. You'll see," Doug said.

He nodded once and went back to his steak, signaling that the matter was closed.

After the meeting, Andie drove to her big sister's house in Malibu, singing along to the radio all the way. She loved this crazy-ass industry, how you could wake up at the bottom of the heap and be back on top by the afternoon. This movie would open so many doors and restore her reputation.

It would be like the last miserable few years never happened.

She pulled up at Cary's triple-story place, set back from the beach and surrounded by palms. Andie jumped out of her car and waved up to her. Cary stood barefoot on her deck in her silk paisley robe. Her dark hair was as hard to tame as Andie's, and it blew around her face in the wind.

"I have big news," announced Andie.

"Come on up. I'm having breakfast."

Unless she was working, Cary never went to bed before midnight. She'd probably been up half the night with her musician neighbors. Andie went in through the unlocked front door, and by the time she got to the deck, a cup of coffee awaited her. A half-eaten croissant and a grapefruit sat on the table.

They hugged hello, and Andie sat down, sipping her drink.

"Well, I thought I was the dramatic one, but you're really milking the suspense. Aren't you going to tell me your big news?"

"I'm still trying to get used to it, myself. I just had a meeting with Dad and Ben. They've offered me *Creature Island*."

"You're directing it?" Cary jumped up and hugged Andie again, coffee sloshing over the side of her cup. "Oops, sorry. I just can't believe it. Honey, I'm so happy for you. I've been worried about you. You're the type of person that needs to be working. You go a little nuts if you're not, like me."

"I know. And I needed something to get me out of my slump. I almost feel guilty about getting handed a dream job on a silver platter like this. I didn't even have to pitch for it. They're really saving my ass," she said, grabbing the pastry from the table.

"Don't feel guilty. You'll have to work that ass off. You've been brought on very late in the game. You've got a lot of catching up to do."

"I know. It'll be crazy. I've got a list of meetings a mile long."

"Dad gave me a heads-up that he might be changing his mind about directing it, but I didn't see this coming," said Cary. "I'm so happy we get to work together. And this means you're going to be working with Ben, huh?"

"The one and only. And Dad's coproducing."

"Hmm."

"What does that mean? Spit it out."

"Nothing, just that they can be a pair of control freaks, especially when you put them together. I hope you're ready for that. I bet they've negotiated to have final cut with the studio already."

"Of course," Andie replied.

It was an afterthought, discussed with Ben and Doug over coffee when they were done with their meal. A director in Andie's position didn't stand a chance of determining which version of the film would make it to theaters. Ben and Doug had developed it and brought it to the studio, and the executives held the purse strings. Only directors who'd proven their money-making credentials, like Spielberg, had the authority to take on final cut responsibility.

"Color me totally unsurprised that they made that clear to you from the jump," Cary said.

"There'll be friction, but I can live with it. We've had our first creative difference already."

"You're kidding, already? What is it?" she asked, picking up the pot to refill their cups.

"They want Skye Buckley for the lead. They're offering it to her today."

Cary stared past her as though trying to picture Skye in the part. "That's a curveball."

"That's what I think."

"It's a great role," she said, kicking the leg of Andie's chair. "Don't worry, I'm not going to start lobbying for it. I know I'm too old."

Andie knew better than to say anything to an actress about her age. Cary had moved onto character parts in the last few years. In her last movie, she played the mother of an actor who was only a decade younger than her. It was one of the many reasons Andie was glad she'd been bitten by the directing bug instead of wanting to act.

Fifteen years separated her from her sister. They shared their father, but he'd married three women and had children with all of them. Their dad had fathered Cary with his first wife when he was barely out of film school, and Andie with the second.

"You're right. It is a spectacular part. I guess Skye Buckley is a decent actress, but she doesn't have the chops. And she's not tough enough."

"I know what you mean. I've only ever seen her in romantic comedies. And all those '80s teen movies, of course. Has she ever done a drama or an action film?"

"Not that I know of. I don't really want my movie to be the one where she's trying to transition into roles with more gravity."

"I wonder why they think she's a good fit?"

"They said she gave a great audition. Maybe she did, but it doesn't mean she can carry a movie like this. It's one of those ideas they've fallen in love with, though. What do you think I should do?"

Cary set her cup down on the table and stretched her arms over her head. "I think you should put your foot down. You're the director now. It's your movie, even if technically they're the bosses. Don't back down just because they offered you the job. You're not some random director for hire."

Cary's advice confirmed what Andie had been thinking. If she gave in too quickly on this, they would think they could tell her what to do about everything else. She was more than grateful to them, but she didn't want to be anyone's puppet. She had to wield at least some influence.

"You're right. Fuck it. Can I use your phone?"

"Go nuts."

Andie went into the kitchen, where a phone sat on the counter. She went through the address book she kept in her bag until she found her casting director's number. They could throw a few ideas around, and she trusted Ellen's opinion. Once they'd worked out some strong possibilities, she could go back to her dad and Ben and tell them there was a change of plan.

After she dialed, she stared out the window, thinking about Skye Buckley. She could be being offered the role right now.

It didn't matter. Until she signed on the dotted line, Andie had time to put a stop to the deal.

It wasn't personal. It was just how things worked.

CHAPTER TWO

Skye laid the phone back in its cradle and ran to the kitchen to find her assistant. She watched Teri unpacking groceries, bouncing on the balls of her feet.

The kitchen was modest, with Skye still living in the Californian bungalow she'd bought with earnings from her teens. It was large enough to house her plants, books, and framed movie posters. She was happy here, so she had no plans to buy one of those Beverly Hills mansions. Many of her child-actor peers had, and she was happy for them, but she preferred it here in Silver Lake.

Teri stacked canned vegetables into rows in the pantry. Her jet-black hair was piled up in a bun, and she wore a leopard print skirt with ballet flats.

She was the most efficient person Skye knew, so it was a no-brainer to hire her when her last assistant left to have a baby. They met when Teri was working for a friend, and over the previous two years, they'd become good friends. At first, she'd felt weird about how close she was getting to someone who worked for her, but it always seemed natural. Teri never slacked off and could switch modes easily from professional to personal.

"I'm nearly done with this. I was going to go through the mail after, unless there's something else you need?" Teri said, looking back over her shoulder.

"I just got off the phone with Helene."

Teri put down the package of crackers she was holding. "Oh my God. Is it a yes for *Creature Island*?"

Skye nodded, and Teri ran over, giving her a high five before they hugged.

"I was sure you were going to get it."

"I wasn't. I'm freaking out. I think I'll go over the script and start working on it this afternoon."

"You'll do no such thing. You still have that bottle of Dom Perignon. You promised we were opening it if you got this one," Teri said, playfully wagging a finger at Skye.

"You know what, you're right. We should. Getting this role is like winning the lottery," Skye said, heading over to the fridge while Teri got a couple of flutes out of the cupboard.

"Oh, come on. That wasn't luck. You worked damn hard to get it, and you went in there so prepared. I don't think I've ever seen anyone work that hard on an audition piece."

Skye had never wanted anything this much. She'd been a fan of the book since reading it as a fifteen-year-old. It still sat on her shelf, dog-eared with underlined passages. She'd never been interested in science fiction before, but *Creature Island* felt like it had been written just for her. On the surface it was a pulse-pounding survival story with wild action sequences, but it was all about fighting corrupt power. She hadn't understood the context at the time, but she'd connected with it thanks to its second-wave feminist undertones. The heroine defeated the bad guy through a combination of smarts and physicality.

She'd always told herself that if they ever made a movie out of it, she had to be Dr. Jessica Foster, no matter how unlikely it seemed. The character had all the qualities she wanted to embody. She was tough and intelligent, sure of herself in a way that inspired her.

Teri popped the cork off the Champagne, whooping at the noise when it shot out.

"I did work hard, but you know what it's like. I could just as easily be crying over losing out. A hundred girls are behind me, wishing they could take my place. I only ever thought I had the slimmest chance."

"Oh, come on. I can't imagine you crying over that. You'd already be working on your next move. But, I much prefer it this way. It's not very often that I get to drink Champagne in the middle of the day."

They took their glasses out to the living area. Teri kicked off her shoes, and they sprawled out on the leather sofa, under a framed *Vertigo* poster.

"You'll come with me on location, right? To the island?"

"Will I spend a few months in paradise? I guess so. It'll be an ordeal, but somebody's got to do it."

"Seriously, we'll be away for months. It's a long way, so it won't be an option to come back here on weekends. I'd understand if you didn't want to be there for the whole time."

"No problem, really. I'm looking forward to it. And I'm so happy for you."

"I'm happy, too. And scared. It's such a big responsibility to be the lead in a movie like this. The whole thing will be on my shoulders."

"It's going to be okay. You're going to nail it. How good is this Champagne?"

"It's delicious. Oh, and by the way, this is a bit of a bummer. Doug McKenzie isn't directing anymore."

"No way. I know how much you were hoping to get to work with him."

It was a feather in the cap for any actor to have a McKenzie film on the resume. When Skye got a callback, she and Teri had had a Doug McKenzie festival, even though they'd already seen all his movies.

"Yeah, and guess what? It turns out I'm going to work with a different McKenzie."

"What do you mean?"

"They've replaced him with his daughter. Andie McKenzie."

Teri coughed, almost spitting out her drink.

"What's up? Did your drink go down the wrong way?"

"Shit."

"What is it? The director change? I'm not too worried about it. I mean, I wish it was Doug, but it could be cool to work with her. She's a super interesting director."

"Cool?"

"What's with all the one-word answers? Is this because of her last movie? *In the Break*? It was a bit of a mess, but I always thought it wasn't as bad as everyone said. You could see she was going for something experimental and different, and she missed."

"That's a generous interpretation."

"I guess, maybe. Either way, the others were excellent."

"It's not the movie, anyway. I can't believe I didn't tell you this when we had that McKenzie marathon. I've really never told you about her?"

Skye put her glass on the coffee table, sitting up straight. "Okay, what's going on? Haven't you ever told me *what* about her?"

"Andie used to date Stella."

Stella was one of Teri's old friends, so they'd met at parties around town a few times. She was a beautiful costume designer who always had another beautiful woman on her arm. Skye felt like a complete novice with women, so it was intimidating to see someone going through them like it was nothing.

"I see. But why is that a problem?"

"Andie was a complete nightmare. I've heard so many stories. They only dated for a couple of months, but Stella was really interested in her. Until she got dumped, that is."

"She was a nightmare, in what way?"

"Cheating. Messing with Stella's head. We hung out as a group a couple of times, and she was a piece of work. It was a few years ago before I knew you. But Stella still talks about her all the time. She was really cut up."

Skye reached for her glass, but the Champagne didn't taste as good as before. "That's disappointing. It sounds like she's a jerk in her personal life. But so are a lot of directors I've worked with, and they've kept it off the set. Do you think maybe she's like that?"

"I hope so. Stella never worked with her, so I don't know what she's like when she's at work," said Teri.

"Fingers crossed she knows what she's doing."

"It's so funny that they hired Doug's daughter. Especially when everyone thought *In the Break* sucked. Nepotism is alive and well in Hollywood."

"You can say that again."

This town was all about where you came from and who you knew. Nobody would think it was strange that Doug was handing off a movie to his daughter, and she doubted any of the actors already cast would pull out. It was something Skye accepted about the business, but she was proud that she'd worked her way up from nothing. When she started, she had no connections in Hollywood.

"Hey, I hope you can still come to the thing? I know you've got lots of work to do now, but Dana's excited to meet you," Teri said.

"Not sure. I'm going to be busy until we go."

Teri was bisexual and seemed to know half the lady-lovers in LA. She'd been a little pushy about Skye getting out there. The idea of being set up made her uncomfortable, but she hadn't met anyone she was interested in on her own. She decided she might as well give it a try, but if there was an out, she was happy to take it.

"Are you sure you couldn't just come out for one night? Claudia says she's super nice," she said, talking about the woman she'd been dating for a few months.

"Well, it wouldn't be fair, right? If I'm going away. I'll be gone for ages. Maybe you could tell her I'm busy with work and ask for a rain check."

Teri smiled gently at her. "If you're not ready, you're not ready. It's all right. But it's just a party. It's not even one-on-one. We'll be there with you."

Skye chewed a nail. Teri was misreading her, big time. It was understandable because she was a late bloomer when it came to this stuff. Just ask Darryl, the man Skye had dated off and on for two years before she finally admitted that she wasn't attracted to men. Now that she had, though, she was eager to meet someone.

Maybe she was being too uptight about the whole blind date thing. Getting the role of her dreams gave her a shot in the arm, and she wanted to take a chance. "You're right. I'll go ahead with seeing her. It might be fun."

"Yay. It'll be great."

The phone rang, and Teri got up to answer it, returning a few moments later. "It's Darryl. Do you want to talk to him, or should I tell him you're out?"

"That's weird. I was just thinking of him, but I haven't heard from him for a while. Maybe I should see what he wants."

A few hours later, Skye was in a cab on her way to meet Darryl for dinner. She'd tried to find out what he wanted to talk about, but he said it was complicated and he'd rather discuss it in person.

She'd changed into a button-down blouse and a skirt, not wanting to look like she'd dressed up for him. There was no way she wanted to send any mixed messages—she'd done enough of that when they were together.

They were meeting at Spago, an Italian place on the Strip that everyone raved about. Darryl was already at their table. The waiter brought her over, and he stood to greet her in khakis and a checked shirt.

As she walked toward him, she realized that she'd long ago stopped asking herself why she wasn't attracted to him. Everyone thought he was such a good-looking guy, with his square jaw and bright blue eyes. He wore his dark hair gelled back and his face clean-shaven.

There were nights when she'd watched him sleeping, wishing she could feel how she was supposed to. Since their breakup a couple of years ago, she'd accepted that it didn't matter what he looked like or how nice he was. She didn't feel that way about him, or men in general. Breaking up with him weighed heavily on her conscience at first, but now she was at peace with it.

They smiled awkwardly. They'd seen one another around and met up for coffee a couple of times, but they'd never quite figured out how to navigate it. She tried to tune out how everyone stared as he sat down across from her. Once upon a time, their relationship was a hot topic in the media.

"How are you?" he asked when the waiter had taken their drink orders.

"I'm not too bad. How are you?"

"I've been doing good. I appreciate you meeting me on such short notice. I know I haven't called in a while."

"That's okay. Hey, I went to see *Hello Stranger* last month. You were so great in it."

"That's nice of you to say."

The waiter interrupted them. Skye had only glanced at the menu, but she didn't want to prolong the evening, so she ordered what Darryl had. Her nerves were killing her appetite. He acted like he had something important to say. He couldn't possibly want to get back together after all this time, could he?

"I had my class this morning. It was a good one."

She nodded politely. He was interested in method acting and would talk about technique and motivation all day if you let him. They took different approaches to the craft, but she'd always admired his commitment.

"And I've started dating again. I think I've met someone special. Her name's Heather."

She exhaled, her shoulders relaxing. "That's great. Have you been seeing her for long?"

"Not long. About six months, but we're having a wonderful time together. It's getting serious."

"That's awesome. You kept that one out of the gossip mags."

"Yeah. She's a private person, and she doesn't work in the business. She's a psychologist. We've kept it low-key."

"I'm really happy for you."

They chatted about Heather until their appetizers arrived. The angel hair pasta with broccoli and goat cheese looked tasty, her hunger returning now that her stomach wasn't in knots. She'd never imagined talking casually about Darryl dating someone else. It was nice to hear he was with someone who cared for him in a way that she never could.

As she spread her napkin over her lap, she finally learned why he'd asked to meet.

"So, I heard you got offered the lead in *Creature Island.* Congratulations."

"Jesus, that was fast. I only found out this afternoon. We're in negotiations. How did you hear?"

"Well, the thing is, I've been offered a role too. I'm guessing you didn't know that?"

"No, Helene didn't mention it. We talked about the director change, mainly."

"She probably doesn't know about me getting cast yet. My agent mentioned that you'd just been offered the part when we went out for a drink this afternoon. I thought I should let you know."

"I should have said congratulations first. I'm happy for you. Which part?" she said, holding up her soda until he clinked his glass against it.

"The pilot. Adrian. I'm not sure how long I'll be shooting for yet. There are some juicy scenes, even if I'll spend the ending lying around playing a dead body."

"You'll be great. I mean, for the scenes when you're alive."

They were both still laughing when the waiter collected their plates. She was starting to see a future in which they might be friendlier than they had been, if not close friends.

"Thanks for telling me about all this. I'll be happy to work together if it's no problem for you?" said Skye.

"Not at all. You're a great actress. It'll be an honor."

She wondered how he felt about being in a supporting role while she was the lead. It wasn't typical for a male star to do that. He seemed excited, so maybe he really didn't care. "Thank you. I'll be honored to work with you, too. Hey, so what do you make of the director change?"

"I was a little disappointed about not getting to work with Mr. McKenzie. You?"

"I feel the same way. Do you know much about Andie?"

"One of the guys in my acting class worked on *In the Break* as a day player. He doesn't have very nice things to say about her."

Skye's heart sank, and as their next course was being laid out, she thought about Andie McKenzie. Skye had been on the phone for most of the afternoon, and the name drew strong reactions. Some of her friends thought she was way too arrogant, while others said she was a genius. Most of them mentioned that she was a womanizer.

Teri took a call from the producer's assistant to arrange a meeting with Andie for the following day. They would be introduced at one of the producers' houses. At least she'd finally get to see for herself what her new director was like.

She was wary about canvasing more opinions, but she couldn't help herself. "What did your acting-class friend say about Andie, exactly?"

"That she was all over the place. Apparently, she went right off the deep end, always late and disorganized."

"Do you think this movie will end up being a mess?" she asked, putting down her cutlery and rubbing her temple. A headache brewed.

"I think we don't know. After all, she's made a few good movies, and her dad and Ben Haynes will be involved. I'd try to not worry about it yet."

She nodded and returned to her food. There was nothing she could do. She should put all this chatter about the wayward director out of her mind. This was the role of a lifetime, and she had to trust herself to work around whatever problems might come up.

She wouldn't let anything Andie McKenzie did get in the way.

CHAPTER THREE

On Friday afternoon, Skye drove to Laurel Canyon to meet her new director. The housekeeper led her into the atrium of Ben Haynes's sprawling mansion.

As she took her seat at the table with Ben Haynes and Doug McKenzie, she couldn't believe she was hanging out with the legendary team. Red and white flowered plants surrounded them, the afternoon sun filtering through the glass doors. It should be heaven, but one thing was getting in the way.

"She'll be here any minute," Doug said.

Attempting to cover Andie's absence, Ben said, "Please, have some sushi. Do you like sushi? Please, take as much as you'd like."

Their frustration was thinly veiled. This was Hollywood, where it wasn't unusual for people to be flaky about appointments. It was another thing for Andie to keep her own father waiting.

The minutes ticked by until she was an hour late, and in that time, Skye asked as many questions as she could think of about Ben's house and Doug's upcoming project. She was running out of small talk, but it didn't seem polite to start a conversation about *Creature Island* without its director.

Luckily, Ben did it for her. "You're going to love working on the island. We're so excited about getting permission to shoot there."

"What's it called, again?"

"Mermaid Island."

"It'll be wonderful. It sounds like a dream, honestly."

He put his hands behind his head and leaned back with a satisfied smile. "It's stunning. White beaches, crystal water, forests, and mountains. Every location we could possibly need, all in one place. It has a private owner. A fellow who happens to love movies. He's thrilled to have us."

"Is there much there, aside from the natural things, I mean? Do many people live there?"

"That's the most wonderful thing about it. It's just the owner, so it's relatively untouched aside from his place. But it has a landing strip and enough infrastructure for us to build on. It's the ideal setting for a movie about a deserted island. We struck gold."

"Wow. I can't wait to see it."

"We've got workers building accommodation for the cast and crew. It's almost done," Doug said. She'd noticed that he was the quieter of the two men. He saved his words, only speaking when he had something important to say.

"Yep. We locked in the deal last year, and we didn't want you all to be uncomfortable, so it will be very nice."

"That sounds like a huge undertaking," said Skye.

"We cut a deal with the owner because he'll be opening the place up for tourists when we wrap. Apparently, it's something he's been considering over the years, and this gave him the push he needed. There'll be a bunch of villas and a hotel."

"And the fact that a movie's shooting there will be a great selling point for tourism?" asked Skye.

"Bingo."

"Hey."

They turned toward the woman who'd appeared in the doorway. She stood with her arms crossed, leaning on the frame. Skye quickly took in wavy black hair, carved cheekbones, and full lips.

Her dark beauty was more startling because of how effortless it seemed. She wasn't wearing makeup, and her hair hung loose and wild. Her long legs were in blue jeans, paired with a black T-shirt. Skye looked down at her own jeans and striped silk shirt, thinking about how carefully she'd blow-dried her hair this morning.

She felt like such a nerd.

"Sorry I'm late," Andie said in a raspy voice, but she didn't sound at all sorry. She didn't even glance in Skye's direction until after greeting the others. Skye stepped forward as Andie finally turned toward her.

"And you must be Skye," she said dryly, holding out her hand.

Skye smiled at her and shook her hand, noticing the deep green eyes. "It's so nice to meet you."

"Nice to meet you, too."

Andie looked intently at Skye. People always said Skye looked different on-screen from how she appeared in person, and she'd never known how to take it. She couldn't shake off the fear that Andie might be disappointed.

Ben put a hand on Andie's shoulder, and finally, she broke her gaze to turn her head toward him.

"We might leave you ladies to get acquainted with one another for a minute. Your father hasn't seen my new Cadillac. Please, enjoy the food."

Andie rolled her eyes as the men went out through the glass doors. "Boys and their toys, right? He collects cars like they were stamps or something."

"Everyone's got to have a hobby," said Skye.

They sat down, and Skye picked up her water glass to moisten her lips, unsure of her place. This felt like auditioning for the role all over again, only worse because it was obvious Andie didn't want to be here. "They were just telling me about the island we're shooting on. It sounds incredible."

Andie crossed a leg over her knee. Her legs were so long. "Yeah. It should be nice. It'll be a tough shoot, though."

"I know. It'll be hard work, but I'm looking forward to it."

"Your role will be very physically demanding. Even with a stunt double, it'll be exhausting."

"That's true. I've never done anything like this before, but I've given a lot of thought to preparing and keeping my energy levels up." Why would Andie assume she hadn't been through all this with her father and Ben? They'd discussed it during their earlier meetings. Skye's petite frame could be misleading, but she'd studied dance throughout her teens. The training was more brutal than most people could even imagine.

Andie made a noncommittal "mmm" sound, and that was it. Skye didn't know what to say, so she asked the first question that popped into her head.

"Do you collect anything?"

"Can't say I do. Do you?" Andie replied, eyebrows lifting.

"Sure. I collect books. And movie posters."

"Really? What kind of books do you collect?"

It was interesting that Andie went for the books instead of asking about her posters like most people did. "Novels. First editions. I have one of *Creature Island*, actually."

Andie reached over to the water pitcher on the table and poured herself a glass. "Oh yeah? Did you get that when you found out about the movie?"

"No, I came across it in a secondhand store years ago, and I couldn't believe my luck. They had no idea how rare it was. But of course, I don't touch it, I've got another copy for reading. I've read it so many times."

"Really."

The skepticism was annoying, even if Skye understood it. It was the kind of thing actors lied about when they were going after parts, like when you said you could do a French accent, knowing you'd be able to work on it later. *Creature Island* was a counter-cultural favorite, and she got that she didn't seem like the target audience. For one thing, she was too young to have read it at the height of its popularity back in the '70s. She didn't know how much older Andie was, but it might be a factor.

"Yes. I read it for the first time when I was in high school."

"Did you? What's your favorite part?"

That was easy. Skye remembered that first time so clearly. While her interpretation deepened as she grew older, her feelings about that scene never changed. She loved how it was adapted into the screenplay. "I always loved the part where Dr. Foster kills Adrian."

"Uh-huh. What do you like about it? In the book, I mean, not the screenplay."

Andie hoped to catch her in a lie, and Skye had to pretend she didn't mind being quizzed. It would make her seem difficult.

"The writing is beautiful. I'd never read something so ugly in such stunning language. It's an amazing contrast. And now I'm older, I can see that those types of scenes are in lots of stories, so it's not that original. But you hardly ever get to see a woman making a choice like that. You never get to see a woman be the hero and kill off the bad guy like that without anyone's help. That was so badass to me."

"Yeah," Andie said, staring at her again. Finally she looked away, her toned arm reaching toward the table for a piece of sushi. She wore a single silver ring on her middle finger.

"What's your favorite part?" asked Skye.

"Actually, what you said."

"Well. That's not very original."

Andie looked different when she smiled, her eyes warm when they met Skye's. She tried to ignore the flutter in her stomach. She was just nervous, that was all.

CHAPTER FOUR

After Doug and Ben returned to the meeting to chat about special effects and locations, they wrapped up. Skye stood, and Andie got up to follow. When Doug made eye contact and discreetly held up his hand, she stilled, her face growing red.

"Let me walk you out," Andie said to Skye, nodding to Doug to show she understood that leaving wasn't an option. She headed for the door with Skye close behind. They silently made their way through the house, Andie wondering exactly how much trouble she was in. The look on her father's face was the same as when she was a kid, any time she got bad grades or stayed out past curfew.

Nearing the front door, she stepped back to let Skye walk in front. As she passed, she caught a subtle shampoo scent, something sweet yet earthy.

Skye had caught her off guard. Though she was in her mid-twenties, she didn't have that wide-eyed ingenue thing Andie had expected. There was something quirky about her, and she knew the source material for *Creature Island* very well.

Andie was intrigued by how much she embraced the story's darker aspects. Skye liked the death scene when even some fans of the book were critical of how it played out. Dr. Foster killed Adrian after finding out that he'd betrayed them all, intentionally stranding his plane's passengers. Detractors argued that she didn't *need* to kill him, that it could be read as a cold-blooded murder. Andie disagreed and it surprised her that Skye did, too.

Then, there were her looks. Most actresses were pretty, but she had an extra something that made it hard to stop looking at her. Her blue eyes changed depending on the light, and her skin was flawless. No wonder she looked so amazing on camera. Andie had no intention of keeping her on, but she wondered how her features would change when her hair was swept up or how she'd look under certain lighting.

They stepped outside onto the lawn, where the drive wound up into Ben's lush, manicured gardens. Next to Andie's yellow El Camino sat a Jaguar with the top down, the silver body gleaming in the sun. Andie whistled, forgetting her lousy mood for a second. "This is yours?"

Skye nodded, smiling at her. "And that's yours? Nice racing stripes."

"Thanks. I guess Ben's not the only one around here with a thing for cars."

"Yeah, but I don't collect them or anything. That car is the only one for me."

"Same here. Well, thanks for coming today. It was nice to meet you."

"You too."

Andie turned to go, then stopped when Skye said her name. Another surprising thing was how her eyes looked sad, even when her expression was hopeful. Whatever made her look like that, she didn't want to add to it.

"Yes?"

"Can I see you again soon to get into the nitty-gritty? It was nice to catch up as a group, but I'd like to hear more about what you want the movie to be."

"Oh, um. Sure," Andie fumbled. Fuck. The last thing she wanted to do was get in any deeper on this.

"Can I ask my assistant to call yours and set up a meeting?" asked Skye.

"I don't have a personal assistant, but I'll give you my card," Andie replied, going to her car and popping open the glove compartment. She couldn't remember the last time she'd given one of these out.

Their fingers brushed as she passed it over, and Andie watched guiltily while Skye tucked it into her purse. This meeting never should have happened. She'd have to screen her calls until this all got straightened out.

"Thanks. I'll talk to you soon," said Skye.

Andie couldn't lie again, so she let the moment pass, waving as Skye got into her car. She took a deep breath. There were so many assholes in Hollywood. They strung actors along and got off on being able to make or break their careers. She'd never wanted to be like them. People didn't always like what she had to say, but they knew where she stood.

She was scowling as she headed back to the atrium, but she pulled it together before the men could see.

"You were late," her dad said, as she was pulling her chair up to the table.

She shook her head. She'd called Ben the day before and told him she wanted to meet about casting. She asked him to cancel the meeting, and assumed they'd done it until her father called her half an hour before it was due to start. He curtly told her that the meeting was going ahead and hung up before she could argue.

"What did you think of her? She's great, isn't she?" Ben said brightly.

"She is great, yes. But as I've said before, I don't think she's right for it. She's too young, for one thing. Nobody's going to believe she's a doctor."

"She can play older. She's your Dr. Foster," Doug snapped.

"No, she's not. She's *your* Dr. Foster. Why did you offer me this if you still wanted to call all the shots? If you want to direct this movie, you should do it."

Doug drew a pack of cigarettes out of his shirt pocket and tapped one out, glaring. He only smoked when he was stressed out, so she supposed she was meant to feel bad about it. "You're acting like a brat. You just want to make your mark. Do it over something else. This is a done deal."

"I'm not trying to be difficult. I'm trying to do what I think is best for the movie. Why the fuck did you hire me if you were going to block me on everything?"

"Watch your tone."

"This is one of the biggest decisions there is to make about this project, and you won't let me make it."

"You need to learn how to compromise. Do you think Ben hasn't overruled me on a thing or two over the time we've been working together? Grow up," he said, stabbing his cigarette in the air.

"I need to compromise? That's funny coming from you."

"You do. And you need to stop running around behind our backs. You think we don't know you've been calling around, trying to recast? You couldn't even wait to meet with us about it again."

Andie's stomach dropped. She'd been very discreet, and she wondered who'd ratted her out. No wonder he was so angry.

Ben held up his hands. "All right, all right. Let's all cool down here. Andie. The studio wants her. I want her. Your father wants her, and you need to remember that he's speaking to you as your producer right now."

"I know."

"Maybe I should've explained this better to you when we offered you the job," said Ben. "You've never done a big-budget movie like this before, and you'll need support to understand a few things. When you take a lot of money like this, you're promising to make a movie that returns that budget. Okay?"

How patronizing, but she had to take the lecture now that she'd been caught. "Okay."

"Sometimes, with a movie like this, you have to cast a star to have more chance of securing a good return. People won't expect to see Skye in a movie like this, and they're going to be surprised at how different she is in the role. People will tell their friends, and it'll get a lot of press. There are many reasons why this movie can be a hit, but this is a big part of it. You see?"

"I see."

"And we've got Darryl Edwards for the male lead. He's playing the pilot."

That, she could see a little more easily. His career was on a high, and she'd liked him in that Vietnam war epic. It would be interesting to see what he did with a villain part.

"Weren't the two of them a couple for a while? Skye and Darryl?"

"They were. And that'll bring people in, too, as well as the fact they were in *Halley's Comet* together. We thought it'd play well."

Andie sighed, then waved her hand in the air, cutting the smoke from Doug's cigarette. Maybe this wasn't the hill she wanted to die on. It would be wise to save her energy for the production. The combination of Skye Buckley and Darryl Edwards was an excellent drawcard, and she could use it to play with the audience's expectations.

And okay, meeting Skye might have softened her a little. She could admit to that.

"I'll stop fighting you on it."

"We don't just want you to stop fighting it. We want you to embrace it," Ben said, his thick eyebrows drawn together.

She laughed and shook her head. He was cheesy, but his heart was in the right place. "Okay. I'll embrace it."

"That's our girl."

Her dad stubbed out his cigarette, and their eyes met across the table, nodding at one another to seal the truce.

Skye Buckley was her leading lady now, whether she liked it or not.

CHAPTER FIVE

Skye stood in front of the mirror in her white dress, wondering if she should cancel this date. She checked the time and decided that calling it off now would put Teri in an awkward position.

They were going to a party in the Hollywood Hills. The woman she was meeting, Dana, was an actress. At least they had something in common. One of her movies came out recently, and when Skye had hired the video, she thought she was beautiful. It was exciting that she was going out with the woman on-screen, but she was nervous.

"Hello?" Teri called out from the front door.

"I'm in here. The bedroom."

"You're about to tell me you can't go out tonight, aren't you?" she said, coming down the hall in a slinky black dress.

"No, I wasn't going to say that. I'm ready to go."

"You look lovely," Teri said, after glancing at all the clothes piled on Skye's bed.

"I didn't know what to wear."

"What you're wearing is great. It's just a party."

"Okay. Thanks."

What she couldn't say aloud, even to Teri, was that dressing for a date with a woman made her incredibly self-conscious. Women never hit on her or even gave her a second glance. Maybe she came across as too straight, especially in a dress like this. She wore what made her feel comfortable, and it might seem forced if she tried a different style. If the lack of attention did have something to do with her clothes, Teri never seemed to have that problem.

"Okay, where did you just go? What are you worrying about?"

"Nothing."

Teri put her hands on Skye's shoulders. "If this is too much, I'll cancel it in a heartbeat. Claudia and Dana will be here any minute, so there's no time to call, but I can go by myself and say you're sick?"

"Thanks, but I'm fine. I'm sure it'll be a good party."

"You make it sound like you're going to the dentist. I'm hoping it'll be a little more fun than that. Even if you don't hit it off with Dana, Tom's a great host. The party will be great. You'll be great," Teri said, and Skye laughed.

"Okay, okay. And you're sure I don't need to worry about anything? Dana knows she can't tell anyone about this?"

"Of course, she knows the score. It's the same for her. I would've never set you up otherwise. And like I've told you, Tom's parties are only for people in the know. There's nothing to worry about. Now c'mon, let's go wait outside."

The party was at the lavish estate of Tom Bennett, a leading man she'd met a handful of times. The ballroom-sized living room was packed with guests, many of whom she recognized. They sat on the white leather sofas and spilled into adjoining rooms.

It was so loud that Skye struggled to hear the conversations around her. She was standing in a group with Teri, Claudia, and Dana, but soon she was left alone with her date. Dana leaned forward, putting a hand on Skye's shoulder.

"I'm getting a glass of wine. Would you like one?"

"Yes, thank you," she said, flushing because Dana's breath had tickled her ear.

"I'll be back in a sec."

They shared a smile. Dana really was cute, with shoulder-length red hair and brown eyes. She had been charming on the ride over here, complimenting her outfit and praising her last movie. When she returned with drinks, she leaned close to Skye again. "I can't hear a thing in here. Should we go outside?"

The deck overlooked a spectacular view of the hills and a large, well-lit swimming pool. Revelers swam, or sat on the side with their feet in the water. It was quiet up here, with only the two of them, but they could hear shouting and music below.

"My God. It's so beautiful," Skye said.

"It really is. Tom must have one of the best views in town."

"Totally. So, how do you know Claudia?"

"We used to date, actually. Just for a little while."

"Oh. Right." She was starting to understand why Teri always said the lesbian scene in LA was a tangled web.

"And Teri's your assistant, right? She's so nice. I think Claudia likes her a lot."

"Yeah, she's the best. I'm very lucky to have her working with me."

While they chatted about their friends, Skye tried to get out of her own head. She couldn't help feeling bored. It seemed that no matter how long they spoke, they weren't going to get any deeper than small talk. She didn't know why, but the connection just wasn't there. Judging by how she kept moving closer, Dana didn't notice how forced the conversation was.

Suddenly, Dana looked around to check they were alone, then slipped a hand behind Skye's neck and leaned in for a kiss. It wasn't bad—she liked how soft her lips were—but she felt numb.

This wasn't what she'd imagined for her first kiss with a woman. Not wanting to be rude or push her away, she let it continue for a few seconds. Then, finally, she drew back.

"Sorry...Did I misread things? Was that not okay?" whispered Dana.

"It's okay," Skye laughed nervously. She didn't want to come across like she was freaked out about kissing a woman. It hadn't felt right, but not because of that.

"Is this because of the movie? I told Claudia it might be weird."

"What movie?"

"*The* movie. *Creature Island*. I heard you were up for it, too. My agent said not to talk about it yet, but let's just get it out of the way. I'm figuring your agent would've told you."

"I'm sorry, I'm confused. It'll hit the trades soon, but I should probably tell you, I booked that. I didn't know you were in the running."

"Now I'm confused. When did that happen? Because my agent called me about it yesterday. He said the new director was interested in meeting with me."

"Oh," said Skye, blood rushing to her face. This couldn't be happening. Andie didn't want her for the movie. It explained why she grilled her about the book, and why she seemed off when she asked to meet with her privately.

"Shit. I thought you knew. What's going on here?" said Dana.

Skye shook her head, wrapping her arms around herself. "Nothing. It's fine. But listen, I think I'd better go. Sorry."

She heard Dana say her name as she turned to go, but she kept moving. Pushing through people, she found Teri and Claudia near the kitchen. Teri took Skye's arm, shepherding her toward one of the quieter areas.

"What's wrong? You look like you've seen a ghost."

"I can't talk about it now. I just came to tell you I have to go home."

"I'll come with you. I can ask Claudia to drive."

The last thing she needed was to be in the back seat of a car with Dana. She couldn't think of anything more awkward. "No. Thanks, but I'll get a cab. You stay and have fun, okay?"

"All right. I don't like to see you leave on your own, though. Call me if you need me?"

"Of course. Thanks."

It was only a fifteen-minute ride home, but it felt like the longest trip of her life. Had she lost the best opportunity she'd ever been given? She'd already told so many people about her starring role. Her two brothers had been teasing her relentlessly. They couldn't wait to see her in an action movie because it would be so much better than her usual sappy stuff.

It was a distant second right now, but she was deflated about the date, too. Though she'd been reluctant about going to the party, she thought she might be interested in Dana. The kiss was a letdown, especially after briefly hoping she might have met someone who liked her back.

Once inside, she dropped her purse on the floor and flicked through her Rolodex until she found Helene's home number. She wouldn't usually call her agent this late at night, but this definitely qualified as an emergency.

"It's Skye. I'm sorry to call you at home," she said when Helene answered in her gravelly voice. She was tough as nails but kind, a woman in the classic Hollywood agent mold. She wore cat's eye sunglasses and always dressed in expensive suits.

"That's okay, sweetie, what's going on?"

"I just got talking to an actress at a party, and she told me Andie was interested in her for the part. Am I getting fired? Have you heard anything?"

"God, this town. I thought I would get away with you being none the wiser."

"Just tell me. Please. Am I fired?" she asked, gripping the receiver.

"It's okay. The part's still yours. But yes, Andie did want to see other actresses for it. It was supposed to be top secret, but it sounds like something got lost in translation somewhere along the line. I caught wind of it. I was on the phone with Ben Haynes not two hours ago. He assures me that's all over, and your deal is going ahead."

"Are you absolutely sure? He promised you that?"

"I'm positive. They're faxing me the contract tomorrow after the lawyers have gone over it."

"I don't like this. What if she changes her mind again?"

"I know this has scared your pants off, but I trust him. He explained that it was all a misunderstanding. There's nothing to worry about. If this actress, whoever she was, hadn't run her mouth, you'd never have known about it."

"Okay. What's her problem anyway? Why didn't she want me for the part?"

"She was just marking her territory, my love. You know how egocentric directors can be. She's been brought on at the last minute. I wouldn't read any more into it than that."

"Thanks, Helene. I'll hear from you tomorrow about the contract, then?"

"Absolutely."

When Skye hung up, she paced the room. She couldn't relax until she got the contract, and she didn't feel like going to bed yet. After a long shower, she put on some sweats and took out her contact lenses. She wanted to relax and watch MTV, but she craved curling up with something sweet. The one glass of wine she'd had should be out of her system. She decided to drive to the Grab and Go a few blocks from her house to pick up ice cream.

Ben & Jerry's would make everything better.

CHAPTER SIX

Andie took her hand off the wheel, rubbing her tired eyes. She'd just spent a few hours chatting with her director of photography, bouncing around ideas. He seemed excited about the look she wanted for the film.

Things were off to a great start. At first, she'd been worried about having so much of her father's team in place. But after her last film, a clean slate was a plus, and she liked the people she'd met with so far. Earlier today, she'd had lunch with her editor, Louise. She had never worked with Doug, but Ben raved about her.

They had hit it off, and Andie was thrilled she was coming to the island during principal photography. Louise would look over the dailies to assess whether they were getting all the footage they needed, to reduce the need for expensive reshoots. Given Andie had never worked with this many special effects, it would be reassuring to have such a skilled editor keeping an eye on things.

She wasn't far from home, but she pulled over to grab a cup of coffee anyway. It was late for caffeine, but she didn't have many vices left, so she drank it whenever she wanted.

Andie was holding her coffee when she saw a woman across the store. Something about her profile was familiar enough to take a second look. The woman was in the freezer section, scanning the shelves before opening the door and grabbing a pint of ice cream.

As Andie got closer, she confirmed it was Skye Buckley. In sweatpants and a baggy sleeveless top, her hair in a low ponytail, she looked very different from when they'd met.

"Hey," said Andie.

Skye stopped walking and said, "Oh…Hey."

Maybe Andie shouldn't have said anything. Skye obviously hadn't clocked her before, and now she was wide-eyed behind her glasses. It was late, and she got that it might not be the best time when you were on a midnight run for a snack.

"Sorry. Didn't mean to startle you."

"That's all right. I just wasn't expecting to see you. Do you live around here?"

"Yeah, I'm in Los Feliz. I was on my way home and wanted coffee. I don't know why, but I love the taste of convenience store stuff," Andie said, holding up her cup. "You?"

"I'm a few minutes from home."

They walked together to the cash register, where a tired-looking guy greeted them. After she'd been served, Andie waited for Skye. She wasn't acting like she wanted to talk, but it would be weird to just walk out on her. At the parking lot, she nodded toward Skye's Jaguar. "I can't believe I didn't notice your car before I came in. It's so cool."

"Thanks."

Skye was clutching her ice cream, not meeting Andie's eye. It wasn't just her clothes that made her seem so different tonight. Maybe Andie's behavior had something to do with the guardedness.

"I don't want to keep you, but I wanted to say I'm sorry I was late to our meeting the other day," said Andie.

"That's okay."

Skye really was lovely to look at, but the way she stared made Andie squirm. Had she been that much of an asshole? She had to make it right. They were working together, and she'd always prided herself on having good relationships with all her actors, even if she'd screwed up on the last movie.

"Your assistant hasn't called me about a meeting, but I'll make that time for you whenever you're ready. It'd be great if we could meet before the table read."

"Sure. I didn't give her your card yet. I'll do it tomorrow."

"Great. I'll look forward to it."

"It'd be good to talk. I haven't done anything like this movie before, but I think I can bring something to it."

"Of course."

The thought crossed Andie's mind that Skye had found out about her attempt to replace her, but that was stupid. There was no way Ben or her father would have told her, and she'd confined her inquiries to just a couple of actresses.

They hadn't hit it off. That was all.

It would get better. Besides, Skye's attitude showed that she had more of an edge than she'd seen the first time. It fit Dr. Foster's character. She didn't look as soft or feminine in those casual clothes, and the sleeves of her baggy shirt were short enough to show strong arms.

Andie quickly looked back up to Skye's face, realizing she'd been caught staring.

"Anyway, my ice cream's going to melt."

"Sure. I'll see you soon."

"Good night."

"Good night."

Andie sipped her coffee and watched Skye unlock her car. Bumping into her was the strangest fluke, but she was glad she'd had the chance to apologize. For the first time, she was starting to feel okay about Skye being cast.

She turned toward her car, thinking that she'd make it work. When they had their meeting, she'd do everything she could to build a positive rapport with her.

The movie was too important not to.

CHAPTER SEVEN

Skye stared up at the ceiling from her bed, worrying about whether her contract would come through today. It was too early to call Helene again, but she'd be a mess until she heard.

Why couldn't she have chosen to do something else with her life? Her parents were both teachers, one of her brothers was a plumber, and the other was in real estate. She should've followed in her parents' footsteps—teaching was an excellent, secure profession.

She gave herself a mental shake, reminding herself how lucky she was to have found success when the odds were stacked against it. Sometimes, it got her down that people like Andie had so much power over her career, but she was just one person.

Thinking about running into Andie at the convenience store made her want to pull the sheet over her head and never show her face again. She wished she'd stayed home instead of going out dressed like that. Andie gaped at her like she was an animal at the zoo.

The sound of footsteps in the hall interrupted her moping, and she sat up, clutching the sheets to her chest. "Who's there?"

"It's me. I'm the only one with a key, aren't I?" Teri called out.

"Come in. And you could have been an intruder."

The door opened, and Teri stood in denim overalls over a T-shirt, her hair gathered up in a scrunchie. Skye squinted into the light when Teri opened the curtains.

"Not an intruder, though you might think so when I tell you to rise and shine, my love."

"No offense, but what are you doing here? It's your day off."

"I'm here as your friend. You didn't hear me knock?"

"Nope."

The mattress shifted under her when Teri sat down. "I was worried about you after last night. Dana told me she's up for your movie."

"Oh, yeah?"

"Yeah. For what it's worth I made it clear to Claudia she should've told me about it, and I'm pretty annoyed that she didn't. I hadn't told her you got it yet, but she knew you were lobbying hard. It wasn't fair to you. I get why you were so upset."

"It was so embarrassing. What else did Dana say to you guys after I left?"

"Not much, but she felt bad. I don't know much about what happened between you two. I can't make you, but if you want, we could go for a walk, and you can tell me about it?"

Staying under the covers and waiting for the phone to ring would only make Skye feel worse. She threw back the sheets and hauled herself out of bed.

They drove to a nearby park and started on a track that wound past a large pond. The sky was bright blue, and the sound of kids playing nearby lifted her spirits. While they walked, she filled Teri in on everything, including how she'd bumped into Andie.

"Well. That's a lot of material. I'm not sure I know where to start."

Skye laughed at the dry tone. Some people might think Teri was only so good to her because she paid her to be, but she knew in her heart it wasn't true. She didn't have to come over today—she wanted to be here, and she always knew how to lighten her mood.

"I felt like such a fool. Dana thought I already knew, and I had no idea. I was walking around thinking that everything was okay, so happy about the movie. And now I've been told not to worry about it, but it feels like a mess."

"I'm sorry. I can understand why this has thrown you. Having a close call like this would scare anyone, and you wanted this part so much," Teri said, taking her arm.

"I hope it's only a close call. I'll feel safer when I get that contract, so I can see it in black and white."

"Helene knows what she's doing. I don't think she would've told you it was okay unless she was sure," said Teri.

"Yeah. I hope you're right. It was just such a rude shock, you know? It was the last thing I was expecting Dana to say."

They came to a park bench overlooking the pond and sat watching the ducks glide over the water, leaving ripples behind them.

"It's such a weird coincidence. Of all the actresses in Hollywood, it had to be the one you were on a date with. It's so weird that you ran into Andie, too. What are the odds?"

"I know. But I guess it wasn't all bad. She seemed serious about meeting up, now that I think about it. I guess she got pulled into line by the producers. At least I know they're behind me. She said to make sure we scheduled a time," she said, rummaging through her purse for Andie's card.

"Good. I hope that means whatever her problem was, she's over it," Teri said, tucking the card into her back pocket.

"I hope so too. Obviously, don't call her today on your day off. She can wait until tomorrow."

"Sure thing. Are we gonna talk about how things went with Dana? Before all this happened, I mean?"

"What did she say about it?"

"Not much. Just that she didn't think you'd see one another again. I take it she's not your type?"

Did she even know what her type was? She'd had crushes on plenty of women, and they were all different. When she tried to picture herself with a girlfriend, there was only a blank space where her face should be. What she did know was that Dana didn't do it for her. She was more attracted to someone tall and dark-haired like Andie, but she shoved that thought out of her mind. By all accounts, she was a terrible person with whom to be in a relationship.

"Dana kissed me, but there was nothing there. Maybe I didn't give it enough of a chance. I don't know. How will I be sure, when I meet the one? Or even someone I'm supposed to keep seeing?"

"You went on a date. That's a great first start."

"There was nothing wrong with her. She seems great."

Teri put an arm around her. "It'll be okay, I promise. Straight people go through all this stuff in their teens, so it's normal to struggle when you're on a different road. But one day, you'll look back on all this as just a bump in that road. And hey, you've kissed a woman now. That's a huge milestone. As for the rest of it, you can go as slow as you need."

"I feel like a baby, but thanks," Skye said, nuzzling into her shoulder.

Teri was only a few years older, but so much more experienced. She was grateful to have someone who'd been through some of the same things.

"Any time."

CHAPTER EIGHT

On her way to Andie's place for their meeting, Skye talked herself into a positive attitude. There was a signed contract now, and Helene had called a couple of times to reassure her she hadn't heard any more rumors. They'd got off to a bumpy start, but she should put it behind her. She was a professional, even if Andie wasn't.

She took in the white stucco exterior of Andie's house, and the vines crawling across the facade. It looked like a restoration, with its antique lanterns and classic architecture. She expected a maid to answer the door, but when it swung open, Andie stood there.

"Hey. Come on in," she said, holding out an arm to show the way.

Skye stared around the foyer as she passed through. She'd seen her share of stunning LA homes, but this place had more personality than most. There was retro-checked flooring, a winding staircase, and a black and white botanical print that she was pretty sure was a Mapplethorpe. It smelled like fresh pine and was immaculate.

Andie walked in front to her back patio. In blue jeans and an untucked white collared shirt, she looked professional and casual at once. Skye congratulated herself on her sleeveless blue dress, thinking she'd nailed the invisible code that went along with a meeting like this.

"Please, take a seat."

"Thanks."

Andie sat on a chair across from her. The coffee table had an ice bucket on top, with bottled water resting inside. Andie slouched like a teenager, but her smile was friendly. Maybe she'd given herself a pep talk about this meeting, too.

"Can I get you anything to eat or drink? Help yourself to water, if you'd like."

"No, thanks. I'm good."

"Thanks for coming over."

"No problem."

"I'm not a big fan of meeting at bars and restaurants. I always find it makes it a little hard to talk, don't you?"

"Sometimes, sure."

Andie leaned forward, elbows resting on her knees, looking into Skye's eyes. For whatever reason, it made Skye shift against the back of her chair.

"I think we got off on the wrong foot when you met me at Ben's. I was a little off that day."

"That's okay."

Andie pushed a handful of hair back, frowning. "All right, look. I'm having this conversation upfront with a few of the people I'm working closely with. My last movie didn't go well. My behavior wasn't great. I don't know how much you've heard, but I'm guessing you know some of the stories."

What was she supposed to say? Yes, everyone told me you're a messy boozehound that ruined your own movie? Skye looked back at her, the gears turning in her mind. Maybe she didn't want to make things so easy for Andie right now.

The truth was that she'd worked hard to try and ignore all the gossip. The problem wasn't that Andie had made some big mistakes in the past or that it led to a career nosedive. It was everything else she'd done in relation to this production. When they met, Skye had wanted to be open-minded and take her at face value. It wasn't too much to ask for the same in return.

"I'm sorry if I'm making you uncomfortable. I just wanted to clear the air," Andie sighed.

The sighing needled even more. Andie was acting like Skye was uncooperative, just because she wasn't kissing her ass. She'd worked so hard to get this role, been unfailingly polite, and had already done so much work to prepare the character. Andie would know that, if she'd asked relevant questions instead of giving her a hard time.

"It's fine. I won't prejudge you if you do the same for me." Whoops. So much for being positive and professional.

Andie's expression changed by a fraction. "I wouldn't say I prejudged you."

Skye had gone too far to come back now. She hoped she wasn't just about to blow it, but she thought about that airtight contract and dove in. "I don't think that's true. You assumed I hadn't read the book. You assumed that I wasn't physically up to the role."

"I didn't get to meet you before you were cast. I was just making sure."

"Well, is there anything else you'd like to know?" She'd never challenged a new boss like this. It cracked something open between them. Andie's gaze slipped up and down Skye's body as though she'd been given permission, and heat bloomed on Skye's face.

"How old are you? Do you think you can convincingly play a woman in her thirties? I don't want to age her down."

"Of course, I can. I'm twenty-six, and it's all about how you carry yourself. How old are you?"

"Thirty-nine. Why?"

"Okay, so you carry yourself with a certain confidence. Maybe you were always like that, maybe not, but people learn who they are more as they get older. That's what I have to show."

Skye had studied body language and expression her whole life, and she could tell when someone was trying to cover something up. Andie was surprised, but she quickly moved to the next question.

"Have you done combat training, and how in shape are you? Are you going to be able to handle the fight scenes?"

"Of course, I have. And I'm very fit. Next?"

"Your ex-boyfriend got a part. Darryl. Is that going to be a problem?"

"Nope. We've talked about it. There won't be any problems at all."

"Good. Anything you want to ask me while we're getting into it?"

Was it just her, or was the friction between them exciting? It almost felt like flirting, which was silly because she was sure Andie would never be into her. All she knew about her love life was that she'd once dated and dumped Stella, who was nothing like her.

"You look like you have something on your mind," Andie said.

"I'm thinking about it."

If she was honest, there were plenty of things she wanted to know about Andie, rather than the film. For example, where did she get that insane level of confidence from? Even with her family connections, it took a lot of guts for a woman to work as a director. There were so few of them, and she was young when she started out. She must've had more than her fair share of challenges.

But showing that level of interest would feel like tipping her hand.

"You know what, I think I'm good. I want to put this stuff aside and focus on the work. Like I said after the meeting at Ben's, I'd like to know what will be different now that you're directing."

"Deal. Let's get to work."

Their eye contact held, and Skye had a swooping sensation in her stomach. The best directors inspired you to do whatever it took to realize their vision. She was starting to feel that pull.

"I want to make a film that transcends the science fiction and horror genres, like the book did. I want people who don't like action movies to love this one, and I don't want the themes to be watered down. I want it to be a wild ride, but not the kind where people turn their brains off. It's got to stay faithful to the script."

"I loved the script, too. I'm happy to hear that."

The script had been penned by the book's author, Cynthia Quinn. Even though she'd never written a movie script before, Quinn had made smart choices. Skye rarely told people, but she'd tried her hand at screenwriting, giving her a greater appreciation for how Cynthia had pulled it off.

"I agree. It's one of the best I've read, and I'll be honoring that as much as possible. I can promise that your character's arc won't be changing one bit."

For an actress, those words were magic. The things you signed on for rarely happened like they were supposed to. Movies started as one thing and became another—and it was all about learning to live with the compromises. Hearing her director say that she wouldn't have to do that was music to her ears.

"Really? I'll be honest. I just assumed some things about Dr. Foster would be rewritten by the time we got to the shoot. There's no love interest, for example. I figured the studio would ask for changes, but is that the kind of thing you want to keep as it is now?"

"That's exactly the kind of thing I'm talking about."

"Wow. I can't tell you what a relief that is."

"She could be iconic, you know? Like Ripley in *Alien*. A woman who gets to be as strong and brave as the men. A leader," Andie said.

"Now you're talking."

The space between them felt alive. Finally, they were getting on the same page. Skye hadn't worked with a female director before, and she'd never thought about what a difference it could make. They could talk about making Dr. Foster the kind of heroine that women deserved to see.

"Can I show you the look book I've been working on?" Andie asked.

"Sure, I'd love to see it."

She grabbed a notebook from the table, then gestured toward the sofa next to Skye. "Do you mind?"

"Not at all."

Skye could smell Andie's perfume when she sat close, flipping through pages. It must be a unisex scent—there were notes of cedarwood or something—and it was so good that she took an extra breath.

They went over the images, Skye's excitement growing as the pages turned. The color palette was bold and vibrant, with Andie envisioning lots of red and yellow against the natural colors of the trees and the ocean. There was a classic tone to the scheme—like when films first burst into color and made such vivid use of it. You also didn't see a lot of scary movies set in the daylight, so it reminded her of something like *The Birds*. She traced her finger over a page. "I love that. It looks like it could be an old movie."

"Glad you think so. That's exactly what I want. The special effects will be modern, but I want to pay homage to old horrors and thrillers. Monster movies too, of course."

"I love old movies."

"Me too. I don't suppose you've ever seen a movie called *Cat People*?"

"I have. If you mean the original and not the remake?"

"That's right, the one from the '40s," said Andie. "See, I believe that monsters are scarier when you make them mysterious. Like how you never see the cat people, and your imagination does all the work. I want to do a lot through the power of suggestion, the idea that things are hiding just around the corner."

"I see what you mean. I like that."

"And most importantly, people are scarier than monsters, right? I don't want to sacrifice character for thrills. Adrian has to be fully fleshed out, and he has to seem trustworthy at first. People who have read the book will know what he does and who he is. But I want the general audience to trust him. I want them to feel the horror of realizing you can't know someone, like what Dr. Foster experiences."

The way Andie presented her ideas was inspirational, and Skye listened with rapt attention most of the time. She kept being distracted by Andie's hands, which were long-fingered and graceful as she turned the pages.

Andie stopped, tapping a picture cut from a magazine. It was of a model, in jeans and a white tank top. "I haven't met with the wardrobe designer yet. I was thinking of suggesting something like this for your character. Keep it like it is in the book. What do you think?"

"That's what I always imagined her looking like, exactly."

"Me too. I'll ask them to make sure it's not too tight or anything. I don't want it to be cheesy, but I like the idea of showing off your arms. That's what Dr. Foster is all about. That beautiful kind of strength," she said, looking down at Skye's bare arms.

Skye was used to people commenting on her body. For her, it was a tool and nothing more. Still, Andie's attention gave her that feeling in her stomach again.

Andie cleared her throat. "I meant because the character is so physically and emotionally strong. I want to emphasize that."

"Sure, I'm not Arnie or anything, but I get it," she said, making Andie laugh.

Skye checked her watch. An hour had passed while they went over the book, and she'd been too engrossed to notice. Not wanting to overstay her welcome, she got ready to leave. Andie walked her out to her car.

"If you have any questions before the table read, don't hesitate to give me a call."

Those emerald-green eyes were overwhelming, and Skye ducked her head, smiling. "Okay, I'll do that."

As she drove away she thought about how much she'd liked talking to Andie. Once they got past the initial awkwardness, they'd spoken as equals. There was a sincerity in how she sought Skye's opinion, which made her hopeful they'd collaborate well.

The meeting made her even more enthusiastic about the project, which she hadn't thought was possible. To her surprise, she couldn't wait to have the chance to talk with Andie again.

CHAPTER NINE

Andie loved table reads. It was exhilarating to have everyone in one place for the first time, starting to develop the chemistry that would fire a shoot.

One of the production assistants had done a great job arranging the read in the back of a soundstage on the studio lot. In the middle of the room sat a long table with name cards. Each place had a fresh, unmarked screenplay next to a bottle of Perrier.

Her seat was at the head of the table, with Skye's on one side and the screenwriter's on the other. Cynthia was already seated, dressed in a sleek black suit, her long white hair flowing over her shoulders. Separate tables lined the walls for the department heads and producers.

They were due to start soon, and many of the actors chatted by a table laden with fresh fruit, sandwiches, cheeses, and potato chips. Andie spotted Skye talking with Sid Redding. They were lucky to get Sid, a character actor who'd lend prestige to the movie.

Skye wore jeans with an open checked top over a T-shirt, her hair in a cute ponytail. They'd met a few times now, and Andie always got a little jolt when she saw that face. She took a moment to admire how her cheekbones stood out, and the blue of her eyes under those arched brows.

Andie hadn't said hello yet, so she made her way over. She hoped things would keep getting better between them—the meeting at her place seemed to have the impact she wanted. Nothing could change that Skye wasn't whom she imagined in the role, but she was reassured that she'd work hard and put in a solid performance.

They agreed about the important stuff, so she decided to accept what she couldn't change.

"Hey," she said as she walked up, Skye and Sid both smiling at her.

"I was just telling Skye here how much I loved *Babysitting Billy*," said Sid. "That movie was funny as shit."

"I assume he's making fun of me. It wasn't my finest hour. I just wanted to work at that point."

"No, I'm really not, I swear. You had great timing. My ex-girl and I used to get stoned and watch it all the time."

"Okay, now I believe you. You'd have to be high to think that movie was any good."

"It's a modern classic as far as I'm concerned. Cheech and Chong have got nothing on you. Now, ladies, I'm going to get some of that food."

Skye looked lost when he walked away, like she didn't know what to say. Andie told herself to be patient. After their rocky start, it might take a while for it to be truly comfortable between them.

"How have you been?"

"Doing good, thanks. Oh my God, is that her?" Skye said, grabbing Andie's arm. She followed her pointed finger over to the table.

"Cynthia Quinn? The one and only. I take it you haven't met her yet?"

"Nope. Wow. Is she the coolest person alive or what?"

Andie looked down at Skye, who still had a hand on her arm, standing close and open-mouthed. It was kind of adorable. It was funny that she assumed Skye was exaggerating how much she loved *Creature Island* when they first met.

"I think she wins the coolest person award, hands down. Look at that suit."

"And her hair. I can't wait until my hair goes gray or white like that. It's so dignified."

"You should go talk to her."

Skye realized she was still holding Andie's arm and dropped it. "Sorry. Just a little excited. I don't know if I can approach her, though. That's way too scary."

"That's okay. But I'm sure she's eager to meet you. She's just sitting over there by herself because she's shy. I'm sure you've heard she's a bit of a recluse."

"I have heard that. It's why I wasn't expecting to see her today. I didn't think she'd come."

"C'mon, let me introduce you."

"Okay, thanks. I should meet her before we start, anyway."

As they approached, Cynthia looked up from her script, a gentle smile crossing her features. In the short time they'd spent together, Andie had been charmed by Cynthia's classic artist's personality—introverted and dreamy.

There'd been no expectation from Cynthia about being involved with casting. When they had spoken about Skye, her reaction was neutral. Andie couldn't help wondering what she thought about Skye playing one of her most precious creations.

"Cynthia, this is Skye Buckley, Skye, this is Cynthia."

Skye put out a hand, smiling shakily. "It's such an honor to meet you, Ms. Quinn. I'm a huge fan of your work."

"Cynthia, please. And thank you, that means a lot. It's lovely to meet you, too. Please, sit."

Andie slipped away while Skye was pulling out a chair. Ben and her father were over the other side of the room, their heads tipped together. They looked like brothers, little boys playing in their own world of games and secrets, breaking apart when she reached them.

"Andie, hey there. Ready to rock and roll?" Ben said.

"Ready as I'll ever be."

"We saw you and Skye talking. I'm so glad we put those problems behind us. We think you two are going to work very well together."

"I think so, too."

"We'll have a meeting afterward to go over any necessary changes. Just the three of us," Doug said.

"Shouldn't we have Cynthia there? I know we agreed I'd handle revisions, but I think we should involve her anyway. Her input could be pretty important. She can explain anything we might be missing."

Andie was more than happy to do the rewrites herself—it meant she could be sure that she honored Cynthia's tone. The screenplay was near-perfect, but they all knew there was no such thing as a finished work. They'd be rewriting to problem-solve all through the production, and Andie's experience with punching up scenes and dialogue would be useful. Cynthia was an excellent writer, but she'd never worked on a film before.

"Eh, not necessary. This would just be a preliminary thing. First impressions, just to hash out some ideas," Ben said.

"Okay, sure."

Andie left them to walk around and mix with some of her actors, answering questions about the script and dealing with a few character ideas. When she was done, she grabbed a cup of coffee and went to the room's perimeter, leaning against the wall. Cynthia was sitting alone again, scribbling in her notepad. Andie scanned the room for Skye, thinking she'd love to hear how their meeting went. When she found that blond hair, she was standing a few feet away and talking to Darryl Edwards.

Andie was happy with the idea of putting them together, as long as any acrimony from their former relationship didn't screw up the chemistry. At least it wasn't a romantic thing, so it was less of a risk. She hoped there wouldn't be too much off-screen drama, but she had a feeling that wasn't Skye's style.

Once she'd started observing them, she couldn't look away. They stood far apart, more like friendly colleagues than former lovers. She wondered who had broken up with whom, and if either of them was still carrying a torch.

"Hey, little sis," Cary said, leaning on the wall beside her.

"How are you doing?" Andie asked, not taking her eyes off Darryl and Skye. Skye nodded at something he said, smiling. At first, she didn't notice when Cary didn't reply. Finally, she looked over to see her staring back at her with a smug smile.

"Having a good look, are we?"

"What do you mean?"

"You're staring at Skye."

"No, I'm not. I'm watching her with her ex-boyfriend. Trying to figure out how well they get along. I'm going to be working closely with them, so I should know, don't you think?"

"Maybe. But I saw you getting an eyeful before when you were talking to her. I was right behind you guys, and I know that look. I get it. She's very pretty."

"It's not like that at all."

"I don't know why you deny it. It's not a big deal if you stare or whatever, as long as you keep it in your pants," Cary said, rolling her eyes.

"Do you have to make me sound like that?"

"I love you, but you've earned it."

There wasn't much she could say to that. Since her late teens, she had jumped from one woman to the next without examining why. She always told herself that she'd settle down if she met someone special, but the day never came. Instead, she allowed herself to revel in the attention that came with Hollywood fame. She knew better now, after all the drama it caused. Over the last three years, she hadn't been with anyone at all.

"Yeah, okay, I know I behaved badly. You can talk. You're not exactly the poster girl for monogamy, yourself. Anyway, that's not what this is."

"Fine, I'll take that. I'm just telling you to be careful because you never know when you might have another Stella on your hands. That broad was crazy."

"To be fair, I wasn't very good to her. I did cheat."

"She cheated on you first. You were a bad combination, but it wasn't all your fault."

"That's what I said at the time. That Stella cheated on me first. I'm not so sure now that it's a good excuse."

Skye was twisting a ring around her finger, looking after Darryl as he turned away. She must have felt Andie's gaze because she looked over, their eyes meeting across the room. Andie smiled at her briefly.

"Well, it's been nice to stand here and go over all my relationship mistakes, but I should probably get this thing going, don't you think?" Andie said.

"You're the boss."

They took their places around the table. Andie signaled to one of the production assistants, Carol, to press the record button on her Dictaphone. Andie uncapped her pen, opened her notebook, and called out to get the room's attention.

"Okay, everyone. Just a few words before we start. Please remember that you don't have to perform right now. This is just about hearing the dialogue and getting a feel for how it's all flowing. Save yourselves for the shoot. I'll be reading stage directions. We'll go around the table first, so you can all introduce yourselves."

It was clunky initially, but the actors loosened up by the end of the first act. It was exciting to hear the script come to life, and she was struck again by how well crafted it was. Cynthia's work managed to be poetic without sounding pretentious.

While making a note about cutting a line, Andie paused, unable to look away from Skye. There was something so convincing about the voice she'd found for the character—her natural pitch had dropped slightly.

They arrived at a pivotal scene between Skye and Darryl. As they went back and forth, Andie was swept up by the moment, goose bumps pricking her skin.

"I keep imagining what my little boy is thinking. How he's doing, without me there to tuck him into bed," Darryl said.

"Please don't talk about him to me. I know what you're trying to do. It's not fair," read Skye.

"Who said anything about fairness? If life was fair, we wouldn't be here in the first place. So, I want you to think about my little boy. Think about how he tells all his friends that Daddy is a pilot and helps keep people safe on the plane."

"It's not my fault that you make a liar of your son every time he says those words. You didn't keep us safe. You put all of us in danger. And for what? To make a little extra money? To make yourself feel big? You should be asking yourself, what kind of man am I? What kind of a father?"

When the scene closed, it took Andie a moment to remember to read the stage directions. They kept moving through the script, but she was still thinking about that last scene. If they were that good together now on first readthrough, she could only imagine how it would play when they did it for real.

When they reached the finale, Andie stood and clapped. The rest of the room joined her.

"Thank you so much, to all of you. This has been wonderful. It makes me even more excited about the shoot. I'm so proud to be bringing this script to life. Thanks, Cynthia."

They gave Cynthia an extra round of applause, and Andie made space for Ben to say a few words. Many of the actors, including Skye, left to get more snacks or socialize in small groups. "That was wonderful. Truly," Andie had a chance to say to her before she left. Skye beamed.

Andie turned to Cynthia, who stared thoughtfully off into space. "What was that like for you? Did it go how you thought it would?"

"I had no idea what to expect, my dear. As you know, I've held out for years on this adaptation. I was just thinking that I'm glad I waited this long because, with this team, the movie will be something special."

Andie could cry happy tears. Not many opinions were as important to her as Cynthia's. "I'm so thrilled to hear that."

"I can't imagine what it would be like if it weren't for Skye. She's the perfect Dr. Foster. She's exactly who I imagined when I was writing the book."

"I'm glad you feel that way," Andie said, trying to cover her surprise.

"She's got Dr. Foster's integrity. I knew it the moment I met her. I can tell when I look into her eyes."

"I'm looking forward to seeing what she does with the part."

Over the next thirty minutes, the room emptied. Andie gathered up her notebook and script and followed Ben and her dad into an office for their meeting.

"Initial thoughts?" Ben said, tenting his fingers.

Andie looked at her father, who leaned back, letting her respond first. She appreciated that he'd stayed quiet throughout the table read. It would be too easy for the lines to blur, for the cast to still treat him as their director.

"I've got notes for some dialogue tweaks. Other than that, the section before the crash feels bloated. I don't think we need to shoot all those scenes. We could pare it down to two or three. But overall, it felt strong to me. What about you guys?"

"I agree," Doug said.

"Great. I think we're all on the same page, mainly. Did you notice how well Skye and Darryl carried off their scenes? They work so well together, I'm excited to see what they're going to do..." Ben trailed off, rubbing his chin.

"That's what I was thinking," said Andie. "But what is it? Are you not happy with someone in the cast?" As far as she could see, there weren't any weak links. It would piss her off if they wanted to make another change after all the turmoil they'd just been through over the lead.

"I think we could do more with Darryl," said Ben.

Andie took down a note, nodding. Darryl was a bankable star, and his role was smaller than Skye's. If she had to throw in a few extra lines so that everyone could feel that the male part wasn't undercooked, she'd do it. It annoyed her that nobody ever suggested this for female stars. Still, she'd been around long enough to know that she wouldn't change it by digging her heels in.

"I'll think about how we can flesh out his character more. Sure."

"Great. Now, what the movie really needs is a little romance. To make it appeal more to women."

Andie wanted to bang her head on the desk. For someone who thought of himself as a vanguard, Ben could be so old-fashioned. "That's a pretty big shift. I don't see how we'd fit that into the story at all. Which characters would you pair as love interests?"

He held out his hands, like the answer was obvious. "Skye and Darryl. They have such chemistry, and we'd be fools to waste it."

"Sure, but..." she said, eyes narrowing. This couldn't be real.

"A relationship between them will add so many layers, don't you think? The heroine and the villain. It could be so complex and wonderful. Groundbreaking, even. Only let's not make Darryl too villainous. It wouldn't be good for the movie."

Andie stared at him, then looked at her father. He was nodding in agreement like it was the best idea he'd ever heard. She looked in between them, so shocked and frustrated that it froze her. They'd planned this all along.

Fuck.

CHAPTER TEN

As Mermaid Island came into view, Andie stared with wonder out of the small plane's window. She'd wanted to visit the location before shooting, but her schedule hadn't allowed it. The ocean was a stunning shade of turquoise, bordered by white sand and green masses of trees.

The journey from LA to mainland Fiji took a whole day, and she'd stayed in a hotel overnight before boarding the shorter flight to the island. As they prepared to land, her stomach kicked with excitement. After a month of stressful meetings and rewrites, it was nice to remember why this opportunity was so special.

"How beautiful is that?" Cary said, leaning across her.

"Yeah. It's something else."

"It's nice to see you smiling. I wondered how long you were planning to act like a surly teenager. It was like when I'd come and visit, and you were too busy blasting your punk music to talk to me."

"And you're still hungry for attention, just like you were then," Andie said, ruffling her sister's hair.

"Seriously, I know you're worried about the script, but the new scenes are good. You've pulled it together so well. It's going to be okay."

Andie gripped the armrest, looking out the window again. She wished she could believe that. Ben and Doug had insisted on the romance, and like Skye's casting, it was a losing battle. They had the studio behind them, and she had no leverage whatsoever.

The only choices were giving in or walking away, and she wasn't about to do that. The movie was hers now, and she didn't give up on things she cared about.

"Do you really think they're good?"

It had killed her to rework the scenes between Dr. Foster and Adrian. They'd demanded that she take out the twist of Dr. Foster killing the pilot. In the original script, and even more importantly, the novel, Dr. Foster discovered that Adrian deliberately crashed the plane so she took him out. That scene was gone now, with the crash a simple accident.

"Of course, the rewrites are good," said Cary. "I know it's a big change but trust me. And trust Dad and Ben. They know what sells."

"What happened to all that stuff about them being control freaks? About standing up for myself and everything? I thought you were on my side."

"I am on your side. I know you did the best you could, and now it's okay to move on."

"I feel like they're taking me for a fool. Like I'm weak, or something. Dad acts like he and Ben have always had these creative disagreements, but I've always felt like Dad's the one calling the shots."

"Who knows? They're forever having their secret chats. They're off in their own little world. They're not used to letting anyone else in, but they wanted you for this. They wouldn't hire someone they thought wasn't up to it."

"I don't know. I'm sure they regret hiring me by now."

"I think you're wrong about that. Either way, you've got to find a way to reconcile yourself to these changes. If you're not in, the rest of the cast will pick up on it. Trust me, if you do that and commit, the movie will be good. From an actor's perspective, the scenes are great. If I were Skye, I'd be ecstatic about the reworking. Her character is much more likable, now."

"I don't think she'll care about that. She's going to be pissed. I had assured her there would be no major changes."

"What do you mean? You haven't talked to her about it?"

"No. I had someone fax the pages to her and Darryl, but I didn't hear from either of them."

"And you couldn't pick up the phone? What were you thinking?"

"Stop giving me shit. I've been run off my feet. Do you know how many meetings I've had? I haven't had time for anything. Skye's experienced. She'll get it."

They were in the middle of a bumpy landing, so Andie took the excuse to stop talking. She should have arranged a meeting with Skye. She'd meant to, but she kept putting it off, partly because the conversation with Cynthia was brutal. When Cynthia sold the screenplay to Doug and Ben, they'd promised her the world. It felt awful to tell her that everything she'd always feared about Hollywood adaptations of her work was coming true and there was nothing she could do about it.

She told herself that seeing as Ben and her father were making her do this, *they* should talk with Skye about the new direction.

She knew she'd messed up. Since instructing an assistant to fax over those pages, she'd felt guilty every day. Still, she hadn't done anything about it.

They deplaned, Andie shielding her eyes from the brilliant sunlight and staring at the mountains in the distance. Her heart was opening, and the beauty rushed in. She could see exactly how the surroundings were going to look on film. Thoughts of studio interference and unhappy actresses melted away.

"Wow," Cary said, turning around to take the view from all angles.

"I can't believe we get paid to work here."

A small group of production assistants, who'd been among the first to get to the island, approached the landing strip. Behind them sat a row of cars, including a couple of station wagons and Jeeps. Carol stood with a bullhorn in front of the new arrivals.

"Okay, everyone. The living quarters are about ten miles away. There are no paved roads, they're all dirt, but the drivers will get you safely to your accommodation. Three to a car. That's three of you, one assistant, and a driver."

While their luggage was loaded into the vehicles, Andie stared at the mountains. She rolled up the sleeves of her white T-shirt, already sweating.

"How are you doing?" Carol asked.

"Good, thanks. Have you taken much of a look around the island?" she asked, ignoring how Carol eyed her.

They'd worked together before, so Andie knew how flirtatious Carol was. She had to admit that she might've gone for it once upon a time. Carol was attractive in a rebellious way, her platinum blond hair dark at the roots and a ring in her nose. She wore ripped jeans and a *Do the Right Thing* shirt.

"Yep. Stunning. I've already been swimming. The beaches are to die for."

She led Andie, Cary, and Sid to a white station wagon. Carol got into the passenger seat, and Andie got in back and settled into the middle. The road hugged the coast, and she drank in the sight of waves crashing down below, breathing in the ocean scent.

"Mmm. I'm going to enjoy this shoot," Sid said, grinning from behind dark shades. "So, what's the story? Do I get a place to myself?"

"It's like there's hotel-style for the crew, but the accomm for talent and high-ranking types like Andie is villas. They're designed for families or friendship groups when this is all over. I can assure you, you're going to be very happy," Carol replied.

"Yeah, but do I have to share, though?"

"Yes, you'll have to share with two or three others. Of course, you'll get your own bedroom, but you share the rest of the villa. I've got it all listed here," she said, opening the glove compartment and gesturing toward a folder.

"Well, let's see it," he replied, clicking his fingers.

She shook her head but passed it back, and he flipped through until he found his name. "All right. Darryl Edwards and Matthew Garfield. I know who the pretty boy is, but who's the other dude?"

"He's playing the passenger who gets bitten by the snake," Andie said, grabbing the folder to search for her name while Cary looked over her shoulder.

"I'm sure they put us in together…Oh good, see, there it is. You, me, Skye, and Teri. Who the fuck's Teri?" Cary said.

"Teri? That's Skye's assistant," Carol replied.

"Shouldn't she be in with you guys then?"

"Oh, I don't know. I guess Skye must have asked about having Teri stay with her."

Andie elbowed Cary. She was being too blunt, even if she had her own concerns. Andie hadn't thought to ask about these arrangements, and she wished she'd known they were putting her in the same villa as Skye. She needed space to work without interruption. As the director, she would be putting in longer hours than anyone.

She considered asking if she could request a change, but it would make her look ridiculous. They were on an island—there were only so many options.

They turned a corner and started descending the mountain. Rows of double-story villas were nestled in the valley. Across from the villas sat a large hotel, topped with triangular roofing. A long pool was at the center, and palm trees circled the little village.

"Wow. I take it back. I'm fine to share," Sid said.

They got out of the car, listening eagerly while Carol pointed out their allocated villas. Sid took off, practically running to check out his place. Cary slung an arm around Andie's shoulder as they made their way toward theirs.

"They really pulled it off, huh? This place looks five-star. I can't believe they got this all built before filming started," Cary said.

"It's pretty amazing."

"I bet you're not happy about sharing with Skye, are you?"

"Oh my God, don't you think it's ridiculous? Why wouldn't they put me in with people from the crew? It's weird to share with the actors. No offense."

"None taken."

"Skye doesn't seem high-maintenance or anything, but what if she has lots of questions and I can't get time to myself? Or if she has lots of friends in the cast, and they come around all the time? That would drive me nuts," Andie said.

"But, no offense to actors, right? Who knows why they've done it this way, but I guess you're stuck with us lowly actors, boss."

"Lucky me."

CHAPTER ELEVEN

Skye wished she could focus on the gorgeous landscape, but she was way too distracted. "What the hell were they thinking? I'm glad they put us together like I asked, but how will we share with Andie?"

"I don't know. Maybe I can talk to someone about it?" said Teri.

"Yeah. Your first question should be, why on God's green earth would they do that? I bet she's not any happier about it than I am."

"I guess part of the reason is that they've split things up by sex, and there aren't that many women on the shoot? Especially women in more prominent roles."

"Yeah, I figured it'd be something like that. Do you think I'd look like I was difficult if I asked for a change?"

"Maybe. It's up to you, of course."

They were nearing the villa, but Skye didn't feel closer to deciding. Smooth white stones were arranged in a path to the front door, and she looked up at the roof thatched with some kind of natural material.

Her stomach was fluttering, and it wasn't just at the beauty of the surroundings. Living under the same roof as Andie made her nervous for reasons she didn't want to think about.

"You know what, who cares? We'll see how it goes. We have already had a weird start. We just patched things up. I don't want to make it weirder. Even if I'm not very happy with her right now."

"Okay, fair enough," Teri said, pushing the door open.

The open-plan space had high ceilings and large windows that bathed the room in light. Glass doors opened onto a back deck, and the living room had inviting gray sofas.

"This is nice," said Skye.

Teri went to the kitchen area and opened cupboards, checking out the cookware. On the way over, they'd been told that they could prepare their own meals if they preferred. They could put in orders for provisions from the mainland to be brought over as often as they liked. Planes would travel back and forth daily, seeing as they had to fly film over to be developed at a Fijian lab. It was the only way they'd have access to dailies.

"I guess Andie and her sister are out, huh?" Skye said after she'd listened for footsteps upstairs.

"Yeah, probably."

"Have you ever met the sister? Cary?"

"Nah. She's a good actress, though, isn't she?"

"Very good. I've always liked her. I wish we had more scenes together."

"Hell, you just might with all the chopping and changing they're doing. Who knows what the next big change might be?"

Skye laughed, but there was an edge to it. All of Andie's promises about preserving story and character were worthless. Obviously, she didn't believe Skye had the talent to perform the original scenes. She was so infuriated that Andie didn't even bother to call and give her a heads-up.

"You know what pisses me off most about those new scenes?"

"They suck?" Teri asked.

"No, they actually don't. There's some promise there. But I'll have to change so much of my approach to make it all work.

She hasn't even offered to work on it with me. It's the least she could do."

"It's not great. It's not too much to ask to go over it with you. It's not like you have a long rehearsal period."

"Exactly. I guess I've got to figure out the new angle by myself, no help from Her Highness. Anyway, do you want to go out for a walk once we've checked out our bedrooms?"

"Absolutely. I want to see the beach up close."

"You're on."

"I'm pretty happy I'm working for you right now," Teri said, flopping onto one of the sofas.

"You're really not too upset about being away from Claudia for so long?"

"I'll miss her, but I don't know. We're not that serious. Not even exclusive. I'm happy about spending the summer here."

"Maybe you'll meet someone on the crew, like a sexy camera operator or something."

"I don't think so. I don't know if I'm in the mood for that. No summer lovin' for me."

Skye grinned. They'd watched *Grease* together twice, Skye confessing that Rizzo was one of her teenage crushes. Back in high school, the movie made her wish she could be suave and popular with girls like Danny Zuko, which should have been a dead giveaway that she wasn't straight.

She launched into the opening bars of "Summer Nights," picking up an ornament from the coffee table to use as a microphone. Teri laughed while she sang—or yelled—both the Danny and Sandy parts.

Skye was at the finale when she caught Teri's eye indicating something behind her. When Skye spun around and saw Andie standing on the stairs, the song died on her lips. Of course, in black jeans slung low on her hips and a white shirt Andie looked the opposite of how Skye did right now—which was like a complete dork.

"Please. Don't stop on my account," she said, trying not to laugh.

Skye put down the imaginary microphone with as much dignity as she could muster. "I didn't realize you were here."

"Clearly. I was just having a nap."

"Sorry if I woke you."

"Don't be. I'd hate to have missed your performance," Andie said, eyes dancing.

"You could have told us you were there instead of sneaking up on us like that."

Andie crossed her arms. "I was coming downstairs. In my own accommodation. I wasn't sneaking."

"You weren't in a rush to announce your presence, either. So next time, just say hi."

"Okay, next time you're giving a concert, I'll happily interrupt."

Teri rose from the sofa, looking back and forth between the two women. She walked over to the stairs and extended her hand. "Hey, I'm Teri."

"Andie. I'm sorry, have we met before? You look familiar."

"We have. I'm a friend of Stella's."

"Right. Small world. Sorry, I remember now. Nice to see you again," she said, flinching at Stella's name.

"Sure. Anyway, we were about to head out for a walk. See you later."

"Later."

Skye's face still burned when they got outside. At a safe distance from the villa, she grabbed Teri's arm. "Oh my God. I want to crawl into a hole right now. I wish I'd known she was up there."

"I was trying to let you know. Don't worry about it, though. Who cares what she thinks?"

"It was so embarrassing. And she just stood there watching me. Do you know how long she was there? How much did she hear?"

"I don't know. I don't know if I noticed her right away. I didn't see her come down. Either way, it doesn't matter, does it? You really stood up for yourself. Good for you."

"Thanks," Skye replied uneasily, knowing she'd overreacted. Andie probably thought she was a drama queen.

She could feel Teri's eyes on her, but they kept walking on the sandy path that led them over a small hill toward the beach. They paused to slip off their shoes, and she wiggled her toes in the warm white sand. Skye suggested they sit down on a large slab of rock, worked smooth by the ocean.

Skye reached down next to the rock and pulled up a handful of sand, letting it sift through her fingers. "Do you think our luggage will be there when we get back? It'd be nice to unpack and settle in."

"Maybe. Hey, Skye? I wasn't going to say anything, but I have to ask. What was going on back there?"

"What do you mean? When I had the world's most embarrassing moment? My new boss seeing me acting like a loser?"

"I mean, what's going on with you and Andie?"

Skye stared out at the ocean. Shit. Her face burned again. "I don't know. I thought we'd worked things out, and she would be honest with me, like with the script changes. But obviously not. I guess she gets under my skin."

"That's not really what I meant."

"No? What are you talking about then?"

"You two were staring at each other like…I don't know. I was picking up on something. It was getting a little hot in there."

Skye could only keep staring at the waves lapping the shore. She was afraid to turn her head and look at Teri. She'd never been so good at acting in her personal life—she was a terrible liar. "I don't like her that way. And she sure as hell doesn't think of me like that."

"Okay. Just thought I saw something."

"Well, you're wrong."

"Sorry. I didn't mean to make you feel weird."

"That's all right," Skye said, bumping Teri with a shoulder. "I think I'll take a nap myself, later. I'm tired from all the travel."

"Sounds good."

Skye settled in against Teri, glad that she'd dropped the subject—even if she wanted to ask a whole bunch of questions. Such as, did that mean that Andie was looking at her like she was looking at Andie? Her heart leaped toward the possibility.

The idea of being wanted like that by Andie made her hot. Was that normal? To not like someone very much, but to find them this attractive?

It was all so stupid. It would never happen, so there was no point wasting any more energy on the whole thing. She was here to work, and Andie was here to direct her. That's all this could ever be.

CHAPTER TWELVE

"Holy shit," Cary said, as they walked into the restaurant on the hotel's ground floor.

"Yeah. Better than your usual craft services, for sure."

It was beautifully decorated with traditional Fijian art, and much larger than Andie had expected. Their meals were served buffet-style outside the kitchen. They filled their plates with fish curry, rice, and flatbread and carried them to a table. Doug and Ben were already seated, and they nodded hello at them but kept talking to one another. After a minute, Cary leaned over to whisper, "Sounds like these two are knee deep in a discussion about their boy movie. I've heard an awful lot about it lately."

"Is it going to be about the lead character being drawn to the crime boss because he's looking for a father figure?" Andie laughed, tearing off a piece of bread.

"Of course. And I haven't heard mention of a single female character."

"That shocks me a little. Where's the nagging wife or ball-breaking mother? Not even a stripper? C'mon."

"What's that about a stripper?" asked Ben.

"Nothing. Great food, huh?"

"Very good. I had the curry too. Delicious."

"Mmm. The catering crew is fantastic. Hey, who made the arrangements for the accommodation? Like, who figured out who's sharing with who, I mean?" said Andie.

"I have no idea. That's way below my pay grade, honey. Why? Is there a problem? You're sharing with your sister, aren't you? Two peas in a pod, you ladies are. You weren't like that when you were growing up, but now, well."

"It's the two of us and a couple of others. I was just wondering."

The guys returned to their conversation, discussing what city would be the best backdrop for their film. Dad was making a strong case for New York, but Ben thought it was overdone and they should make an LA film.

As Andie scooped up a forkful of curry, her eyes fell on Skye a few tables away from them, sitting with her assistant. She was in a loose T-shirt, in glasses with her hair down. They laughed over glasses of wine, Skye lighting up when she smiled, making her look even prettier. It was a big change from how testy she'd been with Andie that afternoon.

Andie hadn't been able to get it out of her head since, and she wondered if Skye's anger was all about the script changes, or something more personal. It was obvious that she and her assistant were close. Had Teri told her some awful stories since they'd last seen one another? Maybe Andie was being paranoid, but she'd been at her absolute worst when she was with Stella.

God, she hated the way her past followed her around. It was humiliating to come across people she couldn't remember because she'd been so out of it.

"How was your swim this afternoon?" she asked Cary, trying to distract herself.

"It was lovely. I can't wait to get in that pool again tomorrow. What are your plans?"

"No pool for me. I'll be working. I've got to go around and look at locations for a start."

"Yeah, it's a shame we didn't get more time here before we start shooting."

"True. At least it's a long shoot, huh?"

They finished their meals and said goodbye to Ben and their father, busily scribbling ideas on a napkin. They passed by the pool, which was surrounded by Sid, Darryl, and some crew members, drinking beer and clowning around.

Darryl called Andie's name, and she slowed, nodding toward Cary that she should go on without her. Everyone loved the notion of working on the island, including her, but it meant she would always be on the job.

"I just wanted to tell you how much I love the rewrites. I was going to get in touch, but I knew I'd be seeing you soon," he said, swigging from his beer bottle.

"I'm glad to hear you're happy."

The rewrites had smoothed out any interesting edges his character had, but she wasn't surprised that he liked them. He had more screen time now, and he'd be playing more of a traditional leading role, with almost as many lines as Skye.

"You did such a fantastic job. That new dialogue? You'd never know it wasn't from the novel. It's seamless."

"Thanks. That means a lot. I'll keep moving because I have to do some work, but I'll catch up with you later, okay?"

"Of course. Thanks again."

Andie felt buoyed. It was nice to be complimented, especially after Skye's hostility. At least someone liked what she'd done.

In her room, she looked over storyboards and made some notes. Production offices were set up in one of the hotel wings, but she planned to spend much of her time here, where she could be alone. The room had a comfortable queen-sized mattress and was big enough for a decent desk. It had a modest sofa and a deck outside. It was a great place to spend a few months.

It was eleven by the time she'd wrapped up, but she was too keyed up to sleep. When she left her room, she could see a strip of light showing under Skye's door. Their bedrooms and a shared bathroom were the only rooms upstairs. Their level was smaller than the ground floor, and Teri and Cary's rooms were downstairs.

Sharing a house with Skye was uncomfortable, but maybe she wouldn't see much of her anyway. After the earlier disaster today, they'd avoided each other.

Nobody was around when Andie went downstairs to make a cup of coffee. She stood on the porch, enjoying the breeze and how this place looked in the evening, lit by tiki torches and fairy lights. There were still plenty of people hanging out by the pool. Craving solitude, she headed for the path to the beach.

The torches made it easy to navigate, and it was even more beautiful at night. As her eyes adjusted to the dark, she could make out the white-peaked mass of the ocean. She was so busy looking at the water that she almost walked right into something. For a second, she thought it was a rock until it said, "Hello."

"Whoops, sorry. And sorry to disturb you."

They might want to be alone as much as she did. Maybe she could walk along the beach for a while. It felt perfectly safe when almost everyone on the island was connected to the production.

"Andie? Is that you?"

"Yeah…Skye?"

"Yep, it's me."

"Oh. Well, again, I'm sorry that I interrupted you." When it came to Skye, she couldn't get anything right.

"It's okay. You can sit down if you want."

"You sure?"

"I'm sure, just don't stub your toe. I'm sitting on a rock."

Andie kneeled on the sand, feeling around until she was sure she wouldn't trip over the rock. It was big enough for them both, and she settled down next to her.

"Is that coffee? I can smell it," Skye said.

"Uh-huh. I take it strong, and black. It's the best smell in the world, isn't it?"

"Not much of a coffee drinker, but it's nice. You can drink it this late and still sleep?"

"Like a baby. Speaking of it being late, what are you doing down here at this hour?"

"I tried to go to bed, but I couldn't sleep thanks to the jet lag. And this is my new favorite place. I found it with Teri this morning."

Skye sounded fine, like she'd forgotten all about how annoyed she'd been when she was caught singing. It was giving Andie whiplash. She figured she might turn on her again at any time. Whatever was going on between them, she wanted to fix it.

"Hey. I'm sorry I upset you earlier. In the villa. I'd really only been there for a moment."

"I was just embarrassed, is all. I should be the one apologizing. I was pretty unreasonable."

"Was that it? There was nothing to be embarrassed about. You were just having some fun. And it really didn't sound bad at all."

"I was acting like an idiot."

"Oh, no way. It was a great performance. The hip thrusting was very effective."

Skye had a beautiful laugh, light and musical. "You can't sing it without doing that part. It's super important."

"I completely agree. Hey…Can I please ask you something?"

"Okay," Skye said cautiously.

"Are you upset about having to share with me? I can talk to someone if that's the case. See if there's anything we can do about it. I'll be discreet. Nobody needs to know but us."

"No. Why would I be upset about that?"

"I don't know, you tell me. I can see you're not happy with me. Is it the new story or something else? I know the changes in the script aren't what you wanted."

"Seeing as you bring it up, I would like to know. The story is so different, and it's missing some of the best stuff. And I thought you weren't going to give Dr. Foster a love interest. What's that about?"

Andie took a sip of coffee, feeling relieved. The changes in the script could be easily explained, unlike her appalling history. She grew so tired of apologizing for her past that it was nice to think she wouldn't have to for once.

"Studio pressure, I'm sorry to say. It's what the producers wanted. I fought to keep things as they were, as did Cynthia, we really did, but we couldn't persuade them. I know it's disappointing."

"Why didn't you call me to tell me that? Especially after our conversation when I came to your house. It sucked, getting those faxed pages without any explanation."

"You're right. I should have called. I'm sorry. There's no excuse."

"So, this has nothing to do with my acting ability? You didn't make the changes to fit around me?"

"The rewrites? No, of course not. You would have been great. I could see that at the readthrough."

When Skye let out a long breath, Andie wanted to kick herself. It hadn't occurred to her that she might think the changes were about her. She'd never want her to think that. It made her feel awful.

"I wish I could believe you," said Skye quietly.

Andie put her coffee mug down, digging it into the sand so it wouldn't fall over. Keeping Skye in the dark about the revisions was wrong, but Andie wasn't a liar. She guessed she couldn't expect Skye to know that, so she took some time to choose her words.

"I'm really sorry. There's nothing underneath it, except that I've been stressed out. It was wrong of me to not take the time. I wish I'd been more considerate, but all I can do is promise it won't happen again."

It was silent. She didn't know what else she could say if Skye didn't accept her apology.

"You took a meeting with me at the same time you were trying to have me replaced."

Andie's stomach dropped. She felt like a deer caught in headlights, and there was no point denying it. She just had to do what she could to fix it. "Okay. That's true. I did want to look at other actresses. I'm sorry that makes you feel shitty, but it's not personal."

"I don't see how it can't be personal. Know what I mean?"

"Yes, I do. But please believe that it was just part of the transition process, with Dad handing it over to me. That's all it was."

"I know I'm never going to be everyone's first choice. That's how it goes. But you sat there and interrogated me. Then pretended we were going to meet and all that."

In a town that ran on bullshit, Andie wasn't used to anyone being so direct. It was usually her forcing people to say what they meant. She usually guessed what people felt about her when they passive-aggressively blew her off. At least this way, she had the chance to clear the air.

When she thought about that meeting at Ben's, Andie cringed. Calling it an interrogation was fair enough. She'd been in a bad mood, and she took it out on Skye. "I wasn't trying to be deceptive, and I didn't mean to give you a hard time. That meeting was just bad timing. I should have handled things differently."

"Listen, I'm not trying to be difficult. I just want to know if it's going to be a problem," said Skye.

"You're not being difficult. You're right. And no, it's not a problem," Andie said firmly.

"And those changes really didn't have anything to do with you thinking I couldn't handle the scenes?"

"Oh my God, no. I was devastated to make those changes. It's the last thing I wanted to do."

"Really?"

"Yes, really. Like I told you, I fought against it. I could either do the rewrites or lose the job, and then they would have gone ahead and done it this way with someone else anyway. At least while I'm involved, I can do everything possible to make sure it's a good movie. Do the book some justice, at least."

They sat quietly, listening to the sound of the ocean. Andie stretched her legs out and rolled her neck, trying to loosen her muscles. She could almost hear Skye thinking next to her in the dark.

"It'll be a different movie to what we thought it would be. That day at your house, I mean."

"It will. Are you still happy to be here, though? Because I really hope you are. I want this to be a good experience for everyone."

"I am. Even with the changes, there's so much excellent stuff in it. I still think it can be good."

"I want it to be good, so badly. Can we meet tomorrow to go over the new arc? I'd like to hear any ideas that you might have," said Andie.

"I'd love that."

"Good. We can think of it as a separate entity to the book. But still try to honor the spirit of it, you know? And please don't think I don't back you because of how things started. It was a rocky beginning, but we can put all that stuff behind us if you forgive me. It doesn't have to mean anything if we don't let it."

"Yeah. You get it, though, don't you? An actor needs to know their director wants them."

"I understand. I *do* want you." The words hung in the air, and Andie wished she could take them back. She hadn't meant them to sound so suggestive. Luckily, Skye was preoccupied with her own thoughts.

"I'm only half serious. But I am an actress. We're known for our insecurity."

"You're not coming off as insecure. This one is on me."

"Thank you for saying that. I take it you thought I was too young? I got that feeling after we met at your place."

"I did. But I know you can pull it off. Like you said, you'll carry yourself differently. I heard how you spoke in the table read, and I know you'll be convincing."

"It's rare to tick all the boxes. I mean, I can't help that I'm a few years younger than you wanted. I've heard every possible reason for not getting cast. Too fat, too thin, too short, too tall, too old, not sexy enough. There's always something."

Andie edged closer to her on the rock. It was hard to imagine someone thinking Skye wasn't sexy, but she couldn't say that. "Sorry that I added too young to your list."

"Don't worry, I don't feel that sorry for myself. I'm lucky to be working at all. I know that."

"Just so you know, the reasons I was exploring other actors weren't anything superficial like that. I just had a different image in my head."

"Oh good, so this wasn't all about my ears?"

Andie burst out laughing, Skye giggling along beside her. "What do you mean? What about your ears?"

"They stick out."

"Did someone really give that as a reason you weren't getting cast in a role?"

"Absolutely. The director suggested I get them pinned back, but I didn't want the part enough to go under the knife."

"That's…I don't know what to say. For one thing, I've never noticed anything about your ears."

"Seriously? I used to get called jughead at school."

"I think you're exaggerating. As soon as we get into the light, I'll check this out for myself."

"Here, give me your hand," she said, and Andie held one out with her palm facing up. Skye guided it toward her. "See? They stick out from my hair."

Skye dropped her own hand. All Andie could think about was how soft her hair was, like silk under her fingers. Skye probably didn't mean for this to feel so intimate. She allowed herself a moment to smooth her palm over Skye's hair, then gently held her ear between two fingers. She could feel Skye staring back at her. They sat still, and finally, she took her hand away.

Had Skye felt it too? That weird sense of closeness? It was hard to tell when she started laughing again.

"See?"

"I see. You're a freak. You should join the circus."

"I wish you'd got a look at some of the guys that say this stuff to me. They could use help in the looks department, themselves."

"I don't doubt that. So, listen. We didn't have the best start, but I mean it when I say that I'm happy with you being Dr. Jessica Foster. If there's anything I can do to make sure we start over with a clean slate and work well together, I'd be happy to do it."

"It helps a lot to hear that the rewrites have nothing to do with me. And I'm sorry you had to change something important to you."

"I think we have ourselves a deal," Andie said softly. It was touching that Skye would even think about how she felt right now. She didn't deserve it. She held out her hand, unseen in the dark. After a moment, she prompted Skye, "Hey. I'm trying to shake your hand. It's that thing a foot or two below your ears."

"Ha."

Skye put her hand on Andie's forearm, using it as a guide to find her hand. The downward slide of her fingers was soft, igniting goose bumps on her skin. When her hand was enveloped in Skye's, they shook on it. Skye held her hand for a beat longer, then laughed softly as she dropped it. Andie shivered at the sound.

In the dark, Andie felt warm, and closer to Skye than she'd felt to anyone for a long time. She enjoyed talking to her so much, partly because she never knew what she'd say next. She put her hand down into the sand, shaking off the feeling. She shouldn't think this way about Skye Buckley, of all people, so she pushed the thoughts from her mind.

The idea of an attraction between them was insane.

CHAPTER THIRTEEN

On the first day of the shoot, Skye woke from anxious dreams. These mornings were always like the first day of school, but she was more nervous than usual. She'd never cared this much about a character. Never wanted to impress her director this much, either.

She rolled over and silenced the alarm, starting to get her head in the game. After the painstaking work of building the character, learning her lines, and rehearsing, it was time for it to all come together. She knew Dr. Jessica Foster inside out, even with all the changes thrown at her. Now, it was time to let all the preparation go and inhabit her as best as she could.

It was still dark, leaving her enough time to shower and have breakfast before getting over to the location for makeup. It was a few miles away, and it was nice not to need to factor in travel time battling LA traffic. She'd slept in only a shirt, and she pulled on sweatpants before leaving her room. The hall light was already on. As she reached the bathroom door, it opened, and Andie stood in front of her.

"Morning. I hope you weren't waiting long?" Andie asked, smiling warmly with those green eyes trained on Skye. She wore jeans, and the cut-off sleeves of her black shirt showed off her toned arms.

"No, not at all."

Skye watched her brush back her hair, focused on those long fingers. What was she thinking the other night, taking her hand to feel her ear like that? It was so embarrassing, but she couldn't stop replaying how Andie had then touched her hair.

When Skye got home that night, she wondered what Andie's lips might taste like. What would it feel like to have those hands in her hair for real? She decided to give up fighting the persistent thoughts about how sexy Andie was. It was strictly a physical attraction, and there wasn't much she could do about it.

"How are you feeling about this morning? Do you feel ready?" Andie asked.

"Yeah. I'm looking forward to it."

"Good. Me too."

Before Andie walked past to get to the stairs, her gaze drifted down Skye's body, spending a long time on her chest. Skye pretended not to notice what was happening.

When she walked into the bathroom, her face was hot. She stared in the mirror. Maybe she should've put on a bra or robe before she left her room. But then, Andie's look seemed appreciative. She shook her head and turned on the shower. It was the first day of shooting on the biggest movie of her career, and all she could think about was if Andie McKenzie was looking at her breasts.

Teri was in the kitchen when she went downstairs, laying slices of pineapple and watermelon on a plate. "Good morning."

"Morning. Thanks for doing all this, but you really didn't have to get up so early," Skye whispered, assuming that Cary was still asleep. She was the only actor shooting today, so Cary wouldn't have an early call time. She hadn't spent much time talking to her yet, but so far, she liked her. She was quite different from Andie—softer, more a hippie type.

"I don't mind making breakfast. I thought I might take a swim after you've gone to work, and I've made a few calls and put in a food order. Unless there's anything you need?"

"No, please, enjoy the beach," Skye said, pulling a stool up to the island counter and picking up a watermelon slice.

"I'll come by later to watch the shoot and see if you need me to grab anything."

"Great."

The toast popped up, and Teri buttered it, taking a slice for herself then sliding the other across on a plate.

"Thanks. Did Andie leave already? I saw her upstairs."

"She was in here making coffee a few minutes ago. I think she's drinking it out on the porch." Teri's voice dropped down even lower. "I'm glad she's making herself scarce, to be honest. I'm trying not to be too rude to her, but I'm just not a fan."

Skye chewed, nodding. "What is it about her that rubs you the wrong way?"

"Same things as for you, I'm guessing. She's so arrogant, for one thing. I still can't believe she didn't even remember me. I met her more than once. We actually hung out. How self-involved can you be?"

"Mmm," Skye said, taking her plate over to the sink. She had no interest in running Andie down. Not anymore. None of this had anything to do with her, so it wasn't her business. Besides, Andie seemed to be genuinely trying to put her past behind her.

Either way, Skye only wanted to think about one thing: the day ahead.

It was showtime.

CHAPTER FOURTEEN

"Cut. Can we get props to help with that?" Andie called out.

Her assistant director, Todd, used his walkie-talkie to call in the props guy, who took Skye's gun. After she handed it over, Skye stood back, stretching her arms. Her hair was tied back in a messy ponytail, faux sweat sprayed onto her chest and arms.

Andie watched her for a second, then looked up at the sky, breathing in the smell of trees and damp earth. They were shooting in a large clearing, surrounded by thick greenery. She was used to shooting in hot soundstages or city streets, so this was heaven. The sun overhead shone brightly, giving the scene just the right amount of natural light. The crew was responding to her well. Aside from the faulty prop gun, everything was flowing just as it should.

Best of all was how things were playing out with Skye. When the cameras had started rolling a couple of hours ago, Andie had watched her transform. She looked like the new action star they'd envisioned together in the white tank top and jeans, all strong arms and cheekbones. Everything about the way she held herself was perfect.

Skye was nailing it. Andie had never been so happy to be wrong in her life.

Ben and Doug observed from their director's chairs set up at the side of the clearing. They hadn't given her a single note yet. At one point, Ben even gave her two thumbs-up. Maybe it would be smooth sailing from now on. She hoped so, anyway.

Andie walked over to Skye to see how she was doing. The scene called for her to run along the path they'd cut into the clearing, then turn around and face the mutant spiders chasing her. They were going to pick up the reverse shot another time, but it was all about her reaction for now. There wasn't much on the page, but the scene was the first time her character did something heroic. It was an excellent way to start.

"How's the angle?" Skye asked, gesturing toward the duct-taped marks set up on the trees.

"Hitting 'em like a pro. You've been lining it up perfectly every time. How's it feeling?"

"Good, good," she said, looking back over her shoulder at the prop master, Clive. He was checking the gun and reloading the blanks.

"Are you comfortable? Do you need anything?"

"No, I'm okay. Thanks."

Andie couldn't shake the feeling that Skye had something on her mind, but she didn't want to nag. "Okay, well. If there's anything..."

Skye looked over her shoulder again, then finally met Andie's eye. "Am I getting it? Is it okay?"

"What, you mean, in general?" Andie felt rusty and stupid about not saying anything sooner. After that conversation on the beach, she should have known Skye could do with the feedback. She promised herself that she'd be more attuned to what she needed from now on. "You're definitely getting it. You're going to be exactly what we talked about that day at my place. It's perfect."

Andie looked into Skye's eyes so she'd know she meant it. They were as blue as the sky overhead. She liked watching how they changed when she smiled.

"You really think so?"

"I know it."

They were still grinning when Clive stepped forward with the gun. "You're all good to go."

"Thanks, Clive. Okay, I'll let everyone know to set up if you're ready to go again?"

Skye ran along the path and into the clearing, again and again. Her energy and focus never flagged, no matter how many times they reset. When they had enough footage, Andie raised her megaphone.

"Okay, great work, everyone. We got it. Can we please get things locked in for the close-up?"

A makeup artist swept in to freshen up Skye's fake sweat. Todd seemed to have everything in hand as they prepared for the next shot, so Andie sat in her chair for a brief rest. Carol stood next to her in denim cut-offs and a hot pink shirt, offering her a water bottle.

"Just what I needed. Thanks."

"You're welcome. It's been a good morning, huh?"

"A great morning."

Carol stood so close that her thigh touched the arm of Andie's chair. It was hard to miss that those cut-offs were very short. Andie looked away pointedly. This project was too important for her to mess around or flirt. Even a rumor could get her into trouble and erode the respect she was trying to earn back.

"A good start is a good omen. Everyone's been talking about how good Skye is in the part. You can already tell," said Carol.

"She is. I'm looking forward to working on the meatier scenes with her."

"I bet. Is there anything else I can do for you?" Carol asked, with an undertone that made Andie look away again and get up.

"No, thanks. Looks like we're nearly ready. I should go check things out."

Todd nodded to her on her way over, letting her know everything was almost in place. Skye stared off into the distance. When she noticed Andie standing close, her look of concentration fell away, and she smiled.

"Hey, again. We're almost ready to go?"

"Yep. I really liked your intensity around the third take. Do you think you can get there for the close-up?"

"Absolutely."

They started rolling, Skye delivering a perfectly calibrated performance without even needing to warm up into it. As the scene continued, Andie noticed something was wrong and called, "Cut."

"What happened?" Todd asked.

"Continuity problem. It's Skye's hair, that lock right there." A piece had worked loose from behind her ear. She was sure it hadn't been there while they were getting the wide shot.

"Do you want me to call someone from hair? Check the photos?"

She shook her head, stepping closer to Skye. "Nah, not necessary, I'm positive. I can fix it."

She reached out and gently pushed the hair behind Skye's ear, searching her hairline and face, checking that it matched her memory. Their eyes met. Until now, she hadn't realized how close she was standing. It took all Andie's energy to not touch Skye's face or cup her jaw. It didn't make sense, especially when they were surrounded by people—she just wanted to hold that face in her hands.

As they stared into one another's eyes, Andie could swear something passed between them. She moved back. "Sorry. Didn't mean to get in your face."

"Oh no, that's fine. But I think you just wanted to get a good look at my ears," she said quietly, so that nobody else would be able to hear it.

Andie cracked up, releasing some of the tension. Still, she felt it again when they locked eyes to share the joke. She glanced around, trying to tune out that people nearby were looking at them.

"Okay, everyone, let's start again."

The rest of the day didn't go quite as smoothly as the morning, but she was happy with their progress. Wrangling fake spiders was the last thing she thought she'd be doing when she became a filmmaker, but goddamn, this movie was going to be fun. The special effects team had nailed the creatures down to the finest details. The spiders were constructed using a mix of puppetry and mechanics, and they were eerily convincing.

She was getting ready to leave the location when Ben approached her. She looked to his side for her father, but he must've left already.

"Hey. Shall we share a car on the way back to the village?"

"Sure."

They slid into the back seat, Andie eying him warily. She was so sick of arguing, even if they always remained on the right side of friendly. It was weird to have friction with someone with whom she'd always had an amicable relationship. Plus, she was in a good mood, and she didn't want it spoiled.

"A great first day of shooting," he said, rubbing his hands together.

"I agree. Skye did a fantastic job."

"Don't worry, kid. I'm not going to say I told you so."

"Okay, let's pretend you didn't just say I told you so. I don't mind. I'm too happy. She's doing great."

"She's very impressive. There is something, though…"

"What is it now?"

"We want this movie to have broad appeal."

"I want the same thing."

"Good. I'm glad we're on the same page."

Her jaw was clenched, and she tried to relax. She knew today was too good to be true. "Can you please just tell me what you want me to change? Get it off your chest."

"Skye's the big draw here."

"I know. Isn't that what we've been talking about?"

"Just don't be afraid to let her be sexy."

"I think she's sexy as she is. I mean. I'm happy with how she's coming across," Andie replied. It was hard to imagine anything more attractive than Skye standing there today, looking powerful and hot as hell.

"I think there should be some tweaks."

"What is it, the outfit? Please don't tell me you want to reshoot today's scene just for the outfit. What she was wearing today was perfect."

"The outfit's fine. Maybe push up the cleavage a little more."

"Jesus, no. I'm not making her into some cheesecake thing. Don't we want the character to be taken seriously?"

"Why wouldn't she be taken seriously? People want to look at beautiful women. You should know that better than anyone."

"Don't bring that into it," she said, scowling out of the window. They were rounding over the hill, and she wanted this discussion over by the time they got back.

"I'm just saying, you could do a lot of things. Maybe even a love scene. That would really show that chemistry between her and Darryl, and it'd help the film appeal to both men and women."

"I think I've already done enough in that area. There's a kissing scene. But thanks for the suggestion."

"Well, if you won't have that, think about an organic way to have a nude scene. Maybe she's having a shower or swimming under a waterfall."

Andie sighed. He was an uncle figure, and this might be work, but it was still weird to talk about nudity with him. She'd never thought she could lose so much respect for him. He'd always had so many lofty things to say about the art of filmmaking, but you'd never know it when he was talking this way.

"I'll think about it." The idea of Skye being exploited made Andie's temper flare. Ben wanted her to spring this on her actress, and she'd never do that.

Andie knew she wasn't perfect. She hadn't always treated women well, but there were lines she'd never cross. She never hit on women who might want parts in her films. That was all so sleazy. She took great care to ensure that her actresses were comfortable at work, and the few sex scenes she'd shot were tasteful. They were only filmed in full collaboration with the performers, and only when they significantly added to the story.

"You should do more than think about it, Andie," he said as they pulled up at the village. "Remember, I'm your producer. I know what's good for the movie, okay?"

"I hear you," she said, nodding at him as he got out of the car. She got out her side slowly, beginning to feel like the most important thing she could do on this movie was protect Skye.

This was their movie, now. It belonged to them, and she wouldn't let Ben or her father ruin it.

CHAPTER FIFTEEN

Andie stood barefoot in the sand, unable to take her eyes from Skye and Darryl as they chatted between takes. They were on a rocky patch of the shore with palm trees in the background. The crew had hauled over a fallen tree as a prop. The actors were perched on the trunk, Skye in the white tank top and jeans and him in a pilot's uniform. His black tie was loosened, and his shirt was stained with fake blood.

When the camera was rolling, Skye acted flirtatiously in an understated way. As soon as Andie called, "Cut," it was like flicking a switch. They looked like polite colleagues, chemistry below zero.

"Quiet on set. Okay, ready to go. Action," Andie announced after waiting for the actors to move back over to their marks.

The camera operator, Frankie, dollied in, using the tracks built onto a platform in the sand. Andie watched with a more critical eye than usual. For the first time in their two weeks of shooting, they were working on one of the revised scenes.

"You have a son?" Skye said as they walked toward the tree.

"I do, Robert. He's a great kid."

"How old is he?"

"He's nine, going on thirty."

"And your wife? What's her name?"

"Nancy. She passed five years ago when Robert was only four years old. An accident. Robert was in the car, so I try to remember how lucky I am that he was okay. I think losing them both would have broken me," he said, looking down at his hand and angling the wedding ring toward the camera.

Skye gestured toward the log, and they sat down. "I'm so sorry. I can't imagine what that must've been like."

"Thanks. It's been difficult, trying to be all things to him. But he's turning out great. He's brave and smart. Loves baseball, just like his old man."

"It sounds like he's lucky to have you."

"I'd like to think so," he said, looking back at her, letting the beat stretch out.

They ran through the rest of the scene, filling it with significant glances and lots of tension. A perfect take.

"That was great. How did it feel for you both?" Andie asked.

"Excellent," Darryl said.

Skye gave her a thumbs-up. Andie searched her face, trying to figure out how Skye really felt about having to do this. She'd done her best with the writing, stitching dialogue from the old scenes with the new. It was impossible to gauge if it was good because all she could do was wonder if Skye thought she was a sellout.

She was letting herself get distracted, so she pushed on. "Great. We'll do one more, just to be sure."

"Can I just have a moment to go over something with you? Alone?" Skye asked.

"Sure, of course. Step into my office," Andie said, nodding toward the water.

Skye smiled and jumped up. They walked until they were out of earshot of the crew, Andie wondering what this was all about. She was still learning how Skye worked, but it wasn't her style to ask for a one-on-one in private. So far, she'd been comfortable asking questions in front of everyone.

"What can I help with?"

"I've noticed Ben and your father aren't watching today. Are they?"

"No. They've flown back to the States for a week or so to take meetings. Why does that matter? Are you nervous about them?"

"No, it's not that."

"Then what's up?"

"Nothing, I just noticed there weren't as many people around. I couldn't see them, but I thought maybe I was missing them, or they were on their way."

"Okay…"

"Yeah. Anyway, for the next take, I'm going to try a few different things. Is that all right with you?"

"Of course. Your instincts are always good. Go with them."

It was hard for Andie to concentrate while she looked into those expressive blue eyes. The smile disarmed her, too. Skye was smiling at her a lot more often these days, and Andie wondered how she'd been able to stand it when she was mad at her. She wanted her to look at her like this all the time.

"Great, thanks."

Andie was still lost about why Skye had pulled her aside for such a minor question. Her brow furrowed as she watched them restart, trying to figure out her angle. Andie sensed Skye's character withholding something, the attraction to Darryl's character gone. The flow-on effect was that he came off as less charming, even slightly stiff.

Andie let them finish, not wanting to throw Skye from whatever process she was working through. "Okay, we're going to do another one, but first, let's take five," she said, ignoring Todd's confused look. She made eye contact with Skye, who understood right away and got up.

"That was a very different performance. I know what you were doing was deliberate because you asked first, but I don't quite understand. I'm trying to figure out what I'm missing?"

"How did you interpret it?"

With no idea where this was going, she gave an honest appraisal. "It kind of felt like you were sabotaging. You threw him off. He had no idea how to respond to you. But you were still good, just different."

"Uh-huh. Keep going."

"The way you were acting made it feel like a different scene. Dr. Foster didn't seem attracted to Adrian at all. She was almost suspicious, I think? And that made him seem darker. More like the book version of his character."

"Good. That's what I wanted you to see."

"It is? Why? I don't think it fits the scene's intention, but I'm happy to hash it out a little. We can take a break to talk if you like."

"You don't have to do that. I understand completely. I just want to make sure there are lots of options."

Skye winked at Andie, looking so pleased with herself it made her heart squeeze. The plan was so clear now, coming at her like a lightning bolt. She grabbed Skye's shoulders.

"Oh my God. I get it now. How did I not get it before? Wow."

Skye shrugged under her hands. "I know it might be an impossible goal, but I thought you might want to try."

Andie stared at her for what felt like minutes, considering the offer. This was supposed to be her comeback movie. She was meant to reestablish herself and take her filmmaking to the next level. What would it mean if she screwed over the people who'd given her a second chance?

"I don't know. Your idea is so risky. But I'm also worried about the movie. I don't think the producers understand how much damage they're doing."

"I've wondered that, too. The book fans are going to be livid. Do you think they get that?"

"No, not really. They're underestimating how much people love it. I keep picturing how it's going to play at test screenings. People will be expecting one thing and get a totally different movie. It's going to backfire. I told them all this a hundred times before we got over here, but they wouldn't listen."

"Then, this is insurance."

Andie nodded, running her hands through her hair as she thought. "I want to try what you're saying, but there's a lot to consider. We'd be doing it right under their noses. Under everyone's noses."

"I know. But I thought if we're discreet, it might work."

"Yeah, but also, I don't have final cut. You know nobody would grant me that privilege when my last movie lost money, and I'm lucky to get hired for this at all. Ben, Dad, and the execs at the studio will all share the decision. I'd never get anything past them, so we'd probably be doing it for nothing."

"But if there's backlash after the test screenings, you've got alternatives."

"That makes sense. Maybe."

"Would we keep it just between us? I don't think it's a good idea to tell Darryl. Not yet, anyway."

"How do you think he'd react? You've worked with him before."

"He might be into the idea of experimenting with the scenes, but he'd go big, even if that wasn't what we wanted. I don't think he could help himself. And he wouldn't be able to keep quiet about it."

Andie looked over to her shoulder, back to where he sat on the log, chatting affably with Todd.

"You really think he wouldn't pick up on it if we kept it from him?"

"I'll tell him I'm trying out different approaches to warm up or switch gears. He's so into the *process* of acting. He'll respect it if I tell him it's something I need to do to get where we're going. That's if he even asks."

Andie bit her lip. She was running the script through in her mind, trying to calculate how it might all come together. "I guess we'll have options for a different cut, which is great, don't get me wrong. But we wouldn't be able to restore it to the original script no matter what you do. It's not like we can shoot that scene where you kill him. Not without everyone finding out about it, anyway."

"That's true. It just came to me. It felt so natural. I guess I hadn't thought it through enough," she said, face falling.

"That scene would have been toward the end. I don't know. Maybe we could work around it, somehow. I'll need some time to really think it through, with the script in front of me," Andie said, rubbing the back of her neck.

"I understand. And I know it costs the production money every time we do extra takes. I'll play it straight if you don't think it's worth it. From right now."

Andie looked at the crew hurrying around the set, ensuring everything was in place for the next take. Being honest with them was important but making the best movie possible had to take precedence over anything else. Even if they couldn't get exactly what they wanted, Skye's offer would add some texture to the scenes. It all might cut together into something midway between the two movies—the one Ben and Dad wanted and the one she wanted.

Taking risks as a director was in her blood. It was better than giving up her vision altogether. "No, I think it's worth it. I'll give it some more thought, but in the meantime, keep doing what you're doing, and we'll see how things shake out."

"Really?"

"Really. Let's see what happens. It'll be fun. And it'll just be between us, at first."

"Deal."

They shook on it, Andie buzzing. She'd never imagined Skye was such a rebel. It gave her the sensation she'd had in the early days of her career, when it felt like she was getting away with something by having the chance to do what she loved.

She wanted to put a friendly arm around Skye but stopped herself. As it was, they were walking so close that their hands brushed. Every time it happened, she felt it like a caress.

They were partners in crime now. Andie liked that more than she cared to admit.

CHAPTER SIXTEEN

That night after putting out a few fires on set, Andie arrived late at the restaurant. Cary had already eaten, and because Ben and Dad weren't around, Andie would dine solo. She found an empty table, sitting down with her tray of pasta salad and a chicken breast.

She planned to eat quickly, then get back to her room to put all her prep notes in front of her. Since her conversation with Skye, she'd been itching to play through different versions of scenes. She was shoving in a forkful of pasta when Carol walked up in those short shorts and a Pretenders shirt.

"Hey. I hope you don't mind if a lowly assistant sits with you tonight," she said, holding her tray with a wine cooler on the side.

"I wouldn't usually allow it, but I'll make an exception just this once."

"What a relief. Maybe I can even make my way up to one of those fancy villas one day."

"You never know your luck. Keep at it. You'll get there."

They laughed, and Andie watched Carol pop the lid off her drink. Carol had been snatching any chance to talk. Andie was doing her best to walk the line of being friendly without giving her the wrong idea, and not just because they were colleagues. She genuinely liked Carol. She was good at her job, and easy to get along with.

"Would you believe that little Angus Harvey just got a three-picture deal over at Paramount? Did you see that one coming when he was in your first movie?" Carol asked.

"No way, I missed that news. He's the last person I would've imagined that happening for."

"I know, but he looks totally different now. He put on twenty pounds of muscle, had his teeth whitened, and cut off his hair."

"I'm trying to picture it, but I just can't."

"It's kind of disturbing."

As soon as Andie finished eating, she stacked her dishes back on her tray. "It's been nice talking to you. I'm going to head on back to that high-class villa of mine."

"The hotel rooms aren't so bad. You should come up and see mine. How about now?" she said, smirking.

"Jesus. I'm going to pretend I don't know what you're trying to say, okay?"

Carol rolled her eyes good-naturedly. "Oh, come on. I'm serious. Come upstairs, we could have some fun. We're both adults."

"I don't do that anymore. Sorry."

Carol took the rejection in her stride, shrugging. "It was worth a shot. What do you mean when you say you don't do it anymore, by the way? Are you into guys now or something?"

"God, no. Where would you get that from?"

"Stab in the dark. Tell me what you mean."

"I mean, it wouldn't be professional."

"This isn't some casting-couch thing, though. I don't want anything from you but a good time. We've known one another for years. You know I'm easygoing. No strings."

"I get that, but it's about staying focused on the production. I'm the director. It wouldn't be appropriate."

"Is that the only reason? For the record, I knew you were probably going to say no. I had a hunch. Do you have a girlfriend back home now? I hadn't heard, but you never know."

"No, it's nothing like that," Andie said, toying with her empty plate, trying to decide how much of herself she wanted to reveal. She talked to Cary, who was understanding when she wasn't teasing. Still, it was different speaking about this with someone who played for her team.

"It's all right if you don't want to talk about it, but we can if you want," Carol said, sipping her cooler.

"Everything went to shit on my last movie. I know you've heard. Everyone has. It didn't look good for me."

"Of course, I did. I just don't see why that has to turn you into a nun."

"It's not just that. I had a lot of fun doing what I was doing for a long time, and then it just…wasn't fun anymore. Do you know what I mean?"

"I'm not sure. I guess I can't help thinking that you're being treated differently because you're a woman. Like, do you think a guy would swear off sleeping with women like this? Everyone would think he was great if he slept around like you used to do. I'm sorry to be blunt, but it seems like you're letting them shame you out of it."

Andie shook her head. "You're right about the double standard. But it wasn't only that. There's nothing wrong with enjoying playing the field or whatever. Like I said, it was fun until it wasn't. I got sick of feeling like I wasn't connecting properly with anyone."

"I don't get it. How are you going to start connecting with someone while you're celibate?"

"I'm not celibate. I want to do things differently. That's all."

"You seem pretty celibate to me, but okay. I'll let you get back to your villa."

They rose from their seats, taking their trays over to the counter.

"What are you going to do now?" said Andie.

"I'll head up to my room, maybe watch some TV. I'm not up for partying during the week. Some of the guys will throw a big one next weekend, though. They've started ordering a lot of supplies."

"I'm surprised it's taken them this long to organize something big," Andie said, pushing open the door to the lobby.

The cast and crew had grown tight quickly. They were far from home and separated from friends and family, so she was happy they were bonding as long as they all stayed on task and kept it to the weekends.

"Yeah, well, I think they're going to make up for lost time. I'll see you around, Sister Andie."

"Smartass. Hey, listen. Thanks for the talk. It was nice."

"Any time."

Andie thought about it all the way home. It wasn't difficult to turn Carol down, but she'd be lying if she said she didn't miss being with women. She missed sex, romance, intimacy. Three years suddenly felt like a very long time. She didn't know when she'd be ready to start dating, but she was prepared to wait as long as it took. The essential thing right now was not mixing business with pleasure. If she followed that rule, she'd be okay.

It would be worth the wait when the right woman came along at the right time.

CHAPTER SEVENTEEN

It was barely past dawn when Skye woke. Over the past month, she'd grown used to early call times and couldn't sleep in, even on the weekend.

Her mind turned to work as she stretched. It was two weeks since she and Andie had made their pact, and the alternative takes were thrilling. She felt bad about keeping it from Darryl, but she loved seeing the look on Andie's face every time she slipped in something hinting at the old script.

She let her mind drift over all those special looks. Thinking about it made her toes curl. After a while, she pulled on jeans and a T-shirt and padded downstairs.

The coffee maker filled the kitchen with the strong aroma she'd come to associate with Andie. The sliding door at the front of the villa was open, and she peered out to see a lone swimmer doing lengths in the pool.

Skye went back to the kitchen and poured a cup of coffee. It was already warm outside, the palm trees rustling in the morning breeze. As she drew nearer, her mouth went dry. Andie was pulling herself out of the pool, and her shoulders looked incredible. They were perfectly sculpted, water beading on her skin.

"You're up early," Andie said, when she realized Skye was there.

"I couldn't sleep. I take it you're the same?"

"Yep. I feel well-rested, though. Is that what I think it is?"

"I thought you might want a cup," she said, holding it out to her.

"You thought right. Thanks so much."

While they talked, Skye fought to focus on Andie's eyes. When she lost the battle and her gaze dropped, she couldn't look away. Andie wore a black bikini, and she'd never seen a body like that. Her legs were long and toned, her thighs and waist curved, her stomach taut. The swimsuit let her see enough of the shape of her breasts to make her wish desperately that she could see more.

When she finally gathered herself enough to lift her eyes, Andie looked back at her with her head tilted.

"That's a nice bathing suit. Where did you get it?"

"This? I couldn't tell you. I've had it for years."

Skye set the coffee cup on a small table between two deck chairs while Andie shook out a towel. As soon as it felt safe to do so, Skye watched as Andie leaned over, toweling her hair. Skye was mesmerized by the muscles shifting under her skin. She'd never wanted to touch anyone this much. She thought about what it would be like to lick the water from her skin, and she crossed her legs, telling herself to keep it together.

Andie wrapped the towel around her waist and sat down next to her. "No coffee for you?"

"No, I don't really drink it."

"How do you keep yourself awake, then?"

"I manage," she said, her heart skipping at how Andie smiled at her. "Isn't it great to have the weekend off?"

"Yeah. I'm not used to how relaxed the schedule is. Indies are always so hectic."

"I've never done one of those. I'd like to, one day."

"It's so different. It's hard because there's never enough time or money, but the trade-off is that you have so much more freedom. I know I might be offered other studio work after this comes out, but I'll never really go mainstream. I like the hustle too much. Maybe we'll work together again, one day, and you'll see."

Skye broke into a smile. Andie enjoyed working with her enough to want to do it again.

"I'd like that. There's a lot of things I want to try. I've never wanted to stay in one genre or get typecast."

"What are your dream projects? The ones you've always wanted to do but haven't had the chance to yet?"

"You mean aside from this one? Easy. There's a book I love called *Shelley*. The main character is called that too, and she's another one of my dream roles. It's about this sheltered woman who moves to New York by herself and gets mixed up with all these crazy scenes."

Andie leaned closer, eyebrows raised. "You like *Shelley?* I love that book."

"You've read it?"

"Yeah, of course. It's so different from *Creature Island,* but I guess it's a cult novel too, huh? You like a lot of those?"

"Absolutely."

"That would be a killer role, by the way. I can see why you'd feel so passionate about it."

"Really? Most people haven't heard of it, or they think it'd make for a depressing movie. Because she doesn't end up happy. And, they say it's too weird," she said, preoccupied with how Andie stretched her long legs out in front of her.

"No way. Sure, some of it's dark, but I always thought the ending was hopeful in an odd way. You know she's never going to be the same, but it's a good thing. Such a fascinating arc."

"I totally agree. Anyway, I'll call you if I ever get it off the ground. Nobody's ever going to make it, but I own the rights."

She'd acquired them three years ago, knowing that it would never get the green light but wanting them anyway. That way, she could protect it and dream about what it might be like to make it. The book was character-driven, without much of a plot. Nobody was clamoring to make movies about flawed women like Shelley, either.

"You're kidding, you own the rights? There's not a screenplay, though, is there? I've never heard anything about it."

"Not officially. Only my own lame attempt at an adaptation," Skye said, fiddling with her hair.

She'd slaved over it, studying formatting and structure from screenwriting guides. She hadn't meant to say anything, but Andie's excitement was infectious. Until now, nobody but Teri knew about it. Everyone in Hollywood had a script, a dream project they wanted to develop. It was the land of burnt-out dreams, and she didn't want to be another cliché, so she kept it close to her chest.

"That's so cool. I didn't know you were a writer."

"I don't think I can call myself that. I don't think of myself that way. Not yet."

"If you've got a complete script, you're a writer. It's no mean feat. I'd love to read it someday if you'd be willing to share it."

"That's nice of you. I'll think about it. I actually have it with me. I didn't want to lug my typewriter here, but I keep a copy with me to make notes on," she said, knowing she wouldn't let her read it. Andie had a reputation for being an excellent script doctor, and Skye felt it would be far too nerve-wracking to have someone with her experience seeing it.

"Okay, well, the door is open. So many people have helped me along in my career, and I'd love to return the favor sometime."

"Thanks. That means a lot."

"No problem. Anyway. Ben and Dad got back late last night, but I'm looking forward to seeing what else you cook up with that genius idea of yours. It's been so much fun. I don't want you to do anything you're not comfortable with, but I think it's worth continuing."

Skye leaned in even closer, noticing how Andie did the same. The air between them thickened, and they looked into one another's eyes. The best thing about this plan was sharing a secret with Andie.

"I could do it in the earlier takes this time, so it looks like I'm just finding my feet. I think I can make it work."

"Perfect. We'll keep checking in about it, and I'll let you know if I ever feel like they know what's going on. And you're still sure that Darryl isn't picking up on anything?"

"Yeah, I'm sure. I don't think he's noticed."

"I'll take your word for it on that one. You must know one another pretty well…because, you know."

Why did Skye have the urge to tell her the truth? She wanted to be seen by Andie, wanted her to know that she and Darryl had never been the real deal as far as she was concerned. She shifted back, then faced ahead. "I don't think we know each other that well. Not anymore, especially. But I'm not worried about him figuring it out."

Skye could feel Andie watching her profile, but if she wanted to ask more, she kept it to herself.

"Fair enough. I hope I didn't intrude just now? I didn't mean to."

"Not at all. I just want to talk about the plan, that's all. It's fun. Like getting to make two movies at once."

"You like breaking the rules, don't you?"

"Nothing wrong with being a little bad now and then." Skye held her breath while Andie stared at her for a moment. She cringed internally at how flirtatious that sounded, but she didn't want to take it back.

Finally, Andie looked out to the pool, still smiling. "There's going to be a big party out here later on."

"I heard about that. Teri tends to know all this stuff before I do. She's so sociable, and she always has her finger on the pulse. I'm just not like that. It's one of the reasons why I'm glad I hired her."

"Right. Teri seems nice, even if she doesn't like me very much."

"Oh, no, she's just a little reserved with new people, that's all."

"It's okay. I know she doesn't, and I understand why. I've been feeling bad that I didn't remember her."

"I don't know..."

"It's okay. I don't want to make you uncomfortable, but it feels like the elephant in the room sometimes."

"I'm sorry about that," Skye said quickly. She considered talking to Teri about being friendlier.

"No, no, please, let me finish," continued Andie. "I've wanted to say something for a while. She doesn't have to like me, and that's her right. A lot of people don't, with good reason. I've had to learn to let what people think of me roll off my back, or I'd go crazy. But it does matter to me what you think, and I know you've probably heard some stuff about me. Haven't you?"

They were still facing the pool, no eye contact, their knees angled toward one another's. Andie sounded as confident as always, but Skye was aware that this couldn't be easy for her. "Yes. I have."

"I'm not going to deny any of it because it's probably all true. I take responsibility for it. I'm not proud of it. I just hope you can see that I'm different now."

"I know."

They'd been shooting for a month, and the most unprofessional thing Skye had seen Andie do was to go along with her suggestion about filming alternatives. When it came to women, she seemed to be alone. Their rooms were right across the hall from one another's, so she'd know. Most of the time, she couldn't imagine what she'd been like before. Maybe she just didn't want to.

"Good. That's all I wanted to say," Andie said, getting up. "I should take a shower. Thanks again for the coffee."

"You're welcome." It meant a lot that Andie even cared what she thought. She wanted to add that, but it felt like the moment had passed.

Skye turned to watch her walk away, staring hungrily. Andie's bare legs were perfect. She dropped her head onto the back of her deck chair, closing her eyes. My God, she had it bad.

She sat that way for a while, seeing Andie's body behind her lids while the sun brightened on her face. She jumped at the sound of feet hitting the cement and water splashing, droplets hitting her face. Someone had cannonballed into the water, and when she opened her eyes, Darryl swam to the side of the pool.

"Sorry to disturb your little nap, there. I couldn't help myself," he said, grinning.

"Ha. No problem. What are you doing out here so early?"

"I just got back from a jog on the beach. Man, couldn't you just live here?"

"I really could."

"And you? Why are you out here at the crack of dawn?"

"No reason. I was just talking to Andie. She was out here swimming before."

"How wrong were we about her? She's nothing like how I thought she was going to be," he said, shaking his head.

Skye realized she wanted to talk about Andie with someone neutral—not like Teri.

"Same here. How are you finding her?"

"I like her. She's super nice."

"Yeah," Skye said, though it wasn't the word she would have used. Kind, maybe. "What do you think of her directing style?"

"She's excellent. Always has great notes but gives you plenty of freedom, too. I feel safe with her."

"I feel safe with her too."

"Yeah. I was thinking about this the other day, trying to put my finger on what it is about her. I figured out that the thing I like most about her is that she's confident. You don't always see that, even when most directors are pretty egocentric. She doesn't need to throw her weight around. You know what I mean?"

"I do. It's like with all that stuff we'd heard, they were talking about a different person. Do you think people can really change, or is she just on her best behavior?"

"Hmm. Can people really change? Whew, early in the morning for a big question like that," he said, flipping onto his back, moving his arms up and down in the water. He came to the side of the pool and pulled himself out, revealing his tropical-print swim trunks.

Skye felt it was the oddest thing in the world that she'd slept with this man. It wasn't like that part of their relationship had gone well, but it was weird to think that it had happened at all. Seeing him in a swimsuit left her feeling indifferent. It was the opposite of the unrestrained desire that slammed through her when Andie got out of the water. He sat down next to her, wiping his face with a hand.

"Can people change for real? I think so, don't you?" said Darryl.

"Maybe. I'm not sure. I guess we change as we get older and learn more. I don't feel like the same person I was five years ago."

"Of course. I'm not the same person I was even a year ago. And I think we're different depending on the people we surround ourselves with."

"You think that? In my opinion, we might act differently, but we're still the same underneath it all." It was almost certain that people would think she was different when she told them she liked women. That she'd changed when she was only being herself.

"That's true. I don't mean that exactly. If you spend time with the right people, like romantically or friendship-wise, you become a better version of yourself."

"Yeah. Maybe you're right."

"Anyway. What are you up to today? Are you coming to this party?"

"Sure, I'll come out for a drink."

"I'll see you there. I'm going to take a shower."

After he left, she thought about what he'd said about spending time with the right people. He seemed a lot different from how he was when they were together. More peaceful and relaxed. It was a little bittersweet. She wasn't jealous that he had a new girlfriend. She only wished she could be as smitten with someone as he was over Heather.

She put her head back on the lounge again, thinking of Andie in that bikini.

Maybe she already was.

CHAPTER EIGHTEEN

Andie left the curtains open while she napped, the sun warming her bed. It was heaven to relax, knowing that the first month of filming was under her belt and that they had some great stuff in the can.

Her confidence about directing a big-budget movie had grown. There were so many moving parts, and she was proud that she was coming in on time and under budget. The plan she and Skye had hatched up should be stressing her out, but instead, it softened the blow of the compromises she'd had to make.

The cast and crew were having a blast, too. The afternoon's party was already underway, clinking glasses and voices drifting in through the open window.

A knock sounded on her door, and she pulled up the sheet. "Who is it?"

"Your sister, who else would it be?" Cary said, pushing open the door. She rested her wineglass on the nightstand and climbed into bed.

"Please, come in," Andie said.

"Thanks, sis."

"Lucky you didn't wake me up."

"Wouldn't care if I did. You've slept enough. Now you have to come and spend time with the gang. Everyone's having fun."

Andie reached for her water glass, propping herself up on the pillows. "I can hear it. Don't worry, I'm planning on mingling when I get up."

Over the past year, she'd grown used to being the sober one in the crowd. She didn't mind most of the time—she had more fun when she was in control—but it could get tiring. It meant listening to people repeating themselves or trying to push drinks onto her. She'd go and hang out to be sociable, but she wasn't in any rush.

"It feels good to blow off some steam," Cary said.

"What would you be blowing steam off from, a tropical holiday? We're four weeks in, and you've barely even worked yet."

Cary grabbed a pillow and hit her sister in the head. "I've been preparing for upcoming scenes, thank you very much."

"Oh, yes, I can see that you've been very busy. How many hours have you logged on the beach, you think?"

"Excuse me, am I supposed to feel sorry for you because you're busy? You're the one who wanted to be a director," Cary said, shouting the last part because Andie had kicked her. "Stop it."

"Okay, okay. I'll stop giving you shit. I'm glad you came early. It's nice to have you around, I guess."

"So sweet. Dad and Ben are down there holding court, by the way. I think I caught Dad flirting with that makeup artist, Angelica. Do you think he's looking for wife number four?"

"Ugh, don't even joke about it. Besides, I don't want him starting another family. Our inheritance is already going to be spread way too thin. Doesn't he know I've got a lifestyle to maintain?"

They cracked up. They'd learned to deal with their father by using dark humor a long time ago.

"Speaking of romance, have you figured out who you're going to have your on-set affair with?" Andie asked.

"Very funny," Cary said, draining her wineglass.

"You could've brought a coaster for that. You're messing up my room. C'mon, tell me. I know someone must've caught your eye."

"All right. If you must know, I think Sid is very charming. And he's been flirting with me."

"Good choice. I like Sid," Andie said, unsurprised. They'd been circling one another since day one.

"And what about you?"

"I don't do that. Not anymore. You know that," Andie said, putting her hands behind her head and staring at the ceiling. It would take a long time for people, even those she loved, to accept that she'd changed.

"Remember when you were juggling those broads on your last movie? That was the messiest thing I've ever seen."

"I know. Don't remind me."

There were good reasons why she didn't like to think about that time in her life. One of the women—a set designer—was an ex-girlfriend. Since they'd broken up, they called one another now and then to hook up. Then Andie had started something new with the director of photography. She thought there'd be no harm in it, that she only wanted something casual. She'd been proven very wrong. When that woman found out about the set designer, she threatened to quit and hold up production.

It was one disaster in a series of many.

"Well, if you change your mind and feel like having a little fun, I think you've got an admirer on the island," Cary said.

"Who, Carol? She's not exactly subtle about it. I've told her that I'm not interested."

"No, Skye."

"Skye? What are you talking about?"

"You haven't noticed?"

Andie shook her head, even if she had wondered sometimes. This morning, Skye's eyes had roamed over her body in a way that made her think twice. She'd dismissed it—straight women got curious sometimes, that was all. They wondered what it would be like to be with another woman, but it didn't mean they wanted to act on it.

"I think maybe you're pretending to not see it, so you don't have to talk to me about it."

"I'm not pretending. I just don't think that it's true."

"She stares at you. Like, all the time. I think she's into you."

"I think she's straight."

"No way. She has a total lezzie vibe."

"How would you know? Since when are you the expert?"

"I have eyes. And you could probably get away with it, you know. Fly under the radar. She doesn't seem like the type to throw a hissy fit if things go wrong."

"That's not the point."

"I think you like her too. Admit it," she said, poking Andie in the belly.

"No, I don't. She's too young for me, for one thing."

"Don't be such a prude. She's not that young. There'd be nothing wrong with it."

"In your opinion. Which I didn't ask for."

Cary laughed, but she stopped pushing it. Maybe Andie was afraid of derision more than anything else. If people knew that she had a thing for Skye Buckley, wholesome and sweet as candy, they'd laugh at her.

Nobody, least of all Andie, believed she was worthy of someone like Skye.

The party was in full swing by the time the sisters got downstairs. People were lounging on the grass under palm trees or hanging around the pool. Empty glasses and bottles were scattered around, and Bon Jovi blasted from a boom box set up on the lawn.

Andie sought Skye out in the crowd and was rewarded with the sight of her in high-waisted denim shorts, the sleeves of her red T-shirt rolled up. Those hips and that waist—she only wished what Cary said was true.

"Well, look at that. My crush is talking to your crush," Cary said, from the side of her mouth.

Andie hadn't even noticed Sid gesturing wildly, making Skye laugh. She shoved Cary's shoulder. "I just told you. I don't have a crush on her, thank you very much."

"Whatever. Let's go over there together and talk to them."

"No."

"If you won't come with me, I have no choice but to assume there's some truth to what I'm saying. The lady doth protest, far too much," Cary said, setting off.

"You asshole," Andie grumbled, trailing behind.

As they drew near, she clocked Skye checking her out again. It was harder to explain this time, because she wasn't wearing anything unusual like a bikini, just ripped jeans and a sleeveless black shirt.

"How's it going?" Skye said, pushing her hair behind her ear.

"Great, thanks."

"Two of my favorite ladies. Y'all want a beer?" Sid asked. He and Skye nursed frosted bottles of Fijian beer, which had been ordered by the case.

"Sure," Cary replied.

"I'm good, thanks," said Andie.

He bent down to fish out a bottle from a nearby ice bucket, opening it for Cary before passing it over. They shared a warm smile as she took it. Oh yeah, Andie thought, it wouldn't be long before something happened between them.

"Party looks like it's off to a good start," Andie said, pointing to a group drinking tequila in the pool. They were lined up on the side, a row of lemons and shot glasses in front of them.

"Yeah. Can't say much for the music, though. Just not my thing," Sid said.

"Agree. They've been blasting that album all afternoon. It's getting tired," Skye replied.

"Someone else has got to take control. You know what? Hold this please, I'm gonna do something about it," he said, passing his beer to Cary. He sprinted to his villa and returned holding up a CD, grinning as he loaded up the player. There were disappointed noises when the music stopped, but they were followed by cheers when Run-DMC started playing.

"Good choice. I love this," Cary said, clinking bottles with Sid.

Andie was sure she had no idea who they were—she always said that nothing recorded after the '70s was worth listening to—but it worked for him. He stepped closer to Cary, and soon they were deep in conversation.

"What about you. What music do you like?" Andie asked Skye.

"Blondie, Kate Bush. Stuff like that."

"Cool, me too."

They'd only just started talking about music when Todd, one of Andie's assistant directors, sidled up to her. When she was given the gig, like so many others he was already on board, and she was still getting to know him. His reddish-brown mustache matched his hair, and his burly build made him look like he could be a teamster. So far, she'd found him efficient, but she was still figuring out his personality. He veered between being too serious and making crude jokes.

"Hey, you got a sec?" Todd asked.

"Um…sure…"

She hoped Skye would stick around, but she slipped away while Todd chatted to her about Monday's scenes.

Andie passed the afternoon circulating, talking to as many of the team as she could. People floated in and out of the restaurant, the staff serving up canapes and pizzas. It was the kind of party where the fun was infectious, the conversations flowing as freely as the booze.

She searched for another chance to speak to Skye, but there was always someone who wanted her attention. Besides, every time she laid eyes on her, Teri clung to her side. She was starting to wonder what that was about. It seemed like such a close relationship, like Teri wanted to be around her all the time. Not that it was any of her business.

When it was dark someone started a bonfire on the beach. Exhausted from all the talking, she saw an opportunity to grab some time on her own. The party had been split in two, and nobody would notice if she left. It was late enough to go to bed, but she didn't want to try to sleep when there was still so much noise. She passed by the crackling fire, letting all the singing and shouting fall away, slowing as she got to her secluded spot.

Her heart thumped. Skye was here. "Hey. Hope I'm not interrupting anything?"

"Oh, no. Hey. Of course not. Stay."

When Andie sat down, she accidentally brushed against Skye's shoulder.

"What is that? What are you wearing?"

"What do you mean?"

"I can feel something fuzzy."

"Fuzzy? Oh, this? What I'm wearing? It's a blanket."

"Good idea," Andie said. It was as cold as it ever got here, her skin pricking in the night air.

"Are you cold? Here, you can have some," Skye slurred.

"No, that's okay…"

She ignored her and draped the blanket over Andie's shoulders, smoothing it down with her hand. "Thanks," she said, grabbing the edge and pulling it around her legs.

"You want some wine?"

She heard the cork being pulled, and there was a strong smell of strawberries and plum. She'd never liked red wine even when she was a drinker, but for a second she was tempted anyway. She liked the idea of having her lips where Skye's had just been.

"No thanks."

"You don't drink at all, do you?" Skye asked after a pause.

"No, I don't. Not anymore."

"Do you mind that I'm drinking? I'm sorry about that. I can get rid of this if you want. I don't care."

"Oh no, not at all. I don't mind, honestly."

"Okay. Good."

"What are you doing down here, all by yourself, anyway?"

She felt Skye shrug against her. "I dunno. I just like to be by myself sometimes. Everyone's nice, but I felt a little out of place. What about you?"

The stars overhead shone brightly, and she could see Skye staring. She looked down, pulling the blanket around herself again. She'd only come to this spot because she'd thought Skye might be here. She hadn't admitted that to herself until now. "The same, I guess. I had fun today, and I don't want to seem like I'm complaining, but I'm not good at being around a lot of people all the time."

"Same here. I come from kind of a big family. Lots of cousins. I was always slinking off to get a moment to myself."

They talked about her brothers, Skye making her laugh by telling her how they'd pranked one another as kids. They hid rotten food in pockets and drew on one another with markers while the victim was sleeping. The way she told the stories, they had never grown out of it.

"You must miss them. I know it's a long time to be away on location. And you're here the whole time. I've got half my family with me, between Dad and Cary."

"I do miss them. I'm from San Diego, and they're still there, so it's always been easy to head home on breaks. But I'm okay. We're all used to my traveling for work. Besides, I have Teri here. She's become like a sister."

"Yeah. Travel comes with the gig, I guess. It's a crazy career we both chose, huh? What made you want to become an actress, anyway? You didn't grow up around it like I did, so I wondered."

"I don't know. I just always loved movies so much. I was a dreamer from when I was a little kid. I started doing it before I understood how crazy it was to think I could make it. But I did. And here we are. And it's a strange business, totally. Weird to think I might've been pulled from this job. I could have ended up on some other movie. I could be in LA right now, or New York," she said. She sounded like she wasn't upset about the attempt to recast her role anymore.

The breeze bought the smell of the ocean and Skye's hair, too. It wasn't enough that their shoulders were pressed together, and Andie wished she could put her arm around her. She sat on her hands, the stone hard and cold beneath her.

"I hope you know how happy I am that you weren't replaced. I can't imagine anyone else doing it now. I was stupid."

When Skye sloppily reached under the blanket and put a hand on her knee, Andie held her breath.

"It's okay. It's okay. We're past all that. We don't need to keep thinking about it."

"All right. Thanks. I just want you to know I mean it," she said, and discreetly moved her knee.

After a long moment, Skye pulled her hand away, wine sloshing in the bottle when she took another swig. "Thanks for saying it, then."

"If you don't mind asking, how did you find out about it, anyway? I always wondered about that."

"Oh, yeah, we never talked about that," she giggled.

"What's so funny?"

"I can laugh about it now, but it was so awkward."

"Why?"

"Okay. I'm going to tell you."

"Okay..." she said, dying to know why Skye was drawing it out so much.

"Dana Rivers told me."

Andie scrubbed a hand over her face. They hadn't spoken directly to one another, but she'd made it clear to Dana's agent that it was top secret. "I had no idea you two knew each other."

"We don't, really. It was at a party."

"What, and you just got talking about it? No offense to her, but she's a loudmouth. I can't believe she did that. Her agent was given strict instructions that she wasn't supposed to talk about it."

"Yeah, she said that, actually."

"And she just went ahead and did it anyway, huh? Plus, I can't believe she told you when you don't even know one another that well. That makes it even worse."

"It wasn't like that. Not exactly."

"Don't worry, I'm not going to say anything. You're not going to get Dana in trouble. I just want to know how it all came about."

"Well...She was worried I'd be mad at her. That's the reason she said it. She thought I might already know or something..."

Andie frowned. Maybe Skye was drunker than she thought because this story made no sense. "I don't understand."

Skye took a deep breath. "We were kind of on a date, actually. It wasn't going that well. She thought the role was the reason why."

Andie didn't know what to say. She had been hanging out in the lesbian scene for years. Her parents were forward-thinking people and growing up around the business meant she had more gay role models than she could count. She wasn't usually this shocked about someone coming out to her, but she could have been knocked over with a feather right now.

"I didn't know you two were dating. I mean, why would I, I guess, I just…" she trailed off, running a hand through her hair.

God, she was so jealous. It never occurred to her to feel like this over Darryl—not when she thought Skye was straight. But Dana Rivers? That was another story.

"Yeah, it was the first date. What a mess. It would have to be one of the worst first dates in history."

"Are you still seeing each other?" Andie said, trying to sound casual, though she had a thousand questions on her mind.

Skye let out a peal of laughter. "No way. Not after that. Like I said, it was the worst first date ever. She really thought I was mad at her from the start, but I had no idea. It's funny now, but it was so awkward when it was happening."

Andie listened while she went over the story again, filling in more detail. "And she was like, don't be mad, let's just get this out of the way and talk about it."

Andie laughed at her dead-on impersonation of Dana, who had a British accent. Soon she was laughing so hard that her stomach hurt.

They huddled under the blanket together, pulled into one another's warmth.

CHAPTER NINETEEN

Skye woke up feeling like her mouth was stuffed with cotton wool, her head pounding. Caught up in the festive atmosphere, she'd had more to drink than usual. A glass of water sweated on her nightstand, and she drank greedily from it.

Last night's conversation with Andie returned to her, making her groan into the glass. Even with her patchy memory, she knew she'd said more than she wanted. Lately, she'd been thinking about slowly letting people in her life know about her sexuality, but she and Andie weren't that close. Telling her about it felt like too much, too soon.

It was the last thing she felt like doing, but she was due to meet with Darryl to go over tomorrow's big scene. Checking the time, she realized the restaurant would have started serving breakfast. A big breakfast would make her feel better, so she forced herself to get up.

When she came downstairs, Teri was tidying the kitchen. She'd drunk even more wine than Skye but didn't look it, all clear skin and bright eyes.

"Hey, you. Want me to make some toast?"

"Thanks, but I thought I'd head over to the restaurant to have a hot one. I could do with some grease. Would you like to come with me?"

"No, thanks. I already had some fruit and stuff. Want one of these?"

"Yes, please," she said, gratefully accepting a glass of orange juice.

"How was your night, anyway? You disappeared for a while."

"It was good, good. I was down on the beach for a while, talking to Andie."

"At the bonfire? I didn't see you guys there."

"No, down the beach a bit."

"Just the two of you?"

"Yep. I was down there at my little spot, and she happened along, so we had a talk."

"Oh, yeah? Anything interesting?" Teri said as she wiped the countertop, eyes darting over to Skye.

Skye looked over her shoulder, checking the living room was empty. Right now, her need to confide in someone was bigger than her fear of what Teri might think. "I told her about Dana, actually. I hope she doesn't tell anyone. You don't think she would, do you?"

Teri paused, cloth in hand. "You told her you went on a date with Dana?"

"I was pretty drunk."

"I have no idea if she'd tell anyone. I don't mean to worry you, but I wouldn't assume she'd do the right thing."

"I'll talk to her. Make sure she understands how private I am, especially about this," she said, sliding off her seat and taking the last mouthful of juice.

"I think that's a good idea."

The restaurant was full of people who looked as rough as she felt, piling their plates with bacon, eggs, and pancakes. She wasn't up for talking to anyone, so she sat in the corner at a table by herself. She was shaking hot sauce onto her meal when she glanced up and locked eyes with Andie, who was putting her empty tray on the counter.

Skye looked back down at her plate. In an instant, she'd taken in Andie's thighs in her tight jeans. She had a flashback of drunkenly laying her hand on her knee. She'd moved her leg away like it burned. Shit. She could feel eyes on her as she shakily sliced up a fried egg.

"Hi."

She knew it was Andie before she looked up. She tried to smile but couldn't quite make it. She did need to speak with her, but she couldn't face it now. "Morning."

"How are you doing?"

"Oh, you know. Tired. Drank a little too much. How are you?"

"Doing good, thanks. A little tired, too, from staying up so late."

"Right," Skye said, fork poised over her plate. Her stomach rumbled, but she was too self-conscious to eat in front of Andie. She'd talked so much last night, and it must've been annoying. They'd sat on the beach for hours, so she had no idea what time they'd walked back up to go to bed.

In the long silence, the smile disappeared from Andie's face. Skye looked down and pushed food around on her plate, stomach lurching. She hadn't meant to act coldly. She just couldn't think of anything to say.

"Okay, well, you have a good day. I hope you feel better."

"Thanks."

As she passed, she put a hand on Skye's shoulder. She leaned down, whispering, "Don't worry. I've got no interest in spreading your business around, okay?"

Skye nodded gratefully. She wasn't sure what affected her more, Andie's touch or how she was looking into her eyes. She exhaled heavily when she was gone, then raised her fork to her lips.

"Sorry. I just woke up," Darryl said, answering the door in pajama bottoms and a white vest.

"That's okay. I can come back later if you want?"

"No, no, please, come in. Just give me a minute. I'll take the world's quickest shower, I promise."

Their living area layout was the same. Skye sat on the sofa, absently picking up a magazine from the coffee table. She rolled her eyes when she realized she was thumbing through a *Playboy*. She was about to set it down when she turned the page and admired a long-legged brunette dressed as a firefighter. She looked a little like Andie. Did this mean she had a type, after all?

She threw it back on the table. Someone was coming down the stairs. Her eyes widened when Cary came around the corner with Sid. She was wearing what must be one of his shirts. It hung almost to her knees, which was lucky because she wasn't wearing much else. Sid, clad only in black shorts, was scratching his bare chest.

"Hey, Skye, what's shaking?" he asked. Cary grinned and waved hello.

"Nothing much. Here to do some work with Darryl. He's just gone to take a shower."

"Well, I am most certainly not working today." He opened the fridge and got out bottles of tomato juice and vodka, making Skye's stomach turn. He bit the end of a celery stick and chewed loudly.

"You want a Bloody Mary?" Cary asked.

"No, thank you."

"Have you seen Andie this morning?"

"Oh, yeah. I saw her at breakfast."

"Your little sister's a cool chick," Sid said.

"She's a brat, but I love her. Don't you love her, Skye?"

"She's great," she said, feeling like her smile was painted on because Cary was looking at her oddly. She tried to shake it off. This hangover was making her paranoid.

By the time Darryl returned, they'd taken their highball glasses up to Sid's room, leaving the bottles and an extra Bloody Mary on the counter.

"Sid and Cary were here. They thought you might want one."

"I can't think of anything worse right now. I had way too much to drink last night."

"I know. Me, too."

"Sorry again about not being ready when you came over. I didn't mean to be unprofessional."

"No problem. We all had a late night."

"Yeah. I actually came back here and talked to Heather for a couple of hours."

"That's nice. What time was it over there?"

"Not sure exactly, but it was morning. She's a saint to listen to me ramble on."

They sat side by side on the sofa, their scripts in front of them on the coffee table. They hadn't rehearsed this newly written scene, and she hadn't done more than learn her lines and make a few notes.

She hoped that they'd be able to work out some good stuff this morning. They'd played a couple before, but not since they'd ended things. As much as she didn't care for this storyline, they had to ensure their chemistry was believable. If the secret plan with Andie didn't work out, they couldn't look like they were phoning it in on the love story.

It was challenging to switch gears toward the romantic arc. Skye hadn't told anyone—not even Andie—but she'd always thought of Dr. Foster as a lesbian. It was probably the reason she'd always related to her. It wasn't explicit in the text, but she'd imagined dropping enough crumbs that people who wanted to see it would be able to.

They ran the scene, working at different angles and figuring out what beats to hit. The second time, they went all the way to the end. They moved together and mimed when they got to the kiss, laughing awkwardly as they pulled away.

Darryl picked up his script and flipped through the pages, not looking at it.

"What's up?" she asked. She thought they were doing a decent job, especially for a rehearsal.

"I wasn't sure if I was going to bring this up today, but…"

"It's okay. Go ahead. Do you want to try it a different way?"

"Listen, I know this probably wasn't what you wanted. You lost some excellent stuff when they made the changes. I can imagine how you might feel about it, which sucks."

"I guess I was a little disappointed. But I like the new stuff, too. Of course."

With those piercing blue eyes, he stared at her. He got up and went over to the kitchen. "Sorry, I didn't even ask you if you wanted anything to drink."

"Water would be great, thanks."

He sat down, putting two glasses in front of them. "Okay. So, Heather told me I should talk to you about this last night, and I think she was right."

"Talk about what?"

"I don't want to offend you, but I've been getting this funny feeling sometimes when we're shooting. That you're more upset than you let on about the changes."

"What makes you say that?"

"Some takes you're just nailing it, and we're playing off one another so well. Then out of nowhere, you do something completely different, and it feels like you're trying to ruin the scene or something. But I know you'd never do that, so I've really wondered about it."

"I don't know what to say," she said, putting her drink on the table.

"I'm not trying to insult you or your performance. Please believe me when I say that. The takes when you're on the money are fantastic. Something's up, though. Tell me I'm not going crazy?"

She listened to him sigh. She'd lied to him so much, and she didn't want to do it anymore. She hated it. "It's not in your head. I'm sorry. I wanted to experiment with the scenes and give Andie the option to dial back our romance in the cut."

He slumped back against the sofa. "Jesus, okay. So Andie knows about it?"

"She does. Just her. I'm sorry. The more who know about it, the more likely we'd be to get caught. With her dad and his best friend being the producers, it's a delicate situation."

"Yeah, I get that."

"Say something?"

"Now, I don't know what to say. I mean, I'm not opposed to doing that. I just wish I'd known about it."

"You're not opposed to it?"

"Not necessarily. That's the movie I signed on for. I didn't get into this business to just please the money people, you know that. I want to make good movies. I want to play character parts and be a good actor."

She slowly turned toward him. "I thought you were super happy with the changes."

"I'm okay with them, but it's not as good. Is it? It's simple, now. Adrian's a fairly straightforward character. No nuance. I liked it better before when it was so different from all the other movies like this."

She looked down at her hands, tracing the line of her palm with a finger. "I owe you an apology. I'm sorry I wasn't honest. And I'm sorry about everything else, too."

"I've thought about all that, a lot. Talked it through with Heather. I'm not blameless. When it came to us, I saw what I wanted to see."

"How do you mean?"

"I ignored anything that went against the story I was telling myself. I knew deep down you didn't feel the same way as I did. Sometimes I guilted you about that. I don't like how I was with you. I didn't want to let you go, and it was selfish of me."

"I don't like how I acted, either. I don't think you were selfish, but I was at times."

When she snuck a look at him, his eyes were wet, like hers.

"I'm happy now. I want you to be happy, too."

"I'd really, really like that," she said, and he gave her a loose hug, one arm around her. It felt so different and infinitely more comfortable, hugging as friends.

"Heather sounds great."

"She is. There's something else. I think there's stuff you haven't been telling me, and it's your business, of course, you don't have to. But I mean it, about wanting you to be happy. In whatever form that comes."

"Thank you," she said, but there was no way she was ready for that.

After patting her on the back one last time, he moved away and cracked a smile. "So, are we going to do this thing or not?"

"Are you for real?"

"I'm one hundred percent for real. I want in. Let's figure out how we can make it work."

CHAPTER TWENTY

Skye jogged to their villa. She wasn't sure whether she was more excited about bringing Darryl into the plan or telling Andie about it. She took the stairs two at a time and smiled when she saw the closed bedroom door, knowing it meant Andie was inside.

Her heart came into her mouth when Andie answered. She smiled at Skye like she was just as happy to see her, even though she had no idea why she was here.

"I hope I'm not disturbing you? I wouldn't have come by to talk to you on a Sunday, but it's important."

"Don't be silly. I'm always happy to talk. Come on in. I was out on the deck, going through shot lists."

Skye followed her outside onto the tiled space that matched her own. On the way through Andie's room, she snuck a peek. It was neat as a pin, a stack of books with the corners perfectly lined up on her nightstand.

Two chairs were pulled together, like she'd been sitting on one with her feet on the other. A notebook, binder, and pen sat on the small round table. She dusted one of the chairs off with a hand and offered it to Skye.

"I was just over at Darryl's place, working on tomorrow's scenes, and we had a very interesting conversation."

"Oh, yeah?"

"Yep. I was totally wrong about it all going over his head. He knew something was up. He asked me about it."

"But you don't look like you're worried about it?"

"No need. He was cool about it. He wants to help."

This morning, Skye had been so worried that she hadn't thought clearly about that closeness last night under the blanket. Although Andie didn't drink, she hadn't made Skye feel silly, then or now. Andie now eyed her with even more intensity than usual. She seemed to be hanging on Skye's every word.

Andie's reputation was so misleading. Sure, maybe she wasn't great with relationships, but Skye felt lucky to have the chance to get to know her. She was so attentive, always making her feel special somehow.

"Darryl wants to help? And you're not worried that he'll give the game away like you thought?"

"Not anymore. I mean, he picked it up pretty early by the sound of it. Even though he was suspicious, he carried on and kept reacting to me as though he didn't know. He thinks he can keep doing that."

"Wow. I'm glad. I mean, *really* glad. That's such a relief. It didn't sit that well with me, for him to not know."

"Me neither. And the best part is, he's eager to film the scene where I kill Adrian."

Andie smiled, but she shook her head. "I'm so grateful that you both want that. It means so much that you were even talking about it. It would be wonderful, but I just don't see how we could get away with that. It'd be so risky."

Skye nodded, having expected it. She was prepared for an argument because they'd gone over everything at Darryl's. "It would be risky, but we can reduce that risk by having fewer people around. We tell everyone that we're doing a love scene and need a closed set. Then, we find some reason to shoot the other scene alongside the kissing scene."

Andie leaned back, Skye staring at her stomach because her shirt had ridden up, showing a sliver of skin. She forced herself to pay attention to what her director was saying.

"And how would we know that word wouldn't get out? I don't see how it couldn't, with something like that. It only takes one person to blab."

"I know, but it cuts any chance way down. We've got a story to tell them. The crew respects you, and Darryl's tight with a lot of the guys. I think between the two of you, we can feel pretty safe. Who would we need?"

"Well, we could just have the three of us, a camera operator, and the boom guy. It's not a love scene, though. Just a kissing scene. I'm not sure anyone would buy the need for a closed set."

"Right, exactly. Darryl said he could spin a story about protecting us both. He'd say that we're self-conscious about being exes but also thinking of making the scene racier than it is in the script. We want the freedom to change it."

"Okay, so take me through this story you mentioned. To stop it from getting out. What would you say?" Andie asked thoughtfully. Her hand was under her chin, and she tapped her cheek.

"We say that it's important to us to shoot the scene, just once, to see how it would've looked. For sentimental reasons, but we don't intend to use it. We stress to them that we don't want it leaking. We just do one or two, so we're not using a lot of film or going overtime."

"Interesting, but do you think you could both nail it in such a short timeframe? It's an intense scene, and we'd have to be so quick."

"We've been working at it all day. I think we can. And Darryl wants to rehearse it with you there so that it's as ready as it can be for tomorrow."

Andie bit her thumbnail and frowned. Skye was scared she would dismiss the whole idea.

"I'd have to talk to Louise about keeping it out of the dailies. That means letting another person in on what we've been doing."

"Do you trust her?" Skye asked. She'd only met the film's editor a few times.

"I think so. It's a gamble but fuck it, I'm in. It means so much that you guys would do this."

Skye got up, loving how Andie rubbed her hands together like she couldn't wait to get to work. Then, Andie reached out and put her arms around Skye, frozen for a moment before she relaxed into it.

Being in Andie's arms stole the breath from her lungs. She smelled like heaven, and she could feel her breasts pressing against her chest. She wondered if Andie could feel how her heart raced. Putting her hands lightly on Andie's back, she resisted pulling Andie into her. Her breath was on her cheek.

She didn't want to let go. It was over way too fast, and as Andie pulled away, their cheeks brushed.

It took everything she had to not turn her head and kiss her.

CHAPTER TWENTY-ONE

Andie barely slept on Sunday night. If the producers knew what she was doing, she'd be in a world of trouble. Her father would be furious, not only because he'd see it as a waste of money and valuable time. He was the great Doug McKenzie who'd helmed modern classics, and she was acting like she knew better. The thing was that earlier in his career, he'd also clashed with the studios. He and his friends had challenged the system, and now he couldn't see that he'd become the very thing he'd railed against.

He should understand that she simply had to do this, even if it was crazy. Skye and Darryl were willing to go out on a limb for her, and that was even more reason to do it. Scenes like this were why she wanted to be a filmmaker. Her greatest ambition was to make a movie that shook people, so they couldn't stop talking about it when they left the theater.

When she was still tossing and turning at four in the morning, she gave up. As she walked downstairs, she picked up a rich coffee smell. Skye stood at the counter with a glass of orange juice. Even first thing in the morning, with her face bare and her hair in a messy ponytail, she looked stunning. Her light blue shirt brought out her eyes, and her baggy jeans looked soft and comfortable.

"Morning. I knew you'd be up soon, so I made coffee. I hope I made it how you like it."

"I'm sure you did. Thanks. You couldn't sleep either, huh?"

"Nope, too excited."

"You want some?" Andie said, after pouring herself a cup. She held out the pot.

"No thanks."

"Why don't you drink coffee, anyway? Some people say it makes them feel jittery—is it that?"

"Not that. I don't know. I just never got into it."

"Try some. This is the best stuff. I brought my own Colombian beans with me."

"I couldn't use any of your magic beans. What if you run out? I'd never be able to forgive myself."

Andie put the pot back on the warmer and fetched a second cup. "I'm getting you some. You need to try these beans, just once."

"Okay, if you insist," Skye replied, going to the fridge and returning with milk.

Andie circled her wrist with fingers, gently pulling her hand away. "No, no, no. I can't let you do that."

"What do you mean?"

"That stuff is criminal. Try it without, and I promise if you don't like it, I won't stop you."

"Pushy. But I will if you want me to," she said, and Andie noticed how her voice curled around the words, almost seductively.

"I have strong feelings about this. Would you like to sit out on the front porch? It's nice out there at this time of the morning."

They sat on the front step with their drinks cupped between their hands.

"Have you tasted it yet?" Andie asked, nodding toward Skye's drink, and blowing the top of her own.

"Not yet," she said, breathing in the smell before taking a sip.

"Do you like it? Do you want me to go in and get the milk?"

"No, I actually do like it. It's bitter, but in a nice way."

"Ah, you have good taste. And listen, again, thanks so much for working things out with Darryl. I can't believe we're actually going to do this."

"That's okay. I didn't really do much, except for getting busted."

"Still worked out. Can I ask you something?"

"Is it about Darryl and me?"

"How did you know?"

"Lucky guess. You can go ahead and ask. I don't mind."

Since finding out about Skye and Dana, Andie was obsessed with figuring out what it meant. She'd never heard any rumors about Skye's sexuality, nor had she ever heard anything that hinted the relationship with Darryl was for show. Did she mainly date men, and Dana was a one-off? Was she open to serious relationships with women, or was she more into guys? It would be rude to ask those questions, but Darryl was a safe place to start.

"Yeah. I've been wondering if you don't mind me asking. You said you weren't that close? But you were together for a while, right?"

"We were together for a couple of years, on and off."

"So, it was pretty serious?"

"Not as serious as he wanted it to be. I guess you might want to know…After what I said the other night…"

"Sorry. I'm so nosy. You don't have to tell me anything," Andie said, taking a mouthful of coffee to shut herself up.

"No, it's okay. I tried to make it work, but I don't feel that way about guys. I feel pretty bad about how I treated him."

Skye's voice shook, making Andie wonder how much she'd spoken to anyone about this. The pressure to keep it quiet must be immense. Her own sexuality was an open secret in Hollywood because she could afford it to be. As a director, she didn't carry the weight of being a straight sex symbol.

"I'm sorry. Don't be too tough on yourself, though. It's not easy. That's what everyone wants from you. It's hard to go against that."

"What about you?"

"I was just thinking about how different it is for me. I've had a few comments and things like that. Sometimes I think it's more about me being a female director than anything else. But things are changing slowly. And people aren't so interested in who I date."

"Sure, but I mean, did you ever do that? Before you were totally comfortable? Try and date men?"

"No, I didn't. I figured out early on that I only like women."

"I wish I could say the same. I think I always knew. It just took me a long time to admit it to myself. I would've saved myself a lot of pain if I'd done that."

"That's the thing about life, though. We can't be totally free of pain, no matter how hard we might try," Andie said, laying a consoling hand on Skye's knee.

Andie knew right away that the touch was too intimate. It was the kind of thing she'd do with a friend, but she wanted it too much for it to be innocent. The moment she realized it, she started to move away. Her stomach flipped when Skye stopped her, putting a hand on top of hers.

They stayed in that heart-stopping pose, Skye's palm resting on her skin and setting it alight. They each stared straight ahead. She wished she knew whether Skye found this comforting, or if there was more to it.

Three years ago, she would have found out by kissing her, right here on the front step. She wouldn't have cared about the risk of getting caught or the consequence.

They drank their coffee, the thrill of Skye's hand on hers not diminishing with time. Skye moved her thumb, playing over her skin. Andie kept expecting her to say something. Maybe when she was finished with her coffee, she would pull away. It was like a timer ticking down, but before she could reach the bottom of her cup, Skye took her hand away and jumped up.

It took a while to register the sounds coming from the kitchen behind them. Andie looked up at her. Skye's face was flushed.

"Teri's up. Would you like another cup?"

"No, thanks."

"Well, thanks for the coffee. You converted me."

"Glad to hear it."

Skye left, and Andie tried to regain her composure. When she shifted, she felt how turned on she was. It had been a long time for her, but it was much more than that. Whatever this was, it had been building without her noticing. Now, there was no putting the genie back in the bottle.

Everything about Skye got her going.

CHAPTER TWENTY-TWO

They were filming up near the tree line, the characters sheltering under the canopy. Andie, Skye, and Darryl had come down late the day before, checking out the area to make sure it would work as a double for the death scene. They hadn't found any reason why it couldn't.

Andie gathered the skeleton crew to talk. True to their plan, there was only herself, one camera operator, the boom guy, and the actors on the set. Carol had cleared everyone from the monitors, relaying that the actors were uncomfortable with being watched as they shot the love scene, even from a distance.

This production was her first time working with both crew members, but she trusted them. Enough, anyway. The camera operator, Frankie, had worked on a couple of her father's movies but didn't seem overly loyal to him. An old-school professional, he just wanted to do his job and go home.

The boom guy, Joel, was less of a known quantity, but he and Darryl were tight. They had a beer together most nights, and she was confident that he'd keep it to himself if Darryl asked him to. Joel and Frankie would only know part of the story, anyway.

When she'd briefed the crew, Andie, Darryl, and Skye stood in a tight circle a few feet away from the set.

"You both all good to go for Plan A? Are there any questions?" asked Andie.

They'd joked about code names the night before. The kissing scene was Plan A, the murder scene Plan B. Skye shook her head, all business. You'd never know they had been holding hands a couple of hours ago.

"Just to check in, when you tell us we've got it, that's when I'll start acting unsatisfied. That's the moment I say I want to talk to you, right?" Darryl asked.

"Perfect," she said, patting his shoulder. He must be nervous as fuck because they'd gone over this a million times last night.

They got into their places, in the sand under the trees. Andie made an effort to forget about Plan B and readied herself to direct them to a successful Plan A.

"We shouldn't be doing this," Darryl said, after a kiss, running his arms up and down Skye's shoulders.

"I know, we shouldn't. I can't seem to help it," she said, hand behind his neck as they kissed again.

Andie cleared her throat. She'd directed plenty of kissing scenes, but she'd never felt this way before. She had to detach because she'd feel jealous if she didn't. It was stupid. They turned on the heat for the camera, but she knew it was awkward for them as well.

Between takes, they pulled away as soon as the word "cut" was out of her mouth, then chatted with studied indifference.

They ran the takes and angles, her discomfort growing when Darryl lifted Skye's tank top over her head. They'd agreed that she would be stripped down to her bra, and he would end up shirtless. They were both happy to do it, partly because it lent more credibility to the request for a closed set.

When Darryl tried to unbutton his top, it got stuck, and they giggled. Andie called for a reset and watched them make out all over again.

This time, when Skye's tank top was off, Andie's gaze slipped. She brought it back up as soon as she was sure everything looked like it should for the camera. Still, she couldn't help catching a glimpse of Skye's taut stomach and the perfect swell of her breasts. She didn't want to take advantage of her position, but Jesus Christ, Skye's body was incredible. She wished she could fill her eyes with it and never stop looking.

"Cut!" she squeaked when they'd been going at it long enough.

There were no assistants around, so she went over to the pair herself. She handed a robe to Skye first, carefully maintaining eye contact.

"Thanks."

Darryl waved the offer away. "Everyone's seen what I've got."

They laughed because it was true. He spent all his downtime hanging out by the pool in his trunks.

"Okay. I think we got it. Well done, both of you," Andie said after they'd nailed the close-ups. If the sequence ended up in the movie, it was the best version they could deliver.

Frankie and Joel looked at one another as if to say, "that's it?" Of course, she'd known they'd question why there'd been a closed set. She was ready for it. She spoke loudly as she approached the actors.

"I appreciate that you were both willing to go further, but I think we've got enough. Did it feel that way to you?"

Skye rubbed her palms on her jeans, and thankfully Darryl barged in. She would have to thank him later for knowing that the guys would buy it more if he took the lead.

"Definitely. It was at just the right level. I don't want to do more than that."

"Yeah, me neither," Skye added.

"But there is something I'd like to run by you. I probably shouldn't say it. Actually, yeah, never mind," Darryl said, frowning thoughtfully.

"It's okay. You can ask. What is it?"

"Well, I know this is a weird request, but Skye and I put a whole lot of work into the murder scene in the early days, before the changes. Don't get me wrong, I love this new stuff, but I don't suppose we could just do a couple of takes. Film it for posterity."

Andie did her best to look surprised, raising her eyebrows. "Oh. Really? It's that important to you?"

"Yeah. I guess I was thinking about it because it's almost a mirror image scene of this one. They're up close and personal, and it takes place at around the same time in the script. Do you know what I mean? I think it'd be so interesting to just try it."

"I was thinking about it, too!" Skye said. "The exact same thing about it feeling like a mirror. That's crazy. I'd like to do it, too. I mean, it wouldn't take long. It'd be cool to do it just for the hell of it."

"Please, Andie? It'd be fun. I won't tell anyone you let us do it. Just to see."

"We don't need anything extra. We could do it right here. Hey, I've even got the prop gun," Skye said. They didn't have to do anything to make that happen. The character had been wearing it in the scene beforehand, so it was still strapped to her ankle for continuity.

Joel and Frankie were standing off to the side smoking cigarettes, but Andie knew they were listening. She stretched and rubbed her forehead. Tried to look like she was thinking about it, calculating whether it was worth indulging the actors.

"What do you think, guys? Do you mind helping out with this? We didn't do many takes, so we can afford the film. It'll only take a little while."

"Sure, why not? No skin off my nose," Frankie said, shrugging.

"Mine neither."

Darryl held his hands up, looking sheepish. "You fellas aren't going to say anything to anyone, are you? I'd look kind of silly. And the suits wouldn't like us spending the time on it, but it'll only take an hour or two, if that. Can we keep this just between us?"

"Scout's honor," Frankie said, looking like he didn't care either way while Joel eagerly nodded along.

Andie feigned thinking it over again. "I never did a shot list, but I think we do a wide shot, close up for the conversation, then a medium. The shot of her firing the weapon can be low, looking up at Skye."

During their workshopping of the murder, they'd agreed that they wouldn't film Adrian's lifeless body. That would mean using fake blood and bringing in more people. She was confident about going around it with reaction shots from Skye. It wouldn't matter that they weren't set up for the gunshot. They could focus on her face and loop in a sound effect.

They started rolling. She could see how nervous Skye was, but she used it. They ratcheted up the tension, showing off a dynamic that couldn't be more different from what they'd done before. She had expected Skye to be brilliant, but she was impressed with Darryl, too. He was genuinely menacing.

When it was time to change angles for the image of Skye shooting the gun, they quickly rearranged everything, barely breaking the flow.

Skye was a powerhouse. Tears ran down her face while her expression remained blank. It was the kind of crying that happened when you didn't even know you were doing it. She walked a few paces and dropped to her knees, the gun falling from her hand. She let out a cry that made Andie's hair stand on end.

There was a long silence when it was finished. Finally, Andie called, "Cut."

Another beat, before Frankie and Joel clapped. "Holy shit. Don't take this the wrong way, guys. What we shot today was good, but that was even better. You should put it in the movie."

"Don't be dumb, Joel," Frankie said, lighting a smoke. "Can't just whack it in there. It wouldn't make sense with the rewrites. I agree, though. That was something."

When they were packing up their equipment to move on to the next location, Andie stood next to Skye. She was staring out toward the sea, drinking from a water bottle while Darryl chatted to the guys.

"Do you think it worked? We got it?" said Skye.

"In normal circumstances, I'd have liked to get more coverage, but I think it'll be okay. I think we got it," Andie replied, adrenaline still coursing through her body.

"That's great. I can't believe it."

"Me neither. I can't tell you how grateful I am for making this happen. I know you're putting yourself on the line for the movie. Thanks again."

"Well, there was something in it for me. That was the most exhilarating scene I've ever shot."

Andie took in how Skye stood with her shoulders back, and her chin tipped up. She looked like a warrior. "You were incredible. Really. It gave me chills."

"Thanks," Skye said softly. She reached down between them, grabbing Andie's hand for just a moment.

When she squeezed, so did Andie's heart.

CHAPTER TWENTY-THREE

Skye breathed in the crisp morning air and savored another mouthful of coffee. She'd worked up a taste for it, but maybe she only liked it so much because Andie made it for her.

"I love that sound. The birdsong. I don't think I've ever paid attention to that at home," Andie said, from next to her on the front steps. They were sitting so close that their thighs touched.

"Me neither. It's beautiful."

Skye had been waiting for this moment all week. Every morning, she set her alarm early, trying to orchestrate time alone with Andie. They'd been working long hours, so she needed to grab the opportunity before starting the day. The only other thing she could think of was knocking on her door at night which would require more courage than she had.

So, there was only the morning, and the plan always failed no matter how carefully she timed things. Either Andie was already at the restaurant, or on the set. More often, Teri was in the kitchen.

Everything had finally lined up this morning. Nobody else was downstairs. When they greeted one another, Andie gave her the same sly smile she'd been shooting her all week when no one was looking. That smile turned Skye's knees to jelly, like everything else about her.

Skye's heart thudded while she prepared to take Andie's hand. Last time, the feeling had been so powerful, and she couldn't wait to have it again. She looked down, charting a course to where Andie's hand rested on her own knee. All she had to do was shift her cup into her other hand so that her right would be free. She started to make her move.

At last, their hands touched. She soared. Andie had reached for her, too.

Andie jumped at the sound of clattering dishes, leaving Skye holding the air. The whole thing happened so fast, and she felt so cheated she wanted to scream. "Every goddamn time," Skye said quietly.

"Yeah, you know that's not an accident, right?"

"What do you mean?"

"I mean, I told you she didn't like me," Andie said, getting up. "Do you mind taking my cup in, please?"

"Of course."

Andie walked away toward the restaurant, with one last meaningful look back over her shoulder. Biting her lip, Skye watched the sway of Andie's hips in her tight, tight jeans. She wondered what it all meant. Was Andie genuinely interested in her, or was she just going along with it for kicks? She'd been with so many women that Skye might only be another notch on her belt. Nobody special.

The weird thing was that she flat-out didn't care. For the first time, Skye knew she had to go after what she wanted. Andie made her understand what it really meant to feel desire, a desire that seemed to be welcomed. Maybe even reciprocated. Nothing could stop her.

She got up slowly, her legs still shaky. Teri ran water at the sink, acting like she didn't even know Skye was out here. Andie was right about Teri not liking her, but it was hard to imagine her going as far as trying to stop them from getting close. Even the possibility of her overstepping like that made her deeply uncomfortable.

"Morning."

"Oh hey, morning. I was just going to start breakfast," Teri replied, closing the tap.

Skye checked the wall clock over Teri's head and then studied her face. Just like that, she knew Andie was right. "I'm surprised to see you this early. What are you doing up, anyway?"

"I don't know. Just woke up and thought I'd better get going."

"Right. You know you don't have to get up at the same time as me, don't you? It's not expected. If I don't have time to get my own breakfast, someone can bring it to me on set."

"I know. It's just a coincidence."

"Okay."

"So…what were you and Andie talking about out there?"

"Nothing."

"Is something wrong?"

Skye paused, not sure whether she should get into this now. She was going off a hunch, so maybe she should cool off before saying anything. Teri had come all this way to the island to work for her without a break, and she'd never put a foot wrong before.

"No, of course not. Just thinking about work, I guess."

"You're out at the lagoon today, right? For that scene where you find a new water source, cos you've been running out of drinking water? It's already looking to be a hot one."

"That's the one. A nice day for me to be getting in the water."

"So, did you want something to eat? Or will you wait until you get to set?"

"No, I'll eat now. I've got time. That would be great, thanks."

As she ate her yogurt and bran, she tried not to stare at Teri, thinking about all the times she'd asked her for relationship advice. Had she invited this by taking her into her confidence so much? Maybe it was natural for Teri to be protective, especially given Andie's reputation.

The problem was the underhandedness. Teri had taken it upon herself to interfere when they hadn't spoken about it. It was like she thought Skye couldn't be trusted to make her own decisions. It couldn't continue. She wouldn't let Teri screw things up between her and Andie, no matter how good her intentions.

Skye loved shooting out here, where the island felt untouched by their production save for their equipment. The sky was powder blue, the water in the lagoon as clear as liquid glass.

"Oh my God, I can't believe it. I thought we would be done for sure," she said, dipping a hand into the water.

"Holy shit. This must be the first lucky break we've got since this whole thing started," Sid said, balancing on one leg while he pulled the shoe and sock off his other foot.

"What are you doing?"

"What do you think I'm doing, Doc? I'm dirty, and I'm thirsty. I'm getting in there."

Dr. Foster leaned forward to peer into the water. She nodded to herself. "Okay, but I wouldn't drink it. We should boil it first, over the fire. It looks safe enough to swim in, I guess."

"I'm going in, too," Cary said, slipping off her sneakers.

The rest of the cast ran through their dialogue and shed parts of their costumes. There were six of them, plus the three principals. They ran or walked toward the water, some of them whooping with joy.

Skye bent to take the prop gun off her leg, but Sid cursed before she could get it off. She stopped, tamping down her irritation. It wasn't his fault, but things were moving slowly today.

"Sorry, guys. I slipped."

"No problem. Let's get you all out and dried," Andie said.

It was a good thing they'd had to stop before she got into the lagoon, so she didn't have to go back to the trailers yet again. After each dip, they all went through a costume change and had their hair blow-dried.

Skye went over to rest under the shade of a palm tree, sitting cross-legged on the soft grass. She wished she'd brought her novel with her today because she didn't feel like talking to anyone.

Carol walked around with water bottles. Skye motioned at her. For a second, it looked like Carol was going to keep walking. It was weird because she was sure she'd seen her right away.

But she headed over, and Skye got up to take the bottle, bringing her closer to a whole lot of skin. Carol had a great figure, and she wasn't shy about it. A black, lacy bra showed from under her low-cut tank top. Skye wondered if she was interested in women—she hung all over Andie in a way that went beyond sucking up to the boss.

"Thanks."

"Anything else?" Carol replied sharply.

"No, thank you so much," she said, smiling sweetly.

Carol turned from her without saying anything more. Skye rolled the cold water bottle along her forehead, looking around until she found Andie sitting in her chair, wearing jean shorts with a rip in the thigh. Even the skin showing there made her hot. This was getting ridiculous.

She was talking to the director of photography, the two of them pointing around the scenery, probably working on angles and framing. Carol walked up to them. Skye could see how closc Carol stood to Andie even from this distance. Andie's reaction was more difficult to gauge.

Skye looked away and uncapped her bottle. If something was going on between those two, the last thing she should be was surprised. Andie was known for sleeping with coworkers. Even if she said things were different now, how could Skye ever know it was true? Maybe Darryl was wrong, and people didn't really change.

The thought of Carol and Andie together made her so jealous she couldn't bear it. She bet they were doing a whole lot more than just holding hands. What if Andie thought she was childish because that was all they'd done?

She ripped out blades of grass until she finished her water, then lay down and threw an elbow over her face. This whole thing was a mess. Of all the women in the world, she'd fallen in lust with someone she couldn't count on. She wished she was into someone uncomplicated, like Dana. It was like her body had a mind of its own, and she had no choice.

A shadow passed over her. When she took her arm away and squinted up, Andie stood there.

"I'm sorry, were you napping?"

Skye sat up, brushing grass from the back of her shirt. "No, that's okay."

"You're not miked, are you?"

"When I'm coming in and out of the water? No, why, should I be?"

Andie crouched and pointed to the lagoon, tracing a line with her finger. "Just double-checking. How are you doing?"

Skye followed Andie's finger, frowning. "I don't get it. What am I looking at?"

"People could be watching so, we're talking about the scene. But I want to talk about some other stuff with you."

"Oh, right. Of course."

"Is that okay with you?"

"Sure. Whatever."

She had an awful feeling Andie was about to tell her she wasn't interested and that it had everything to do with Carol. Why else would she come over here to speak with her, right after the two of them were talking?

When she glanced at her, a half-smile was on her lips. "What are you mad about now?"

"I'm not mad."

"I think you are, and I'm going to take a wild guess and say it has something to do with Carol. I saw you looking over at us just now. Am I getting warm?"

"Maybe."

"Well, I know she has a certain energy around me, but just so you know, I'm not interested. She knows that."

"You're not?" Skye said, looking back at the lagoon when she remembered they were supposed to be talking shop.

"Nope. I might be interested in somebody else, but see, it's a complicated situation."

"It is?" she said, her heartbeat accelerating. Oh my God. It was mutual.

"Yes. And I have a lot of questions. And I'm not sure what's going on. Every time I think I might be about to figure it out, we get interrupted."

"I was thinking about it this morning after you left. I don't know why I didn't see it, but I think you're right about Teri. That she's doing it on purpose."

"Exactly. It's funny if you were wondering about Carol because if anyone should be jealous, I think it should be me. About Teri."

Skye was so shocked she forgot what they were doing and stared right at her. "Teri? Wait, what are you saying?"

"Have you two ever been a thing? Because she acts like it."

"That's way off base. We're just friends."

"I don't think she knows that."

"It's not like that. She's just protective of me."

"I don't know either of you that well, but it seems like more than that to me."

"Well, you're wrong," Skye said, but she was reeling. She'd never thought about it, and it sounded crazy, but something about the idea stuck. She tucked it away to think about later.

"Okay. If you say so. Well, I was wondering if we could find some time to talk. Somewhere we won't be interrupted by Teri or anyone else. Where nobody's watching."

"I could come to your room tonight. Or the other way around? After everyone else has gone to bed."

"Oh, my. You are forward." Andie smirked, and Skye was a goner. "Stop looking at me. Look at that crane over there, instead."

"Then stop saying crazy stuff. And you're looking at me, or you wouldn't know I was looking at you. Besides, that's not what I meant. It was just to talk."

"I thought of that, but I don't think it's a good idea with Teri downstairs, probably trying to listen. It's too tempting, as well."

"What, you think we can't resist doing something if there's a bed in the room? Speak for yourself," said Skye.

"I am. I'm not going to pretend I wouldn't find it hard to keep my hands to myself."

Skye picked out another blade of glass, twirling it between her fingers. The way Andie talked turned her on so much that it was overwhelming. "Okay, so where, then? The rest of the villa is completely out. Teri always seems to know when I'm up."

She snatched a look at Andie, who kept an eye on the crew. Those full lips were irresistible. Would she really get the chance to kiss her soon?

"The pool? Early in the morning or something?"

"I don't know. We could try, but someone always wants to talk to you. We'd probably get interrupted." Over Andie's shoulder, she could see Todd striding toward them. They still had some time, but not much.

"What's up?"

"Speak of the devil. Todd's coming. I'll try and think of something and let you know. Maybe the beach? That rock we sat on?"

Andie drummed her fingers on her leg, looking back over her shoulder. "Nah, too close to where people might hang out. What about right here? Nobody will be around tomorrow. We could walk here from the villas. It's not that far."

"Okay. What time?"

"In the morning, before they start the party. I'm usually in my room, so nobody would look for me except for Cary."

"And she's pretty busy with Sid, now."

"Exactly. We'll walk here separately. 11 a.m. See you then?"

"Yes," she said quickly just before Todd arrived, walkie-talkie in hand.

"Hey, ladies. Just got word that they're all dry and nearly done with makeup. Another ten."

"Great, thanks. We were just talking about Skye's body language as she gets near the water," Andie said smoothly.

"Cool," he replied, raising the walkie-talkie to his mouth when it started crackling.

They passed a look back and forth. In those green eyes, Skye could see her own feelings reflected. They wanted one another, and it made her stomach do somersaults.

Waiting until tomorrow was intolerable, but there was no other way.

CHAPTER TWENTY-FOUR

Andie checked her watch, quickening her pace. She hadn't left the villa as early as she had wanted. She'd had to shake off Cary in a chatty mood, having come home from Sid's place to shower.

There was just enough time to pick wildflowers on her way. When she arrived at the lagoon, she had a small pink and yellow bouquet.

Skye sat on the grassy bank, under the same tree where they'd talked yesterday. As she grew near, Andie felt like she was flying. Over the years, she'd forgotten how pure and simple this could be. A beautiful woman was waiting for her, everything between them fresh and new. Anything was possible.

"Hey, there. These are for you," she said, holding out the flowers and enjoying how it made Skye smile.

"Hello. Thank you. They're lovely."

Andie sat down next to her. Now she could look at Skye properly, and not having to hide it was a relief. She liked how she looked in the sun, her lips full and pink. Her skin was radiant against her floral summer dress.

The way she fiddled with the straps of that dress made Andie think she was nervous. She was scared too, but it was a good kind of fear. Like when she rode a motorcycle or drove too fast.

"Did you have any trouble getting away?" Andie asked.

"No. I told Teri I was going for a walk. She was on her way to help with setting up the party," she said, putting the flowers down in front of her and arranging them neatly on the grass.

"I hope you haven't been waiting long."

"Not too long. So, you said you had a lot of questions you wanted to ask me."

They were jumping right into this. That was okay because Andie had been thinking all night about what she wanted to say. She moistened her lips, noticing how Skye's gaze followed the movement.

"I was pretty surprised when you held my hand. Especially when you did it a second time. I didn't think you liked me. Let alone in that way."

"That wasn't a question."

"Was I wrong? About you not liking me?"

"I guess I changed my mind. But I always thought. Well, I thought you were attractive."

It surprised Andie how much she liked hearing it said aloud. Skye's actions had started to make it clear, but it was different hearing the words. "I'm happy you changed your mind."

"You didn't like me either."

"No, it was never that. I like you more now that I know you. But there was always something, I guess. You didn't notice me looking at you all the time?"

"I wasn't sure why. I couldn't tell what you were thinking."

Skye was staring at her mouth again. Andie told herself to be mature. Keep it slow and do what she came here to do. "Well, now you know. And I'd really like to act on it, but like I said, it's complicated with the movie."

"We'd have to be very discreet. I get that. That's fine."

"I think it's a little more than that," Andie said gently. "Don't you think it's a huge problem, our roles? Me being the director, and you being in my movie?"

"I guess on paper, sure. But it doesn't feel like that to me. You treat me like an equal, so I thought that was how you felt."

"Of course, I see you as an equal. Other people might see it differently. But either way, it's too risky. Look how hard we had to work to find time to talk to one another in private. As you know, I've made a bad name for myself in the past, and I need things to be different for this one. Not just for me. It's for you, too, and for everyone involved in the production."

"Okay. What are you saying, exactly?" Skye asked, pulling her legs underneath herself.

"That I'm very interested, but I think it's important to wait until after we wrap. When we get back to LA, I'd love to take you on a date."

The reaction wasn't what Andie had hoped for. Skye shook her head. She waited, wondering what she'd said wrong. Skye was so sensible and level-headed. She'd assumed she'd feel the same way about not doing anything right now. "What is it?"

"I'm not sure how to talk about this."

"It's okay. You can be direct. Let's get everything on the table while we can."

Skye stared out at the water, and Andie felt like she was going under. Something was wrong. The beautiful harmony that lived between them as they worked or talked was gone.

"I'm not sure I'll want that. Dating."

"Oh. You don't think you want to go out? You're not interested?" Andie asked, wondering if she was pulling off the neutral tone she was trying for. She was crushed. She'd spent all night talking herself out of so many worries. She went over the idea that it might be inappropriate even after they were done, that Skye was too young for her, Skye was too good for her. She'd only plucked up the courage for this because she thought it was a feeling that couldn't be pushed away.

"I wouldn't say that, exactly. I mean, I'm not sure."

"I'm trying to figure this out. Are you trying to tell me you just want something casual?"

"I think so? I'm sorry, but yes, I think so. I'm not looking for anything serious," Skye said, sounding relieved that they were coming to an understanding.

"You don't have to be sorry. You're just being honest."

Those flowers—Andie wished she could get rid of them. They just sat there, looking as stupid as she felt right now. The rejection felt like karmic justice. After all the women she'd hurt, she was learning what it was like to be on the other end. She'd never imagined how shitty it felt, and she wondered if any of those women had liked her as much as she liked Skye.

"I guess we want pretty different things, huh?" Skye said.

"We do. Please, don't look so worried. It's okay. I promise I won't treat you any differently because of all this. I wouldn't do that."

"Thank you for saying that. Same here, of course."

"At least we cleared things up, huh? We know where we stand," Andie said, flatly.

"Yes."

Andie crossed her legs, staring out at the lagoon. She wanted to get up and walk away, but she didn't want it to look like she couldn't handle it or needed comforting. She didn't want to lay a guilt trip on Skye, so she had to deal with the hurt and humiliation later.

"So, are you going to the party again?" said Andie.

"I guess so. You?"

"Yeah, for a bit. I'll get around and say hi to everyone, at least."

"Cool. I was just thinking. If you change your mind about what I said, you can let me know."

Andie grinned despite herself. Well, well. She never would have expected this, not from Skye. "Same to you. The offer will still be open after the shoot. I'm sure."

"Okay. I guess I just thought that we could try things out to see if anything was there. I don't know how either of us can be sure we're really interested when we haven't even kissed or anything. That's all."

"I don't think I have to kiss you to know I'm attracted to you."

"Sure, me neither. That doesn't mean we'd have chemistry. You can't know that until you try."

"Wow, really?" Andie laughed.

"What? Don't laugh at me."

"Sorry, I don't mean to. I'm not laughing at you. It's just that I think you're trying to get me to make out with you."

Skye lifted one shoulder. "Is it working?"

They dissolved into giggles. There was something clumsy about how Skye was approaching her, but it didn't turn Andie off. It was more charming than anything. If she had to guess, she'd say she was used to being pursued, and she didn't have a lot of experience with it being the other way around.

The laughter died down, and they locked eyes.

"It might be working, yeah."

Why try so hard to be good when Skye had already made up her mind about her? Andie's bruised ego was loud, urging her to show Skye what she was missing. She could never want to hurt Skye, but she liked the idea of leaving her sexually frustrated. It would even things up between them and restore some of her wounded pride. "I guess there's no harm in one kiss when there's nobody around. It would give you something to base your decision on, for when this is all over. What do you think of that?"

Skye moistened her lips with her tongue, and Andie's stomach dropped. She was only human. How could she resist a woman like Skye?

"Sure. It makes sense," Skye said, blinking fast.

"It's just a kiss. No big deal, right?"

"No big deal."

"Okay. Here goes."

Andie got up, moving the flowers out of the way and kneeling before Skye. She took a moment to appreciate how keen and willing Skye looked, sitting there with a flush on her collarbone above that pretty dress. She put a hand on Skye's waist and shifted forward, Skye's eyes fluttering closed, her own following a second later.

Time stopped. There was the taste of mint and perfume, Skye's lips as soft as they'd always looked.

At the first, tentative contact, Andie knew she'd made a huge mistake. This was why she didn't drink anymore. She could never stop at just one.

They slowly tasted one another's lips, and she heard herself sighing into Skye's mouth. It had been so long since Andie had had this, and maybe that was why she thought she'd never felt this way. Skye pushed Andie's hair back and didn't let go, holding her face in her hands.

They drew apart slightly, made eye contact, and kept going. Skye ran her hands down Andie's arms and then stunned her by slipping her tongue into her mouth. It made her tighten her hand on Skye's waist, her stomach plunging.

Andie tasted that plump lower lip like she'd always wanted to. Skye's arms circled her neck, and she sighed.

They stopped only to look at one another again, in wonder. Skye must be thinking the same thing—that it was shockingly good between them.

"This is so pretty. You're so pretty," Andie said, playing with the strap of Skye's dress, grazing her soft skin.

Skye pulled at her, gently pushing until they were lying down. The palm trees swayed overhead, and the sun warmed Andie's back while their kisses grew deeper and longer. She wished they could stay here all afternoon, tucked away from the world.

Skye flattened her palms and pressed them into Andie's back. She used one hand to prop herself up, keeping her weight off Skye. Still, it took every ounce of her will to stay back and keep the other hand from wandering. Skye's thigh was so close, and she kept thinking it was right there, under her dress. She had a feeling Skye wouldn't stop her, and she barely had the strength to stop herself.

They paused again, and Andie trailed a finger over Skye's cheek. "Should we go back?"

"Okay, if you want to," Skye said breathlessly, and her lips looked so inviting that Andie dipped toward them.

"I didn't say I wanted to," she said, between kisses.

Skye laughed, putting a hand behind her neck. "Well, I don't want you to do anything you don't want, but we're already here. Just another minute?"

"Really not sure what's giving you the impression I don't want to," Andie said, sliding her hand up Skye's waist, then resting it on her face. She kissed her forehead, then her temple. Their lips joined again, soft and sweet.

"I'm sorry," Skye said, voice thick.

"What for?"

"That I gave you the wrong impression about today…"

She ran her thumb over Skye's lower lip then kissed her quiet. "It's okay. I know you didn't mean to, and I'll be all right. You feel so good."

"So do you," she said, holding Andie closer.

Skye wrapped her legs around her. Andie's nipples tightened, tingles spreading over her whole body. They each parted their lips again, melting into one another.

The sweetness fell away, the kiss turning toward a roughness that made Andie wet. Wetter, actually, because she'd already been turned on. Skye was pushing her breasts into her, and it was all she could do to not grab them. She wanted to fuck her right here by the lagoon, and Skye was acting like she wanted that, too.

Her tongue was in Andie's mouth again, and she grasped her ass with both hands, pulling her tightly against her. Their legs were entangled, and they moved against one another until Andie almost forgot why she shouldn't be doing this.

She dropped her head into the crook of Skye's neck and tried to slow her breathing. Jesus. She'd told herself she was doing this to get Skye worked up, but she was the one crawling out of her skin. She kissed Skye's neck and felt her shiver, then rolled onto her back.

"I'd better go."

"Okay, sure," Skye said, fingers tented over her forehead.

"Are you okay? I mean, are we okay?"

"Of course. I'm just going to take a minute."

"Gave you something to think about, huh?"

Skye reached up and pushed Andie so hard she almost toppled over on her side. "Okay, I'll leave you to it." She grinned. She reached for the flowers as she got up. "Have a nice afternoon."

"Where are you taking them?"

"I'll toss them on the way back."

"No, it's okay. You can leave them."

"Oh. Okay," Andie said, touched. She laid them back down at Skye's side.

All the way back to the villa, Andie traced her lips with her fingertips. They still tingled. She should feel very, very bad about what she'd done, but how could she, after a make-out session like that?

It wasn't her style to chase after a woman too intently. In the old days, she'd never had any trouble bringing them to her bed, nor did she struggle to move on if she made a pass that didn't work out. Skye was the exception to every rule she'd ever had. She couldn't let herself think that it might never happen between them.

Their kisses told her that Skye wanted her, at least physically. It wasn't enough, but it was a start. When the timing was right, she'd woo her. Maybe if Skye could see how much she'd changed, she'd be in with a chance.

Her watch told her that it was well past noon, so they'd been out there longer than she'd thought. They'd be serving lunch, so she cut through the grounds toward the restaurant. She filled her stone bowl with Kokoda salad and carried it to her father and Ben's table.

"How are you both?" She wondered if they were aware that their safari suits matched, except Ben's was beige, and Dad's was khaki.

"Doing well, honey, how are you?" Ben said.

"Very well, thanks," she said, gathering up a forkful of fish.

"We did want to check something out with you, though. We've been hearing some strange stuff the last couple of days."

"Oh, yeah? What kind of stuff?" she asked, keeping her eyes trained on her food.

"Probably just rumors. But you could clear some things up for us."

"You know how it is, with gossip on film sets. Whatever it is, I'm sure it's nothing."

"Maybe."

She needed time to think. She shot a look at her dad, who still hadn't said a word. "Anyway, if there's something you need, couldn't we talk about it on Monday? It's the weekend. Time to unwind, right?"

"What kind of work ethic have I taught you? You're in production, no matter what day it is. End of story," Doug said, closing his eyes while he talked. It was almost as clear a warning sign as if he'd lit a cigarette.

"Fine. What is it that's so goddamn important?"

"People are saying that Skye and Darryl seem off in some of their takes. We didn't know whether to put any stock in it. But then we were talking about when we watched the dailies before we left for the States. There's something there, we think."

"So?"

"Can you tell us anything about it?"

"I can't see how that warrants any discussion. Skye and Darryl are both actors who like trying things out. Or, sometimes, they take a little while to warm up. Is that a crime?"

"Of course not, but we heard it was happening all the time. Particularly in their more meaty scenes together. Don't pretend you haven't noticed it."

Andie caught the thread and flooded with relief. She glanced up from her food to double-check. They were pissed, but not furious like they'd be if they knew what was really going on. Now, all she had to do was grab that thread and pull. "Okay, sure. You got me. I have noticed. It's not easy for either of them."

"Did they have a bad breakup? I heard they had a bad breakup," Ben said. He leaned forward eagerly, the old gossip. She wasn't above exploiting that, even if it was ridiculous that he was asking these questions now, instead of during the casting process.

"Quite bad, I think," Andie said.

"Who broke up with who?"

"I'm not sure. They're both pretty quiet about it. I mean, it's not like I'm going to ask them. It seems like it's very raw. They're both totally professional, to be clear."

"But you're sharing with Skye, and you know, you're both girls. She must've said something."

She looked around, pretending to check for eavesdroppers. "Just that he broke her heart. He's got a new girlfriend, you know."

"Oh, the poor thing. That must be awful for Skye. They broke up a while ago, though, didn't they?"

"Yeah, but I think maybe he started with the new one while they were still together. Skye didn't say that, but I heard a rumor. It fits. Sometimes she's a bit cold toward him," she said, sipping from her water glass. That part was just to be an asshole. Starting an affair had always been Dad's number one strategy for getting out of a relationship.

"Hmm. I didn't realize things were so messy. They both seemed fine with the casting, but maybe they were just saying that. Maybe we made a bad call here."

"No, not all," Andie rushed to answer. "She's wounded, but I don't think it's hurting the movie as much as you might have heard. You must've seen all the good stuff in the dailies, too."

"That's right. Plenty of good stuff, but we haven't watched them all. The love scene, for example. Louise didn't have the dailies ready in time," her father said.

Bless that woman, Andie thought. She must've been extra cautious with keeping the footage separate.

"So, they don't always hit the mark, but I'm not worried. They're just uneven, but I'm keeping a close eye and making sure we get enough for Louise to cut around it."

Ben looked at Doug before he spoke. She'd love to ask if he was ever allowed to express an opinion without getting permission first, but she bit her tongue.

"I'm glad we talked. Will you update us if things change? If things come to a head and you think it could end up hurting the movie?"

"Yeah. Of course, I would do that. I didn't mention it previously because I felt confident, but if anything were to change, you'd be the first to know."

"Okay, good. We all need to keep out ahead of this. If I can suggest it, it might be a good idea to put a little more energy into Skye. She's sharing a villa with you, so cultivate that relationship. Make her feel important. Pay more attention to her. What's so funny?" Ben asked.

"Nothing. Sorry, I was thinking of something else. Sure thing. I'll give some thought to how I can keep things going well for her. I'll see you guys later, okay?"

Scooping the last bite of Kokoda from her bowl, Andie pushed back her chair. She wanted to get back to her room to have some time to think. They'd distracted her from delicious thoughts of Skye's arms wrapped around her, Skye's lips on hers.

She wanted to live in that memory for as long as she could.

CHAPTER TWENTY-FIVE

After Andie left, Skye lay on the grass for over an hour, watching the leaves dance against the bright blue sky. Her dress brushed against her sensitive thighs, her arms were covered in goose flesh, and she was as wet as rain.

The kissing had blown her away, and she wasn't embarrassed about throwing herself at Andie. It was worth it, and she'd do it again in a heartbeat. Besides, there was something in how Andie looked at her that made her feel like there was no need to be self-conscious. She loved that.

When she finally returned to the villa, she slid open the glass door to see Teri perched on the sofa, paging through a magazine. "Hey."

"Hey. What's with the flowers?"

"Nothing. I picked them on the way back from my walk."

"I brought you back some Kokoda from the restaurant. Thought you might be hungry."

"Thanks. Is it in the fridge? I'll grab it. You don't have to get up."

"That's okay. I'll get you some water."

Skye stood at the counter, digging into her lunch. They were served the Fijian-style raw fish dish often, and she loved the coconut taste. "I thought you'd be out partying by now. I walked past the pool, and it looked like it was going to be another big one."

"I thought I'd head over a little later. Where have you been, anyway?" Teri asked, setting a glass of iced water in front of Skye.

Her tone was light, but Skye kept chewing a piece of fish instead of answering. She couldn't get Andie's earlier words out of her head. She didn't know whether to believe Teri had a thing for her, and she sure as hell wasn't going to ask. Either way, she was starting to see possessiveness in Teri that she'd never noticed before.

"I went out for a long walk on the beach."

"Oh, yeah? By yourself?"

"Yep, just me. It's a beautiful day out there."

"Where did you get the flowers, then?"

"I didn't just go to the beach." Skye looked down, thinking that if she asked another question, she wouldn't answer. This was turning into an interrogation.

"Do you want to come out to the pool? I heard someone's setting up a cocktail-making station. There are a few ex-bartenders in the crew," Teri said as she stacked some plates.

"That sounds nice, but I'll go out later. It's been a big week. I might go work on my script for a little while and read."

"Cool," she said. She opened her mouth like she wanted to say more, but then turned from her to put a glass away in the cupboard. "I'll see you out there."

In her bedroom, Skye sank onto her mattress, thinking about that kiss and everything they'd talked about before it happened. She wished she could give Andie what she asked for and agree to date, but it wouldn't be fair. They'd be on the island for another six weeks, then the shoot would move to the studio lot in LA for two weeks. That would mean two months of Andie thinking they had a future when she couldn't say for sure that she wanted that.

It would be stringing her along.

It was so complicated. She wanted to spend time with Andie and desperately wanted to touch her. But it would be stupid to try to be with a woman everybody knew was a cheater. The whole world knew that she'd played women off against one another—that she seemed to enjoy casting women aside. Lots of women. Skye didn't want to be one of them and have her heart broken. Andie said she'd changed, and she desperately wanted to believe it, but there was no way to be sure.

Whoever Skye dated would hopefully become her first girlfriend, and she couldn't choose a woman who might not be good to her. After all that time figuring herself out, she wanted to make the right decisions. She wished she could talk to somebody about it. She'd wished that so many times lately, but instead of talking to Teri, she was up here hiding in her bedroom.

She wanted to see what the party looked like, to help her decide if she wanted to go down there. As she stepped outside, she heard voices and realized Andie and Cary were on Andie's deck, only ten feet away. Shit. She felt like she was intruding and almost turned and walked back inside, but it was too late. They'd already seen her.

"Hey! Come over here. I've got a jug of the best mojito you've ever tasted," Cary said, looking relaxed in a white dress with the straps of her striped bikini showing. Skye hesitated, not wanting to crash their party. Andie gave her a subtle nod.

"Okay, thanks. I'll be over in a minute."

"My bedroom door's unlocked. Just walk on through."

"And bring a glass," Cary added.

She was heading toward the stairs, but she realized Teri would give her the third degree if she went to the kitchen. She couldn't go down there again without inviting her up. There was a water glass on her nightstand. As she was taking the last mouthful to empty it, her eye fell on her draft of *Shelley*. She grabbed it before she could change her mind.

On the way through Andie's room, she stared at the bed for a moment. It smelled so good in here, like her shampoo.

When she put the script—ragged from being carted around everywhere she went—on Andie's ordered desk, it felt like she was messing it up.

"Hey. Glad you came over," Cary said.

"Thanks for asking me," she replied, holding out her glass so Cary could fill it.

Andie got up, waving a hand over her chair.

"It's okay, I can stand."

"No problem. Please, take it."

"Thanks."

Cary was busy pouring drinks, so she couldn't see how they were looking at one another. Andie's gaze was appreciative, warm, and sexy all at once. She wished they were still under that tree, and she knew Andie was thinking the same thing.

"Bottoms up," Cary said, clinking their glasses together.

Andie leaned against the deck railing and crossed one ankle over the other, her back to the party. She held out her empty hand, miming cheers with them. Skye grinned, eyes drifting down to her sun-browned forearms. Her skin was so soft, and she couldn't wait to touch it again.

"So, you were at Darryl and Sid's place the other day," said Cary.

"That's right. Darryl and I were working on a scene," said Skye, turning her head away from Andie and sipping. Cary was right. The mojito was perfectly balanced, not too sweet or too bitter.

"You two seem to still get along pretty well."

Skye flicked her eyes over to Andie, not wanting to talk about her ex-boyfriend in front of her. "Yeah, we do."

"That's good. Do you always date within the industry?"

"Yeah, I usually do. It's not like I have a requirement or anything, but it's hard to meet people otherwise, don't you think?"

"I see what you mean, yeah. And you're single now, aren't you?"

"Yes, I am."

"Are you a serious relationship kind of a gal? Like, are you looking to settle down?"

"Cary," Andie warned.

"Shush. I'm just making conversation. Getting to know my costar."

"Not everyone likes talking about their love life as much as you do."

"Anyway, like I was saying, I mainly date other actors too, and I love love, but I've got no interest in long-term stuff," said Cary. "I move on once the heat dies down. I got serious with a bank manager when I was younger, though. We nearly got married."

Andie rolled her eyes and pointed at Cary. "Oh, how she loves this story."

"Shush, you. I was in my midtwenties, and my career was taking off. I was starting to make a name for myself, outside of being the great Doug McKenzie's daughter. I met this guy just after *Fire Down Below* came out," Cary said, opening a silver cigarette case. When she put a rolled-up smoke in her mouth and lit up, Skye realized from the smell that it was a joint.

"How did you meet him?" Skye asked.

"In a bar on Sunset. His name was Luke. He bought me a drink, and he was utterly charming. Handsome, charismatic, well-dressed. The whole package. He swept me off my feet. He was older than me, and square as can be, but I didn't care because I thought he was very sophisticated," she said through held breath, holding the joint toward her.

"No thanks."

"Anyway, he asked me to marry him when we'd only been dating for six months, but I said yes because I was head over heels. The only thing left to do was to introduce him to the family. So he met my mom, which went great, and then I took him to meet Dad and Antonia."

"That's my mother," Andie said.

"Uh-huh. If you don't know the ins and outs of the McKenzie saga, Dad married Antonia after my mom. He had Andie and our brother Louis with her."

"Where's your mom now, Andie?" Skye broke in, wanting to know everything about Andie's family.

"She lives in Spain. She's an artist. Mainly sculptures. I spent a few months over there with her last year," Andie said.

"Yeah. Andie's mom is the coolest. Anyway, when I took Luke over there to meet them, Andie was ten years old. Ten going on thirty. She was always like that, and we were always very close. So we have a nice dinner, everyone gets along and everything, and when it's time for the kids to go to bed, we're all setting up in the living room to have a few drinks. I go in to tuck her in and talk to her before she goes to sleep."

"Do you know that you tell this story the exact same way, every time?"

"Shush," Skye said this time, and they all laughed. She was intrigued to hear what Andie was like as a kid, and it was sweet watching the two sisters tease one another. She always wished she had a sister.

"Thank you, Skye. Now, she's in bed, and I'm sitting there, about to say good night. I ask her what she thinks about Luke, and she says that he's very nice, but she doesn't think I should marry him. So I say, what do you mean, you don't think I should marry him? And she says, you're too different. I think you should marry an artist, like you. I ask her why she thinks that's important. And she goes, when I grow up, I'm going to marry an artist because that's what I'm going to be, and we'll go all over the world together making our art."

Cary stubbed out her joint on the corner of the table. Skye shot a look at Andie, whose eyes were fixed on Skye's face, as though she wasn't listening to the story anymore.

"So what happened then? With Luke?"

"That's the thing. When we got home that night, I told him what I thought was just a funny story about my cute little sister, but it started this big fight. It came out that he'd assumed I'd give up acting for at least a few years to have babies with him, and I'd already decided I didn't want kids. So, it turned out Andie was right about not marrying him."

"I love it when that's the moral of the story. But maybe the moral of the story is don't agree to marry someone you've only known for six months. Especially when you haven't talked about kids yet."

"Hey! When are you ladies coming down here?"

Skye and Cary got up and looked over the railing. Sid stood underneath the deck. "You better come on down before I bring the party up there."

"Are you going to come?" Skye asked Andie. Cary was already turning, heading for the door into Andie's room.

"Thanks, but I might get some work done before I join you all."

She knew she wasn't supposed to, but before she went, Skye ran her fingers down the length of Andie's forearm. Andie's fist clenched, but she held back her hand.

"Okay," Skye said softly, turning to leave reluctantly.

CHAPTER TWENTY-SIX

Feeling like a mess, Andie stood and watched her walk away. All she wanted to do was take Skye into her room, lock the door, and take off that sundress.

She gathered her notebook and binder to take them inside, knowing that Sid and Cary would nag her all afternoon if she stayed out here. She was about to set her things down on the desk when she saw the script.

She stared at the title page. Skye must have snuck it in here on her way through. This was a big fucking deal. When Skye told her she'd written it, she'd been so curious, but she didn't get the feeling she was ever going to be allowed to read it. She ran her finger down the edges and then flipped through it. There were lots of notes in the margins and crossed-out lines of dialogue.

What did it mean that she was trusting her with this?

She carried it over to the bed and propped herself against the pillows, taking a deep breath before turning to page one. She was afraid to read it. She'd been handed countless scripts, and it was rare to find a good one. If this one wasn't one of the good ones, she respected Skye too much to lie to her. Yet, she couldn't stand the thought of hurting her feelings, either.

Two hours later, she'd ignored Cary's begging to join them and hadn't moved. She closed the script and rested it on her stomach, collecting her thoughts. After a few minutes, she grabbed her notebook to jot down some ideas.

She ran down the stairs, knowing that Skye would be as anxious to hear her opinion as she was to give it. It was dusk, and the crowd around the pool had thinned since she'd looked down on it from her deck earlier. Skye was nowhere in sight.

"Hey, boss lady, who are you looking for?" Carol asked as Andie passed her group, a couple of women from Makeup. Andie greeted them distractedly.

"Skye. Have you seen her anywhere?"

"Probably down at the bonfire. A bunch of people went down there a little while ago."

"Great, I need to talk to her about something."

"I bet you do." Carol winked. Luckily, the makeup team had split off to talk amongst themselves and didn't see.

"I don't know what you're getting at, but this is work-related."

"If you say so. So much for you not doing the dirty anymore. Skye's gorgeous, though. I'll give you that."

"I told you, it's not like that."

"All right, well, I'm pretty sure she's down there. But if I see her around, I'll let her know you're looking for her."

"Thanks," she said tightly, setting off. For a moment, she considered telling Carol that she shouldn't talk to the director like that. It wasn't Andie's style, but she could do with reminding.

The fire on the beach shot up bright sparks against the darkening sky. Skye sat with a blanket wrapped around her shoulders. When she was sure she had clocked her, Andie nodded ahead toward their rock and walked on. After a few minutes, she spotted Skye making her way down the beach toward her. Her shoulders were hunched. She waved, wanting her to see that there was nothing to be afraid of.

"Do you think anyone saw you follow me?" Andie asked, remembering Carol's wink. She hoped Carol hadn't passed on any gossip to the makeup women after she left.

"No, I don't think anyone noticed me leave. They're all pretty drunk, anyway," she said as she sat down.

Andie reached underneath Skye's blanket, seeking out her hand and interlacing their fingers. "Hey. You don't have to be scared. It's all right."

"Tell me what you thought."

"It's excellent work, Skye. I couldn't be more impressed."

"Really? You think it's good?"

"Yes, really."

When they looked at one another, the connection felt so powerful that Andie had to look away. If she didn't, she might try to kiss Skye again. Holding hands out here was one thing, but anything more would be crazy.

"You're not just saying that because of…"

"No. Please, trust me," she said, and hoped Skye could hear the underlying plea. The one that said trust me about everything, not just this. Trust that I could never hurt you.

"Thank you. It means a lot that you're saying that."

"It means a lot to me that you let me read it."

"How much more work does it need? You can give it to me straight," she said, squaring her shoulders.

"A lot. But don't let that get you down. They often do. The tone, though. That's what matters, and it's beautiful. That's something that can't be taught. You've got natural talent," she said, and Skye held her hand more tightly.

"Would you help me with it?"

"Of course. I'd be thrilled to. I'd love to give you some notes to help you rework it. Then, I think one day, you could get it produced. I believe that. Especially after this movie comes out. You'll have a lot more bargaining power, then."

"I can't tell you how happy I am that you like it. Thank you so much."

They watched the water together, not letting go of one another's hands.

There was so much Andie wanted to say, but she bit her tongue. She was already fantasizing about them working as a team to bring the script to life. The problem with that, of course, was that they were in this weird stalemate about their future. She hoped Skye would say she wanted to date, after all.

If she pitched to direct Skye's movie, she'd be giving up on any chance of them doing that for a very long time. They couldn't date while they were working together, with no guarantee things would work out between them. She didn't want that kind of drama on set now, or on her next film. Still, the idea of the two of them collaborating again was thrilling. Andie loved everything about directing Skye—their conversations, the shorthand they were building, and their shared understanding of what made for good cinema. It was a dream to develop a partnership with an actress she could work with across multiple projects.

When Cary told the story of what she'd said as a kid about traveling and making art with someone, it sounded like a dream she hadn't known she had all these years. Maybe the dream was only waiting for someone like Skye to come along, to remind her.

Working together might not be an issue if they were in a committed relationship. A lot of couples managed it.

It was a lot to hope for, but she had this moment.

Skye held her hand, leaning over to rest her head on Andie's shoulder. She closed her eyes and listened to the water, more content than she'd ever been.

CHAPTER TWENTY-SEVEN

Skye stretched after being helped out of the harness by the stunt coordinator, rubbing her sore shoulders. She'd been up in a tree for half the morning. Dr. Foster clung to a branch to fire her pistol downward for the scene, aiming at a snake.

Andie and the AD, Todd, stood at the tree's base, examining the animatronic reptile. It was painted black with a red belly, and its big black eyes had been creeping Skye out all morning. The thing must be eight feet long, and its rubber exterior looked all too realistic.

Andie prodded it with her foot. "This thing looks great, but we have to resist showing too much of it. Like I keep saying, it's scarier if you don't see the whole thing."

"I heard Spielberg is doing a movie where the dinosaurs are going to be completely computer-generated," Todd said.

"I heard about that. Anyway, let's talk to Frankie about lifting the frame even more. We just want to see the snapping jaws and get a sense of how big it is."

"Sure thing. Hey, you think they made it look like a giant cock on purpose?"

Andie didn't reply, nor did she look happy when Todd laughed at his own joke. She crouched down to look at the snake from different angles, opening and closing its jaws.

They hadn't noticed she was there, so Skye listened, stretching her arms. She loved watching Andie work. When she was in deep concentration and frowning like that, she looked sexy as hell. Her wild dark hair fell into her face, and she pushed it back impatiently.

"I guess that's why she's running away from it, huh? It could be an interesting subtext. Though she doesn't seem the type who would run away from one because it was too big."

Andie shot up to her full height. "Who do you think you're talking to, Todd? I don't want to hear that kind of shit."

"C'mon, it's a snake. Is there anything more phallic than that? I'm just joking around."

"I know, but like I said, I don't want to hear it, okay? It's completely inappropriate in the workplace. Or anywhere else. Show some respect. Don't talk about her like that."

"I wasn't talking about Skye. I was talking about the character. And it was just a joke," he said, hands on his hips.

"I don't care. It's not funny."

"Okay, sor-ry," he said and stalked off, muttering to himself. Andie watched him go, then noticed that Skye had been standing behind him.

"Hey, you," Andie said, face brightening.

"Hey."

"Did you hear all that? Sorry."

"It's okay. I appreciate you standing up for me."

"Of course. He should know I'm not going to laugh at things like that. But he's probably calling me a man-hater right now."

"Oh, he's definitely calling you a ball-breaker."

"Even better. You're doing great up there, by the way. Are you feeling okay? Like I said, we could be using your double more."

"Thanks, but I know we need to see my face as much as possible, and I want to do it. I'm a little sore, but I'll be fine.

Hanging off a tree will look easy tomorrow when we're doing that group scene."

"Sure, there are some big moments for your Dr. Foster. We can make time to catch up if you like? I thought we could talk about *Shelley*, too. I've got some ideas. We can hit two birds with one stone."

Skye had given her the script a week ago, but she hadn't expected them to work on it any time soon. "That's so kind, but we don't have to talk about *Shelley*. I wanted you to read it, but I know how busy you are. There's no rush."

"It's no trouble. We should finish filming by nine or so tonight. How about a late dinner? I could have the restaurant send something over to the villa, and we can work at the table? We can discuss tomorrow's scene and *Shelley*."

"That sounds great."

As the stunt coordinator helped her get back up in the tree, Skye couldn't wipe the smile off her face. She loved that Andie was paying her extra attention. She hoped it meant they might get the chance to kiss again. It was easy to picture it turning into more—the two of them working and joking at the table, then maybe slipping outside for a walk to be alone.

Being with Andie again was all she'd been able to think about, and she couldn't wait to be close to her.

CHAPTER TWENTY-EIGHT

It was closer to ten by the time they'd wrapped for the day and seated themselves at the large rectangular dining table, with foil-wrapped bowls of lamb stew. Skye tried to ignore how Teri hovered, puttering around the kitchen and then taking a book into the living room. Skye had to remind herself that it was her house, too.

"I feel like I've got the monologue down, but I'm a little nervous about it," she said after a mouthful of the tender lamb.

"I understand. It's a big moment. Is there anything you want to explore that might help?"

A wave of tenderness swept over Skye when she noticed the dark circles under Andie's eyes. You'd never know she was exhausted from the way she looked back at her so attentively. If she didn't think Andie would brush it off, she'd end the meeting and tell her to go up to bed.

"I can tell you how I was planning on playing it, and you can tell me if I'm on the right track?"

"Sounds good."

"The way I interpret it, Dr. Foster's covering up some serious fear in this scene. She feels like she's got to hold it all together and be the rational one, but she knows something is happening that can't be explained. Right?"

"Exactly," said Andie. "She's trying to hide how scared she is while everyone else is losing it, and that's making her even more scared. But she would never show that. She's too controlled, and she knows that if she does fall apart, everyone will really lose their shit."

"How much do you think she suspects Adrian's betrayal by this point?" Skye said, lowering her voice so that Teri wouldn't overhear.

"A lot. I think of it as a moment of someone losing their faith, in a religious sense, I mean. She's clinging on, but she knows she can't do it for much longer. The blinkers are falling from her eyes. Once that happens, everything will change, forever."

"I like that. That's the kind of angle I was thinking of," said Skye, talking at a normal level now. She usually told Teri everything but decided from the start that it was too risky to let her in on their plans.

"Good. And I'll just highlight that the camera's going to be on you most of the time. There'll only be a few cutaway reactions from the group. We're going to keep pulling in tighter as you run through the monologue," Andie said, holding her hands like she was framing the shot.

"Okay."

"I want the audience to be totally engrossed in what you're saying. It'll keep amping up the tension, so nobody will be even thinking about the fact that you're all in danger. They know something's creeping up on them, but they're not thinking about it because they're only watching you. Then bang," she said, clapping her hands.

Skye jumped, then laughed at herself.

"Oh, great, sounds easy. Make people think only about my face, not the giant spiders and snakes."

"I'm positive it'll work. People will be so busy looking at that tremendous face. That's what Ben calls it. Tremendous,"

Andie said, throwing her hands up like he did when he talked about Skye.

"Okay, okay. Enough," she said, though she was so tickled by Andie's compliment she couldn't stop beaming.

"If there isn't anything else you want to talk about for that scene, we can move on?" Andie said, tapping a finger on the script for *Shelley*.

Skye nodded toward Teri. She hadn't been watching her the whole time, but she could swear she wasn't turning the pages of that book.

"Damn, I don't have the notebook I need. I'll have to go up and get it," Andie said, raising her eyebrows and nodding upstairs.

"I'll come with you."

It felt like they were teenagers, running away from a chaperone as Andie led her out to the balcony. As soon as they'd settled into their chairs, Andie started to get up again.

"Sorry, I forgot to turn the light on."

"Don't worry about it. There's enough light from inside. Hey, I'm sorry about that, and thanks for the rescue. I don't want her to know we're talking about *Shelley*. It was weirding me out how she was sitting there listening to us."

"I noticed, and I get it. It's okay."

"So, you said you had some ideas?"

"Yeah. The main thing is, I'd drop the voiceover narration. You don't need it."

Skye thought about that for a second. The book was all about the character's internal monologue, so it had been a natural choice when writing the screenplay. "I'm not sure about that. Wouldn't the audience be confused without it?"

"Not necessarily. Think about it. Maybe reread what you've written through that lens. Anything Shelley's thinking can be communicated through your performance."

"You think so?"

"I'm positive. A good director would make sure of it."

They sat quietly, looking out over the twinkling lights of their little Fijian island village. They had an early morning the next day, but Skye didn't want to sleep. Out here in the dark, she couldn't think of any reason why she shouldn't say what was on her mind.

"I want that to be you. If you're interested, I mean. I'd love you to direct it."

The silence before Andie answered felt deafening. "I'm flattered, but I don't want you to feel you have to say that because I offered to help you. The offer to help with the script comes with no strings attached."

"I know. I can't think of anyone I'd rather do it."

She heard Andie breathe out slowly. "You know how it is. Your script could be in development for years. This is your baby, and things might change. Keep working on it, and we'll see what happens. Keep me on your wish list."

"Okay."

"I've got some other notes, but that's the most important. Start thinking about that one, and we'll go through the others in more detail later."

"Sounds good," Skye said, rising and going over to the balcony railing. She was scared that Andie was about to ask her to go. Her tone had changed, and Skye wasn't sure why. She'd hoped she'd be excited about the prospect of them working together again. The aloofness surprised her, especially after she'd asked to talk about this.

A few night owls hung around the pool, like always. Voices drifted over, but they were too far away to make out the words. She heard Andie get up, and she held her breath. Skye didn't have to turn around to know that she was coming closer. Everything in her was alive to Andie's every move.

When Andie put her hands on her shoulders, she closed her eyes.

Over the last week, she'd been shocked by how they'd managed to act like nothing had happened. Andie was completely normal, even when they saw one another in the villa and nobody else was around. The looks she always gave her had gone up a notch in intensity, and that was the only tell.

"Are your shoulders okay after today?" Andie asked, rubbing lightly.

Skye moved her head forward, inviting her to keep going. If she stopped touching her, she might lose her mind. "Not too bad."

Andie squeezed her shoulders. She needed those hands on her, and she was standing so close that her front grazed Skye's back. Without meaning to, she let out a quiet moan.

She wasn't sure whether she moved backward or Andie moved forward—it might've been both of them. Andie was pressed against her back now, and Skye gripped the railing so hard her knuckles turned white. Andie's hands rested on the railing, on either side of hers.

They were still, and she was afraid to move and break the spell. She was already so excited from the feeling of Andie's body against hers.

"This is so difficult. Is it hard for you, too?" Andie said, her breath hot against Skye's ear.

"Yes," she said, her bottom lip caught in her teeth, turning her head. Difficult wasn't the word for it. She couldn't look at Andie without wanting to kiss her. All week, she'd been telling herself that Andie kissed women all the time, so it probably didn't mean much to her. She loved hearing that she was wrong, and she wasn't the only one struggling.

Andie's forehead rested against Skye's back. She lifted one hand from the railing and put it on Andie's, threading their fingers together. Their joined hands moved together until they were on her hip, and she pushed back into her even though they couldn't get any closer.

They stood like that for a while, breathing hard. She was keenly focused on the softness of Andie's breasts against her back. Skye watched the people down by the pool, reassuring herself that nobody could see them up here. At this point, she wasn't sure she even cared.

Finally, Andie took her other hand off the railing in front of them. It was on Skye's waist, then sliding with delicious intent up her stomach, barely touching as it moved up her torso. Andie paused when she reached her chest. Though Skye wished she'd stop for longer, her touch was delicious as she ran a palm over her breast.

The hand kept moving until it was under Skye's chin, tipping her head back.

Their lips molded against one another's. Skye opened her mouth, and their tongues slipped together, making a liquid fire in her belly.

She shivered, feeling Andie's hands on her hips. There was nothing in the world like being kissed the way Andie kissed her. It was slow and deep, and it shot a bolt of desire through her that was so strong it felt like her knees might give out.

Skye put an arm up and behind Andie's neck. Andie sighed, hips jutting into her.

She was turning toward her when Andie drew away breathlessly. "I'm so sorry," she said, taking a big step back.

"There's nothing to apologize for. I wanted you to."

"This is why I said it was a bad idea to have meetings in my room."

"Do you want me to go?"

"Not really, but you should," Andie said, shoving her hands in her pockets.

Skye waited for a second, hoping she'd change her mind, then pushed off from the railing. "I'll go get all the stuff from downstairs. Do you want me to leave yours outside your door?"

"Yes, please. I'd appreciate that."

"No problem."

Skye walked downstairs in a daze. That first time making out hadn't been a fluke. She was just as turned on this time, even though it only seemed to last an instant. Why did they have to stop?

Teri hadn't moved from the sofa. She flicked through the channels on the TV with the volume down low.

"Hey, you're still up," said Skye.

They'd drifted apart so much since getting here. Skye had been avoiding her, which gave her a pang of guilt now and then. They used to be so close, and Teri helped her so much. She'd started to wonder what it would be like when they left the island. It was hard to imagine Teri still dropping over on her days off.

Teri got up and switched off the television. "Yeah. I was just thinking about getting to bed."

Skye gathered Andie's binder, notebook, and script into a pile. "How was your day? Did you get to the beach or anything after work?"

"No, just a swim in the pool. Do you need a hand with all that?"

"No, that's okay, thanks. I'm just leaving Andie's stuff outside her door."

"What were you guys working on just now?"

"Tomorrow's scene. It's a big one."

"Right," she said, that skeptical tone reminding Skye why she'd been avoiding her in the first place.

"Okay, well, I'll see you in the morning."

"I don't want to keep you, but can we talk?" Teri said, her forehead creased with concern.

"Okay. Sure, of course."

They went to the living area and sat on the sofa, a few feet apart. She wished she were anywhere else. She'd never been great at these conversations, but this one was a long time coming. Ignoring a problem until it went away rarely worked.

"I know you're getting sick of me asking you all those questions, but you know why, right?"

"You don't like me spending so much time with Andie."

"I'm just worried about you."

"I know, but I'm a big girl. I can take care of myself."

Teri looked down at her hands, her expression sour. "I know you don't want to hear this. I remember what it's like when you have your first real crush, but I just don't want to see you getting hurt."

Skye looked out the window at the flames on tiki torches dancing in the dark. It was well-meaning, but that didn't make her feel less patronized. Crush sounded so high school. It also made it sound like it wasn't a mutual thing, and the last half hour had only made it clearer that this was a two-way street.

"I appreciate your concern, but it's not your place to tell me who to spend time with. I'm sorry to say that, but that's how I feel."

"Maybe not, but I wouldn't be a good friend if I didn't tell you I think you're making a big mistake."

"We're not even doing anything." She couldn't meet her eye. It wasn't easy to lie right to her face, especially when Teri was one of the people who knew her best in the world.

"I don't know exactly what's going on, but I can see how much you like her. It's like you've forgotten everything we know about her."

"I'm telling you, it's not like that. Andie is my director. We have a professional relationship, and it's not uncommon for people working together to get really close. That's just how it is. You've been on movie sets for years, so you should know that better than anyone."

"I know you have to work closely with her. Of course, I know that. I'm just telling you if you think she's different than everything you've heard about her, it's not the case. Charismatic people like Andie are very good at showing you the side of themselves they want you to see. I'm sure all the women she's screwed over thought she was great too, at first."

"It's just work," Skye said, her fight gone. It was like Teri had extracted all the worst, private fears from her heart and spoken them aloud.

"Okay. Just know that no matter what happens, I'm here for you."

This would typically be the part where they'd hug, but Skye couldn't bring herself to do it. "Thanks. I know you're coming from the right place."

"I'm glad you can see that."

They smiled at one another tentatively, but Skye couldn't let it go. "I appreciate your concern, but I don't want to keep talking about this, okay? I'd really like it if you'd just drop it."

Teri's smile faltered, but she nodded. "Okay. I will. I promise."

As she ascended the stairs, Skye had a bad feeling that this would not be the end of it.

CHAPTER TWENTY-NINE

Andie needed to get it together. The woman who'd kissed Skye on the deck was the old, reckless version of herself. It scared the shit out of her.

She spent her days avoiding being alone with Skye and her nights lying awake, thinking about how close she was across the hall. Once thoughts of tiptoeing to her room and kissing those soft lips took root, she struggled to get them out of her head. She traced her own mouth endlessly with her fingers, the memory of their kisses so intense she could feel them.

To resist the temptation, she forced herself to remember the humiliation when her last film premiered. The thought of ruining *Creature Island* was enough to pin her to her mattress. Second chances for women in Hollywood were rare. A third chance would be impossible.

On Saturday morning, a week after that kiss on the deck, she was doing laps in the pool. Exercise helped her burn some of the built-up nervous energy, so it felt more important than ever. When she stopped at the end to catch her breath, she realized

Skye was by the pool. She swam to the edge and climbed out, shaking water from her hair.

"Morning," she said, grabbing her towel to cover up. Skye was staring at her thighs, and she liked it too much.

"Good morning. I haven't seen you around much lately," she said, perching on a deck chair.

"Yeah. It's been a busy week. How have you been?" she replied, sitting down on the chair next to Skye.

"Doing good, thanks. I was wondering, we were talking about *Shelley* last week, but we didn't really get to finish."

Andie broke away from those intense eyes. "Right. We could set up a meeting if you like. I'm sorry I hadn't brought it up after that night…just, you know. Busy."

"Of course, I get it. So, you're happy to talk about it again?"

"Absolutely. I think we should meet at the production offices, though. Would you be okay with that?"

When Skye looked at her, she was poking her tongue in her cheek like she was trying not to laugh. "Are you sure that's necessary? We live in the same villa."

Andie cracked a half-smile but nodded. "Yes. I'd like to meet you there. I think it's important."

"If that's what you want."

Andie smoothed her towel over her legs. If Skye kept looking at her like that, she would lose her resolve. "I think we should."

"Okay. Of course. Is everything all right?" Skye searched Andie's face, trying to read her. It felt cruel to leave her wondering, but she couldn't get into it here, where they could be interrupted at any moment.

"It's okay. I do want to talk to you about *Shelley.* We should do it today. It's still early. Why don't we meet after breakfast, say ten o'clock?"

"You sure? I didn't mean we had to talk right now. I just wanted to see if everything was okay."

"I'm happy to," Andie said, getting up from the deck chair. "I've got to take a shower, but I'll see you there." She could feel eyes on her all the way back to the villa. She wanted to turn around and meet them, and feel that lovely rush of knowing how much she was wanted, but she walked on. She had to be stronger than this.

Like many other things on the island, the production offices were earmarked for repurposing after the shoot. It meant that they looked like hotel rooms with missing furniture. This room had only a large rectangular oak table, a mini fridge, and a coffee station. A painting of a fishing boat hung on the wall, over where the bed would be.

Andie arrived right after breakfast to get some extra work done before their meeting. By nine thirty, she was sitting at the table with a cup of coffee, staring at the clock.

The hands were just about to tap ten when Skye appeared, wearing a plaid shirt with rolled-up sleeves, golden hair framing her face. She knocked on the open door. Andie's heart contracted at how pretty she looked.

"Morning, again," she said, smiling warily before closing the door behind her.

"Good morning. Thanks for coming to see me."

"Of course. Thanks for offering."

Their eyes met across the table, setting off that mysterious spark. It made Andie want to throw away all her resolutions. It made her want to do whatever Skye wanted. She was gathering herself to start talking when Skye jumped in.

"I think you're right about the voiceover idea. That's one of the things I wanted to tell you. I reread the script with your advice in mind, and I think I can see how it would work."

"That's great to hear."

"When I get home to my typewriter, and I have the time, I'm going to redraft. I'm looking forward to it. I've got some ideas about getting the information across in other ways like you said. Before I do that, I'd love to hear what other ideas you might have."

"I'm glad it was helpful," Andie said, wishing so hard that they could sit here and dig into developing the script. Every interaction between them was so loaded that she had no choice but to address the unsaid.

Skye sat expectantly, hands clasped in front of her. Andie stopped herself from reaching across the table to take her hand. She hated it when she looked scared. "I'm afraid you may not like what I'm going to say."

"All right. I thought things were a little off, out by the pool. What is it?"

"I've been thinking about it a lot this week. About the script and about you asking me to direct it."

"That's what I want. You've already helped me so much, and you're the best director I've ever worked with."

Andie took a beat to steel herself against how good that made her feel. She couldn't let anything distract her. "I asked to meet with you here because I need to make it clear that I can't be an option for you as a director. I can't let you think there's any hope of that happening. I'm sorry."

"Oh…"

"Don't take it the wrong way, please. It's not about the script. The script is very good, and I believe that you will make it great. It's just that when we talked about it, it's like you hadn't thought about what it would mean. For us."

It was a good thing that she'd been thinking for days about what she wanted to say, because Skye's silence was unnerving. If she hadn't scripted this in her mind, she wouldn't know how to go on. "I'm saying that you know nothing can happen between us when we're working together. So when you tell me that you want me to direct the movie, all I can hear is that you're telling me you don't ever want to date. That hurts. But you don't even acknowledge it."

Skye shook her head, staring down at the table. "I'm not trying to hurt you. I've been honest about not wanting to go out. I told you that the first time we talked about it."

Andie tipped her head, trying to get Skye to make eye contact with her. She refused. "I know. That's the problem. Sometimes I wish you'd be a little more upfront about *why* that is. I think I know, but I need to hear you say it. I need to know if there's any hope."

Nothing. Skye stared at the table as if the answer was written across the top. Andie was starting to feel shitty for forcing the issue, but she didn't know what else to do. If they didn't work this out, her feelings would keep growing. Things had already gone too far.

"I know what I am. I know what people say. I've been with more women than I can count. There's probably not much you could say that would surprise me. Just tell me. What is this for you?"

"Okay," Skye said, bringing up her gaze until they were eye-to-eye. Andie could see that she didn't want to say it, but she did anyway. "I'm attracted to you, but I don't trust you."

Andie took a deep breath before replying. She'd known. Of course, she'd known. It still felt like being punched in the stomach. "Okay. Fair enough. And there's nothing I can do to change that, is there?"

"I don't think so."

"And the kisses, and everything. That was just fooling around. Nothing more to it for you."

Skye shook her head, looking back down.

Honesty was what Andie had wanted, and she ignored the lump in her throat. She couldn't blame her for telling the truth, and at least she couldn't keep lying to herself and clinging to false hope. She nodded brusquely.

"All right. There it is. I'll give you the rest of my notes for *Shelley*, seeing as I've already worked on it. And if you want any help coming up with a director wish list, I'd be happy to do that. As you know, any connections I have won't do much good right now. Maybe that'll change when *Creature* comes out. Either way, Dad might be able to help. I can talk to him if you'd want that."

Skye's hands were splayed out on the table, but she wasn't staring down at it anymore. She stared at Andie.

"I'm sorry if that disappoints you," said Andie. "I couldn't keep living in this in-between zone with you. I want to keep things simple between us. I guess we were both hoping the other would change their mind, but it's clear that's not going to happen. So it's not good for me to spend as much time around you anymore. Can you please say something?"

"I feel like you're using *Shelley* against me."

"What do you mean?" Andie had anticipated hurt and disappointment. She hadn't imagined that Skye was going to be angry.

"I'm saying I don't want to be with you, so you don't want to help me anymore. It's like you're trying to punish me."

Why didn't she understand? How could Skye think she was motivated by some kind of revenge? "I never promised to direct the movie. I told you to think about it. I said I'd help with the script, and I have. I'll give you my notes."

"Why did you think I gave you the script in the first place? You didn't guess what I wanted?" she said, letting out a disbelieving laugh.

"My understanding was that you wanted me to read it. I loved reading it, but it has to end there. It's not that I don't want to work with you. I *can't* work with you."

"You could if you wanted to, though. You're fine with us working together now. We've been working together great, actually. Why couldn't we keep doing it? Why does that have to change?"

They sat there long enough for the silence to grow uncomfortable. Finally, Andie pushed back her chair. If Skye didn't know what was wrong with what she'd just said—that it killed her to be around her without hope of more—she wasn't about to sit here and spell it out for her. Andie had laid herself bare enough.

"I'll put the notes down on paper and get them to you. If you want me to talk to Dad, let me know. That's all I have to say for the moment."

She left Skye sitting by herself at the table. This time, she had no desire to look back.

She took a long walk along the beach then sat facing the ocean. Watching the waves fold over on themselves soothed her.

So, that was it. It was over before it started.

They'd been careful this whole time, and she was sure Skye wouldn't tell anyone—not even Teri. They'd be able to finish the project on professional terms. Nobody would ever know that they'd kissed. She'd gotten away with it, but that didn't make her feel any better. She'd finally met someone she cared about, but they didn't care back. That was life, but she'd screwed up royally by opening herself to this kind of hurt.

When Andie got back to the village, she gave the crowd by the pool a wide berth. She couldn't think of anything worse than mingling. As she slid back the door to their villa, she braced herself for seeing Skye or Teri, but only Cary stood in the kitchen, singing a Bob Dylan song.

"Hey, little sis. What's cooking?"

"Nothing. It's my nap time. I'm going upstairs."

"I've barely seen you the last few days. At least stay and talk to me while I have this sandwich. I had a craving, so I made the kitchen give me supplies," she said, licking the knife she'd just used.

"What is that?"

"Cheese and peanut butter. Two of my favorite things, so why not have them together?"

"Because that's disgusting."

"Do you want one?"

"Yes," Andie said, her stomach rumbling.

Cary plated the sandwiches and took them over to the coffee table. Andie slumped onto the sofa and looked at the stairs, wondering if Skye would come down while they were eating. She hoped to make it to her room before then.

"Hey, this isn't actually that bad. It's better than when you used to make those banana and mayo things," Andie said, peanut butter sticking to the roof of her mouth. Cary had laid it on thick.

"Yeah, well. You used to eat those too, if I recall. Anyway, how are you doing?"

Andie shrugged and took another bite. "You know. Busy as hell. I'm happy with how things are going, though. Can't complain. What about you?"

"One of my favorite shoots ever. Sid and I are having a ball. Hey, you look tired."

"Gee, thanks."

"Well, you do. You're working so hard. You're going to have to promise me that when this is all over, you'll have a little fun."

"What, the type of fun you're having with Sid, you mean?" she said, looking to the stairs again.

"That's exactly what I mean. And you can stop looking. There's nobody here. They're both out at the party."

"I keep telling you that I won't be doing that anymore."

"So, what, you're just going to stay by yourself forever?"

"Maybe. I don't know."

"Don't you ever get lonely?"

"How would I have time to get lonely? I'm surrounded by dozens of people every day. I don't get a minute to myself."

"C'mon. Don't stonewall me. Be real with me. I'm your sister."

Andie blinked a few times, fast. Her throat was thick, but she didn't want to cry. It was so silly to cry over something that would never work out anyway. Yet she felt like if she started, she might not be able to stop.

"Fine. Sure. I get lonely. There's not much I can do about that right now. I don't get why you're asking me these questions. You're not that much different than me. It's not like you're in any hurry to settle down. Since the banker, you've never been serious about anyone."

"That's because I'm happy with what I'm doing. I like having affairs, and I like my freedom. But sometimes, I wonder what we'd be like if we had better role models in our parents. Nobody in this family seems to be able to hold down a relationship. Louis is the only one."

"I wonder that too. I really wonder how different I am from Dad." She lay down, her feet across Cary's legs, the plate with the half-eaten sandwich on her chest.

"There's nothing wrong with you or with any of us. You just need to trust yourself more. If you want to have affairs, do it. If you want to settle down in a relationship, do that. But you're just standing still."

"It's only been three years, Cary. It's not that long."

"It is if you've met someone that you like. I'm trying to say you should go for it with Skye. How long will you let the past hold you back like this?"

"We've been through this. There's nothing between us."

"There is so. I can see it. Why won't you talk to me about it? You used to tell me everything."

"Because this is more than just about me. You might not understand some things about this," Andie said.

"Give me some credit. If you're trying to say she likes girls and doesn't want anyone to know that, I get it. I'm not going to tell anyone. I swear."

"You especially couldn't tell Sid. You couldn't tell anyone. Do you understand?"

"I understand. It's a pinkie promise," she said, grabbing Andie's little toe and wiggling it back and forth.

"All right. Well, yes. There is something there, but it's not going to happen. I tried."

"You tried? Oh my God, what happened?"

"Shush, I'm trying to tell you. She's interested in fooling around, but she doesn't want anything serious."

"And you do? With her? I knew it! I knew you liked her. I could always tell by the way you looked at her. And the way you try to not look at her."

"I know it's not realistic or right to start a relationship now, but I asked her if we could date when we got back to LA after the movie's finished. She's not interested in that."

"But she wants to fool around with you?"

"Yep."

"Huh. I would've thought it would be the other way around. She seems like she would be the serious relationship kind, and you're the female Warren Beatty."

Andie kicked her, and Cary grabbed her foot again. "I am not."

"You used to be. So, why doesn't she want to date? Is she one of those chicks who just likes to play around with girls now and then?"

"Does she seem like that kind of person to you?"

"No, not at all. But you never know."

"I don't think she is. The problem is me. You're not the only person who thinks I'm like Warren Beatty."

"I feel bad for saying that now," Cary said, covering her mouth.

"Don't, it's fine. Some things were never meant to be, I guess. She's not getting past it. I have to move on."

"Screw her. If she can't see how great my sister is, she doesn't deserve you, anyway."

Andie wished she could push aside her feelings with a pat statement. Cary was only trying to help, but it wasn't that simple. "It's not her fault. She doesn't owe me anything, and she's entitled to feel that way."

Cary's eyes were so warm. It made Andie want to cover her face and hide.

"You really, really like her, don't you? I've never seen you like this before."

"Yeah. I do. I don't know what it is about her, but it's got its hooks into me."

"Then you have to keep trying."

"No way. I know when enough is enough, and she's been clear. I have to respect that."

"Do you want me to talk to her? I think I could do some good. I could explain to her that she's got nothing to worry about with you. I can see how much you've changed. I know you better than anyone," she said, so earnestly that Andie couldn't make fun of her like she usually would.

"That's really sweet of you. But no, I honestly think it'd make things worse. She'd be upset with me if she knew I'd talked to anyone about it. And she's made up her mind. Why would I want to push someone into something like that? If she doesn't want me, then I have to move on."

"Aww. Come here," Cary said, noticing how close to tears she was.

Andie let her big sister hold her, telling herself that this was her one indulgence. From now on, she had to pull it together and move on.

She didn't have a choice.

CHAPTER THIRTY

"Cary, get out. I'm sleeping," Andie groaned later that night.

Cary had crawled into bed with her, pulling the sheet away. She appreciated that she was trying to give her extra support after their heart-to-heart, but this was too much. She had no idea what time it was, but it felt like she'd been asleep for hours. It was still dark outside. She could hear yelling and the tinkle of glass smashing on the ground, but that didn't tell her much. These parties could go all night.

Cary didn't answer, only letting out an obnoxious laugh. She rolled over, squinting into the dark, her heartbeat picking up its pace. That laugh didn't sound like Cary. Someone was lying on their back, peering up at her, and the big mop of dark hair was missing.

"Who is that? Why are you in my room?"

"It's me. Why haven't you come down to the party? You usually come down, at least for a little while."

"Carol?"

"The one and only."

Andie put her hand on her forehead and lay back down, her heart rate slowly returning to normal. At least it didn't seem like she was in here to make a pass. She was just lying there, exhaling alcohol fumes.

"Jesus Christ, you scared me. What are you doing in here?"

"I told you, I wanted to see what you were doing."

"What do you think? I was sleeping. You can't just come and get into my bed. How did you even know this was my room?"

"Why not? It's not a big deal. I figured out this was your room because I see you sitting out on your deck all the time. I'm being a good friend to you."

"By waking me up in the middle of the night?"

"Exactly. Checking that you're okay."

There was no point arguing with her when she was drunk off her ass. Maybe she'd have to start locking her door. Between Cary and now this, her room felt like Grand Central Station.

"Okay, well, I'm fine, as you can see. I'm tired, though, so I was getting some extra sleep."

"You're working too hard. You shoulda come down and played cards with us. We played poker. You know who's really good? That camera guy, Frankie. What a shark. He hustled a lot of money out of everyone."

"Thanks, but it's only one party. They've started throwing them every single weekend, now. I'll come to the next one. Okay? Carol?"

She poked her shoulder, then shook her, but she didn't stir. The glowing numbers on the clock radio told her it was nearly three in the morning. She'd never get back to sleep here, not with Carol snoring like that. She slipped out and grabbed the blanket folded up on the end of her bed, wrapping it around her waist.

The house was quiet and dark—everyone else must be either still at the party or in bed. Grateful for the comfortable sofa, Andie quickly fell back to sleep to the fridge's hum, with the blanket wrapped tightly around her.

Light slanted in over her face. After a moment, she sat up. Carol looked back at her sheepishly, trying to tiptoe her way to the door without waking her up, and failing.

"Morning," Andie said through her laughter. Carol's shirt and miniskirt were rumpled from sleeping in her clothes, and eyeliner was smudged halfway down her face.

"I am so sorry. I was mortified when I woke up in your bed. It took me a while to figure out whose room I was even in."

"You don't remember coming in?"

"Not really. Patches, but that's it. I wasn't too awful, was I?"

"No. I mean, you snore, but it was fine. You fell asleep after talking to me for like, thirty seconds."

"Thank Christ. I woke up terrified. And, with a banging head."

"Turn around for a sec," Andie said, wrapping the blanket around her waist. "I'll go put on some pants and then make coffee."

"Oh, that would be great. Thank you so much."

"No problem."

When they were sitting on the sofa again, Carol apologized for the thousandth time. "I'm not looking forward to doing the walk of shame today. I'm going to have to beg forgiveness from quite a few people. Maybe you have the right idea after all, with not drinking anymore."

"It does have its benefits. Waking up and being able to remember everything is a big plus."

"It's really cool of you to make me coffee and everything instead of booting me out on my ass. You're all right, Andie McKenzie."

"What kind of hypocrite would I be if I gave you a hard time? I've done way worse than falling asleep in someone else's bed."

"Touché."

They were still sitting on the sofa when Teri emerged from her bedroom in her sleep shorts and tank top. She walked a few steps into the living area and stuttered to a stop, her eyes trained on Carol.

"Good morning."

"Hey," Andie said, barely containing her dislike.

Teri seemed to know and get along with everyone. In another life, they might've been friends. In this one, though, she couldn't stand her. If she had an employee who interfered like she did, she would have fired them long ago.

"Morning. This is not what it looks like, I promise," said Carol. "I stumbled into Andie's room last night, and she was kind enough to come down here and sleep so that I could pass out in her bed. I acted like I was at Spring Break or something."

"That was nice of you," Teri said.

"Not really. I don't think I would've been able to get her to move. I couldn't wake her up. She was snoring like a bear."

Andie didn't like the look Teri gave them when Carol shoved her shoulder. She hadn't done anything wrong, and she was done with people's assumptions. "Is something wrong?" she said sharply.

"No. Nothing at all. Excuse me, I'm going to take a shower."

As soon as Teri left the room, Carol giggled. "Oooh, icy. You seem like you hate each other. Why?"

Andie didn't bother to deny it, just shaking her head to show that she wouldn't talk about it. Her annoyance faded now that Teri was out of her face, and her heart sank. She should've been nicer and put more effort into getting her to believe them.

This could get her into some serious trouble.

CHAPTER THIRTY-ONE

Skye filled her tray with scrambled eggs, bacon, and orange juice. The eggs tasted rubbery this morning, and she picked at them and yawned. All night, she'd done her best to mix in with the cast and have a good time, but she'd been miles away. Trying to act like nothing was wrong exhausted her. Plus, it didn't work.

It was hard to fathom how things had become so screwed up. Andie was basically telling her she wanted nothing to do with her. It hurt so much, more than she could remember anything hurting for a long time.

She hated knowing that she was hurting Andie, too. She could see it on her face, and it made her feel sick.

She felt stupid for believing that they were already doing something special with *Shelley*. Nothing thrilled her as much as feeling like she and Andie might become a team. Maybe she didn't have the whole romantic part of their relationship worked out, but she loved knowing that they'd see a lot of one another. That they'd keep having these great conversations about writing and filmmaking. That she'd get to look into those heart-stopping emerald eyes all the time.

She had to pull it together and get on with the rest of the shoot, but she didn't know how she would manage.

"Are you okay?" Teri said, leaning over and brushing a piece of lint from Skye's shirt.

She pushed eggs around on her plate. "Yeah, just a little tired."

"Me too. I woke up early. I noticed you got up a little later than usual. I was surprised the noise didn't wake you up."

"Noise? What noise?"

"Maybe we could go for a walk after breakfast? We can talk about it then."

She didn't feel like it, but she didn't feel like doing anything else, either. "Sure."

They quietly walked along the beach. Skye's apprehension grew with every step because Teri had the vibe of someone with an agenda. This wasn't going to be a casual chat.

"Should we go to your rock? I know how much you love it there."

"Sure," Skye said, but in her head, she was saying that it was *their* place—hers and Andie's.

They sat down, Skye shivering. It was a cool morning, the sun barely peeking out from behind the clouds. "So, what did you want to talk to me about?"

"It's an awkward situation. You said you didn't want to talk about Andie anymore, but I don't think I have a choice."

"Okay. What is it?"

"I heard voices this morning in the living room. When I went out there, Andie and Carol were sitting on the sofa."

"Oh. That's weird."

"I thought so, too. It didn't look good, Skye. I'm sorry."

"How do you mean? What were they doing?"

It had never been a secret that Carol was interested in Andie. Skye had believed Andie when she said she didn't feel the same way, but Carol *was* good-looking. Andie could have changed her mind, especially now. That sick feeling in her gut intensified. Andie wouldn't do anything, would she?

"Carol slept over. In Andie's bed."

"They said that?"

"They gave me some story about how Carol slept in Andie's bed and Andie slept on the sofa, but they looked pretty cozy. It didn't seem very convincing to me."

Skye didn't know whether she would vomit or cry. Could Andie have been so annoyed with her after yesterday morning's meeting that she'd do something like this to hurt her?

She tried to piece it all together. She hadn't seen Andie at the party, even though she'd looked for her all night. She'd worried about her. As for Carol, she hadn't thought to pay her any attention at all, so she had no idea when she might've left.

"So, did it look like the sofa had been slept on?"

"Nope. I didn't see blankets or anything."

"And how did they act?"

"I don't know. Andie was rude, like always. They were drinking coffee. They were definitely a bit flirty, though."

"Right. Anyway, I'm not sure why we came all the way out here to talk about it. It's not really any of my business. Or yours."

As the shock started to wear off, Skye realized the story didn't make sense. Why would Andie work so hard to restore her reputation, only to blow it all up? If she was upset and did something impulsive, why wouldn't she work harder to hide it? She'd always been so worried about people knowing about them, especially Teri. Why would they just be sitting there, on the sofa, for anyone to see?

"Skye…"

"No, really. They're both adults. They can do whatever they want." She didn't want to argue about it, not when Teri could accuse her of being naïve. She knew how it would make her look.

"I know how you feel about her."

"I don't feel any kind of way about her," Skye said, unable to stop herself from raising her voice. Teri cared about her, but it also felt like she was enjoying this. She'd wanted a reason to drive a wedge between them. Now she had one.

"Hey," Teri said, taking her hand. She looked into her eyes, and Skye felt herself calming, just a little. Teri thought she was doing the right thing, even if she was getting this all wrong. She didn't know Andie like Skye did.

"I'm okay, I'm just super tired, and I told you that I don't want to talk about this anymore."

"I felt like I should tell you. I thought it was important. Come here. I'm sorry."

As Teri put her arms around her, Skye realized she wasn't sure what she was apologizing for. It could be about the state of their friendship or because she was the bearer of bad news.

Teri rubbed her back. Still thinking about Andie, it took longer than it should have to clock how strange it was, the way Teri lingered over the kiss on her cheek. There had always been ease between them that way, but this was different enough to make her pull back.

Teri put a hand on Skye's jaw. "I don't want things to be weird between us. You know that I really care about you, don't you?"

"Of course. I care about you, too."

Teri ran her thumb over Skye's jawline. Skye desperately hoped this wasn't what she thought it was. When Teri leaned forward, Skye put her hand on her chest, shaking her head. This time, there was no way she'd go along to spare her feelings like she had with Dana. She'd promised herself she'd never do that again.

"What are you doing?"

"Nothing. I just thought, maybe…"

Skye stood up unsteadily. Andie told her this was coming, and she'd kept pushing it out of her mind. It was too shocking for words. "I need to get out of here. I have to think."

Teri reached for her hand, but she pulled it away. "Wait, don't go. Let's talk about this."

"What would make you think that would be okay? I thought we were friends. I don't think of you that way, and I didn't think you thought of me like that, either."

They faced one another, the waves crashing in the background.

"I'm sorry, okay? I just got caught up in the moment."

"What moment? There was no moment."

"You've never thought anything was going on here?" Teri said, gesturing between them.

"Not that I knew of. You were always trying to fix me up with women. I don't get it."

"I don't know how to explain that."

"Try, please. I don't understand, and I'd really like to know."

Teri bit her lip, throwing her hands up. "I don't know. I guess I just thought that it was all really new to you. You seemed to want to get out there. I thought maybe when you'd done that, and you were feeling more confident, that might be the time for us. But I didn't mean to do this now. I really didn't."

Skye shook her head. So, Teri thought she could set things up for her to practice with someone else, and then they'd have something? It disgusted her. "But we work together. We're friends. We couldn't."

"I don't think you care about that as much as you're pretending to," Teri scoffed.

"What's that supposed to mean?"

"I think you know what I mean."

Skye hugged herself, shaking her head again. She wished she could press rewind on the last ten minutes and erase the whole thing. She covered her face with her hands. "I don't know how to deal with this."

When she took her hands away, Teri's face crumpled. She wasn't crying, but she was close. "Are you going to fire me?"

"No. Maybe. I don't know."

"Can you wait until I find something else?"

"Wait. I didn't say for sure that I was firing you. I need time to think about it. It'd be for the best if we weren't sharing the villa while I'm working that out."

"Okay. I can talk to Carol. See if they can swap someone out of a hotel room, and I'll move over there. I'll do it today. I swear."

"Thank you. And, Teri? I need you to promise that whatever you think you saw between Andie and Carol stays with you."

Teri stared at her, eyes colder than she'd ever seen them. "That's your main concern right now?"

"It's important. I won't be telling anyone about what happened today, and I expect the same from you."

"I understand."

As Skye walked away, she had the strangest urge to laugh. She couldn't wait to get off this island, back to her family, where her world might feel normal again. It was like the island cast a spell that made them all lose their minds. She was chasing Andie like a teenager, and now she found out that Teri had been chasing her.

The sooner she got back to the States, the better. Maybe then, her heart would heal from all of this.

CHAPTER THIRTY-TWO

Skye rounded the bottom of the stairs and looked around warily. She'd thought about staying in her room until the driver picked her up for work, but she didn't want to hide. If Andie was still here, she was outside on her deck, anyway.

She looked back toward Teri's room with a mixture of relief and sadness that it was empty now. Grabbing a grapefruit from the fruit bowl, she sliced it neatly in half and sprinkled sugar on top. She ate it standing up at the counter. As she finished it and was wiping her mouth, the door slid open and Andie walked in wearing a faded black shirt and jeans.

Slowly, Andie put her cup on the counter and her hands in her pockets. She was so gorgeous that Skye felt a stab of remorse about everything. How could she give that up willingly? It wasn't fair that she looked like that.

"Hey," said Andie.

"Morning."

"Would you like to join me for coffee?"

"Thanks, but I'm okay. I just had breakfast."

Without replying, Andie went to the coffee machine and poured herself a cup, but then she turned and leaned against the counter. "I don't want to nag you. But I'm not asking to be nice or anything. I like having coffee with you."

"I thought you didn't want to spend as much time together anymore."

Andie smiled, and it made Skye's pulse quicken. Goddamn it. She was supposed to be mad at this woman.

"It's just coffee, and we're still working together. We could talk about what we're doing today."

"You're pretty good at getting what you want, aren't you?"

"Not always."

The air between them was so thick that Skye had to look down at her feet to get it together. "Okay. Go on then, pour me one of your magic-bean coffees. Thanks."

When they sat on the wooden stairs, a couple of feet separated them. Skye looked at the shape of Andie's thighs, and her long fingers holding her cup. It hurt to have her close and know that she couldn't reach for her.

"So. Killer fish. It should be an interesting day," Andie said.

"I've always been scared of piranhas. That part freaked me out in the book. Before I read it, I saw that movie *Piranha*, so I was primed already," Skye said, with an exaggerated shudder.

"I loved that movie. It was a lot of fun. I went to the drive-in to see it with Cary and Louis."

"I loved it too. When a movie scares me, I watch it again and again until I know all the tricks, and it doesn't scare me anymore."

"So, how many times have you seen *Piranha*?"

"A lot."

"Really? I didn't think it was that scary. I get scared more by supernatural stuff, I guess. Possessed kids, haunted houses. Stuff like that."

"Are you kidding? I was scared to go in the water after I saw it. And it's not like I was little. I was already in my teens when I saw that."

"Someone should've told you that there aren't any piranhas in California," said Andie, laughing.

"You never know when someone might release them into the open waters. That was my theory, anyway."

"Of course. You're right. I can see that you're not going to need much direction today to look scared out of your mind."

"Nah, I don't think so."

They sipped their coffee in companionable if somewhat awkward silence, giving Skye time to think. When the film was finished, they might promise to keep in touch professionally and run into one another at events and parties. That was the best-case scenario for them. It could never be the same as having Andie here in the early morning when it was quiet and nobody else needed her. All of Andie's attention was on her, as if everything she said was funny and fascinating.

"I couldn't help noticing that Teri moved out yesterday afternoon. What's that all about?" Andie said, breaking into Skye's thoughts.

"Nothing. She was supposed to swap with someone with a hotel room, but it turned out they had a couple of extra rooms from people going home early. So, it'll just be you, me, and Cary for the rest of the shoot."

"I see. Why did she move over there, though?"

"I asked her to."

"Is everything okay between you two? I know you're good friends. Seems weird that she'd move out now unless there was a problem."

"It's fine. I just started to feel a little crowded, you know? I thought it was for the best." She still hadn't decided what she would do about Teri. She'd been such a rock to her personally and professionally, and Skye needed more time to wrap her head around it all.

Andie ran a hand through her hair. "Okay. Maybe this is an arrogant question for me to ask, but it doesn't have anything to do with me, does it?"

"Not arrogant. But no, it's not about you."

"I think you know why I'm asking. The timing is interesting. She wasn't too happy with me yesterday morning. She told you about it, right?"

"Yeah. She said that you and Carol were sitting on the sofa when she came out. Something about Carol sleeping in your room."

"That's right. Carol crawled into my bed. I had no idea she was coming. It was kind of scary, actually, because I just woke up from a dead sleep and she was there. I didn't even know who it was at first. I could see that she was drunk right away, and I told her she shouldn't have just shown up like that. She passed out, and I came right downstairs…"

Andie's voice was trembling, her knuckles white around her mug. Skye had never heard her sound so nervous and almost put a hand on her knee, catching herself just in time. "Hey. You don't have to explain yourself to me. It's fine."

"Can you look at me for a sec? Please?"

Skye turned her head. She didn't ask why, only looked, and their gazes met and held. Her heart thumped. Until this endless beat of looking into Andie's green eyes, she'd been able to lie to herself about the depth of her feelings. This pain wasn't just remorse—it was heartbreak.

She'd had a hard time admitting to herself that she was falling in love.

Andie looked down at her coffee, speaking softly. "Thank you. I wanted to see if you really believed me. I think that you do. You have no idea what that means to me. What makes you so sure when Teri wasn't?"

"I know you better than she does."

"Yeah. You do. So, she told you, obviously. How many other people do you think she's told by now? I've been trying to not worry about it, but it's hard not to. I don't know what I was thinking, asking Carol to stay for coffee. I should've gotten her out before Teri saw her. I know how suspicious it probably looked."

"None. I've made sure of that."

"How do you mean? Did you manage to whip up a nondisclosure agreement since yesterday?"

"Don't worry about it. We have an agreement, and I'm certain that she'll honor it."

"Thanks. I don't know what to say."

She snuck another look at Andie, fingers practically twitching to reach out and grab her hand. It was as though her body had forgotten the events of the last forty-eight hours.

"You don't have to say anything. It's what anyone would have done."

"We both know that's not true. If it was, I wouldn't be in such a mess in the first place. There's your ride," Andie said, nodding toward a car approaching their villa.

"I'll see you there."

"Looking forward to it. I promise you, there aren't any actual savage fish in the lagoon. I'm not looking to get sued."

"Ha, ha."

Skye backed toward the car, unwilling to cut this moment short. Andie grinned at her, looking her up and down lazily. Perhaps she shouldn't be so happy about it because it was selfish, but it made her heart sing. She still wanted her. That hadn't changed.

Finally, she turned away.

CHAPTER THIRTY-THREE

Andie checked her watch for the thousandth time. They were behind, and the color of the sky worried her. They'd been blessed with perfect weather so far. It hadn't rained once, but it looked like their luck had run out. She hoped it would hold until they got the next scene. She checked in with Todd, whose eyes were on the monitors.

"We're running out of time."

"Yep."

"Looks like it could come on suddenly. Can you please get someone to make sure the vans are ready to go and all equipment's tarped and covered up?"

"Sure. I think the guys have already started, but I'll check it's done."

"Thanks."

She went to Skye, who was having special-effects makeup applied to her leg. Her pants were rolled up, and she stared down at the fake wound, seemingly fascinated by how gross it looked.

"How are you doing, terror-wise?"

Skye grinned at her over the head of the makeup artist. "I'm having a ball. It took everything I had to wade into that water, though, after all that talk this morning."

"It looked great. You really sold it."

"Thanks. What's up? You look kinda worried."

Andie pointed up at the sky. "We've got an hour tops before the sky opens. Sometimes I wish we were in LA, shooting in a big tank or something."

"You don't mean that."

"Not usually. Right now, I do. We can't afford to lose the time."

"Hey, can I take a break, please, Angelica?"

Angelica—an enthusiastic horror nerd—put a final touch on the wound with her brush. She'd been having a blast with all the fake blood today. "Actually, I'm all done here. It looks fuckin' sick. What do you think, Andie?"

"I agree. Excellent work, Angelica. Disgusting," she said, slapping her on the back before she walked away.

Andie crouched, so they could talk without being overheard. "There's not much time to do both sets of takes. If we don't finish before it starts raining, we're screwed. We have to move on tomorrow."

"And this scene is crucial in sowing the seeds for Dr. Foster knowing that Adrian's sabotaging the group. The suspicion about why the fish are in there when they weren't before was always a big clue. Right?"

"Exactly."

They sat still for a moment, thinking.

"We can do it. I'll convey suspicion in the close-ups, giving enough to cover it. Then when we move out, I can do the normal takes. I know it'll cut together if I do it right." Skye was always so smart about knowing exactly what they needed to make both sets of shots work. Complicated relationship aside, Andie would give an arm and a leg to work with her again.

"Okay. I know you can do that. Let's get this in the can," Andie said, offering up her hand for a high-five. Skye gave it with a smile.

True to her word, Skye did fantastic work with her facial expressions. As she used a rag to bandage another actor's wound, those eyes communicated so much. Her eyes darted toward Darryl.

"It doesn't make sense. We swam in here only yesterday, and these things are so fast and vicious. How could we have been in here and not attacked then?"

"I don't know," he said, hinting at defensiveness.

Andie took Skye and Darryl aside when they had it. "That was perfect," she whispered, looking up at the sky. "You think you can change gears and get the next part done in as few takes as possible?"

"No pressure," Skye said.

"Oh, don't be ridiculous. You're prepared within an inch of your life," Darryl ribbed.

"So are you."

They were both right. It came off flawlessly, and they only had to stop once because the actor playing the unconscious victim sneezed. As if on cue, the sky forked with lightning. Moments later, it poured down thick sheets of rain. The cast was quickly bundled into cars. The crew ran around, gathering equipment and packing everything into the vans.

"You all right, boss?" Frankie shouted as he ran past her.

"Yep, thanks. Just sticking around to make sure there aren't any problems." She was getting soaked, but all she cared about was that they'd nailed it. Regardless of the problems between her and Skye, they worked together like a dream.

A couple of drivers waited nearby. Andie looked around, astounded at how quickly they'd squared it all away. Todd approached her, wet shirt sticking to his front. "I think we're all good here. Thanks for being so on top of everything. I feel like we pulled off the impossible today."

"Right," he said tightly. She figured he was desperate to get away so he could take a hot shower, but then he gestured toward the cars. "Can we get in and talk?"

"Sure."

As they slid into the back seat, she brushed wet hair back from her face, wondering what was so important that it couldn't wait until they'd dried off. Todd was good at what he did, but she doubted she'd ever work with him again—they just didn't click. For example, he had no radar for the right time to talk. The driver pulled out, and he turned to her.

"I'm going to need you to tell me what the fuck is going on with this movie."

"What do you mean? Everything's going great."

When he wiped the water from his face, he angrily flicked droplets all over the car. "I'm your first AD. I'm supposed to be right there with you. I've never had a director pull the kind of shit you're doing with me."

"Just tell me what your problem is."

"You're up to something. You, Skye, and Darryl. I want to know exactly what you're doing."

"Excuse me?"

"I've been trying to ignore it for weeks and get on with the job, but I've figured you out. You three are working together on arcs that aren't supposed to be in the movie anymore."

"I don't know what you're talking about."

"The weird takes? Do I look stupid?"

"What's brought this on, Todd? It was a good day. We got everything against the odds. Can't we just enjoy it?" she said breezily.

"Even when we were on such a tight timeline, they messed around. You know what I'm talking about."

"Whatever you think you saw, you've got no right to question me on it."

"I walked in on Louise looking over dailies a couple of weeks ago, and I only caught a sec, but I knew it must be from the day you shut down the set."

"So what?"

"Well, she turned off the monitors real quick and got all funny. That's when I started to know you were hiding something. I wasn't sure until today."

If it were anyone else, she might level with them and try to bring them over to her side. It wouldn't work on him. They'd never built up a good relationship like she had with Louise, so she had to flat-out lie. "You're being paranoid."

"I don't think I am. I've noticed how you keep me out of those conversations with the cast. I've been watching."

They were nearing the villas, and she had no idea what to say. What could she do? Offer him a bribe? Beg him to not tell anyone? The thought of doing either of those things made her sick. "It's perfectly natural for you to not be a part of every conversation I have with my actors. You're being ridiculous."

"I know what I've seen."

"No, you don't. And if you don't mind, I'd like to go and shower."

"I heard you were a pain in the ass. Still didn't figure you'd be this bad."

"You're so far over the line it's not even funny," she said, watching the muscles in his jaw twitch.

"Just so you know, I will be talking to Ben and Doug. As soon as they get back."

She paused as she reached for the handle. The producers were due back on the island the following day. "Are you fucking kidding? Did you just tell me you were going to tell my dad on me?"

"They're the bosses. It's not my fault you got the job because of who your daddy is," he said, pointing his finger at her.

"Oh, nice," she said, slamming the car door behind her.

She walked toward her villa with her stomach churning. She hadn't handled that well at all—she'd let her temper get the better of her. Todd wasn't going to let this go. That was obvious.

What was she going to tell Skye?

It was all over. She was utterly screwed.

CHAPTER THIRTY-FOUR

Skye ran toward her villa in the pouring rain. She'd been transported to the production offices for Angelica to remove her wound makeup. She'd refused a lift to her place, loving the feel of water on her skin after a humid day.

With the wet weather likely to continue all evening, their night shoot was canceled. She couldn't be bothered going out to the restaurant. She was looking forward to making grilled cheese, hanging out in her sweatpants, and curling up with a good book.

The door was wide open. As she stepped inside, it only took a glance to see that something was very wrong. Andie sat on the sofa in her wet clothes.

"Are you all right?"

Andie shook her head. Her hair was plastered across her face, which held a frightening blankness. She knelt on the ground in front of her.

"What's going on?"

"It's over. I'm fucked."

"What do you mean? Is this about the stuff with Carol? Did Teri tell someone?"

"No, it's way worse than that."

"What's happened? Did someone get hurt today?"

"It's Todd. He figured everything out, and he's going to Dad and Ben with it. I might as well pack my bags. They'll know tomorrow, by the end of the day. There's nothing I can do."

"Oh, no."

Andie slumped back on the sofa, staring at the ceiling. "It's hopeless. I thought about getting out ahead of it, just fessing up and telling them. Going over to the hotel and seeing if I could get them on the phone. But I can't seem to move."

"Do you think that would help?"

"Probably not. But it means I wouldn't just be sitting around waiting to get fired."

"You really think they'll fire you?"

"Of course, they will."

"But…" Skye was about to say, but he's your father. Andie looked down at her, shaking her head like she knew what she was thinking. It made no difference.

"This is all my fault. It was my idea. I can't let them fire you. I couldn't live with myself."

Andie shot up and grabbed her hands. "Don't say that. I'm the director. It was my call. I'm not going to have you feeling bad about this."

"We have to stop it. I'll threaten to walk. I think Darryl would do the same. He really respects you. They can't fire us all."

Andie was holding her hands so tightly. "You're under contract, Skye. I can't let you do that. I'm replaceable. You're not."

They fell silent, and Andie let go of her hands. Skye wished she hadn't. She wanted to put her head on Andie's lap or hold her. She couldn't bear it if she were ripped away. At least now, they saw one another every day, and she wasn't ready for that to change.

"Do you want to go and call them? I'll come with you. I'm with you, every step of the way, and I'll take full responsibility." She couldn't let this happen. If Andie was fired from the movie that was supposed to be her shot at reviving her career, she might never work as a director again. That would break Andie's heart. Why had she ever suggested this plan? She'd wanted to impress her, not put her whole career at risk.

"I don't know. I just don't know. I don't even know what time it is there or if I'd be able to reach them."

"That's okay. Why don't we both take a shower, and I'll make us something to eat while we talk about it. We'll figure this out together. I saw Cary at the hotel before I left, and she said she was going to Sid's. We've got the place to ourselves."

"Yeah. I could really do with a shower. That'd be good."

"You take the upstairs shower. I'll take mine down here."

It felt good to do something, to have a purpose. They climbed the stairs together. Skye would take care of this, start trying to make up for all her mistakes, take care of Andie.

Downstairs, she showered quickly. By the time Andie emerged, red-eyed but looking calmer, Skye had fixed them a couple of grilled cheeses and poured coffee. She laid everything out on the dining table.

"Thanks for making that, but I don't think I can eat."

"Just have a little."

"No, thanks. I'll have some coffee."

"You should eat something. I bet you didn't have lunch. It'll help."

Andie smiled softly at her and picked up the sandwich. Skye bit into her own, holding back. She was anxious to talk through a plan, but they had all night.

"I keep expecting a knock at the door. Like I'm going to get dragged out of here. Even though there's no way they could know yet," Andie said after a while.

"Are you sure Todd's really going to do this? Is there any chance it was an empty threat?"

"He was pretty fired up. I'm sure he will. I guess they'll demand to get their hands on the footage Louise cut from the dailies when they find out, and there's nothing Louise will be able to do. She'll have to show them, and they'll see the Adrian death scene. I don't know how I ever thought this wouldn't happen, that we could hide something so huge from them. I guess I got carried away. I was stupid."

"You weren't stupid, Andie. You had a plan. You wanted to do something special. So did I."

"I know."

Andie looked so broken it hurt to look at her. For the first time since they'd come back to the villa, Skye wondered if she was the right person to help. Things were so complicated that she couldn't even hold her like she needed. "Do you want me to get Cary for you? Maybe she can help."

Andie put her head down on the table for a moment.

"Thanks, but that's okay. I don't want to drag her into it, not yet anyway. She'll find out soon enough."

Skye leaned over, putting her hand on her shoulder. "Do you want me to leave you alone? I don't want to crowd you or anything."

"I don't want you to take responsibility for this. I'm already going to be in trouble. There's no getting around that," Andie said, brushing the question aside.

"But it was my idea," Skye said earnestly. Taking the blame was the only way they might save Andie's neck. They could chalk it up to Skye being demanding. If they kept to the original story about Skye and Darryl wanting to do the scene for fun, they might get away with it.

"It doesn't matter. Don't you see? I'm already in trouble. There's no point getting you and Darryl in trouble, too. I know I'll get replaced, and you guys can finish the movie without getting involved. It's better this way. That's what I want."

"No. I want to do it together."

"I'd really rather you stay out of the whole thing. Okay?"

With a stormy expression Skye stared at the table. Still, she wouldn't back down just because Andie was getting annoyed. "No, it's not okay. I'm not prepared to go along with that."

"Why not?"

"Because it would be wrong. It's a lie. I'll take the consequences, whatever they are, but I have to be honest."

Andie leaned over and grabbed Skye's plate, stacking it on top of her own. She went silently to the kitchen. "Thanks for dinner. I'm going to try and get some sleep."

It wasn't even eight o'clock. Skye understood that Andie was scared and exhausted, but it stung. This might be one of their only chances to talk like this if it went as badly as Andie thought it was going to.

"So, that's it? Discussion over?"

Andie leaned against the sink, folding her arms. "Yes. I don't want to discuss it anymore. You're not listening to me. So, what's the point?"

"I'm listening. I just disagree with you."

"Yeah, well. We've never agreed on everything. What's new?" Andie said, heading toward the bottom of the stairs.

"Why are you talking to me like this? You're being so flippant." Skye was embarrassed by how desperate she sounded, but she couldn't help it. She wanted to beg Andie to stay, to stay down here and let Skye hold her.

Andie paused, hand on the banister. "I don't mean to be flippant. I can see you're trying to help, and I'm grateful. But I just want to be alone right now. Good night."

"Night," Skye said stiffly.

She sat at the table for a long time, listening to Andie's footsteps above her. For a while, she had really felt like they were in this together. She hated that Andie was in her room by herself, just waiting for the other shoe to drop.

Why couldn't they stay up together, brainstorming solutions like they had so many times before? They made such a good team. It couldn't end like this.

Sighing heavily, Skye turned off the lights downstairs and got ready for bed feeling hopeless, knowing that sleep would elude her for a long time. It would be a miracle if she slept at all.

CHAPTER THIRTY-FIVE

Andie's jaw was so tense it made her head hurt. Her memory caught on one thing then another, trying to find the exact moment she could have used better judgment and prevented all this. Her conclusion was that she couldn't have stopped herself. She was a born fuck-up. Take Skye, for example. If anyone was off-limits, it should be the star of her redemption movie. She'd never learned a thing.

She wondered if she would have done all this if it weren't for Skye. Maybe, in some strange way, all she was trying to do this whole time was impress her. She wanted to be the maverick, show that she could stick it to the studio, refuse to let them impede her creativity.

It had backfired. Even with the alternate takes and secret shooting being Skye's idea, Andie was so ashamed. She'd thought she was smart enough to get away with it, but she wasn't. She'd told herself that she was nobly fighting for her vision, but she was a fool.

The humiliation from her last movie was nothing compared to this. Getting thrown off a film by her father would be a new low.

She kicked off the sheets. When she was with Skye downstairs, she wanted to be alone. As soon as she'd left, she wished she hadn't. Nothing felt right.

She slipped on the boxer shorts she slept in sometimes. It was so quiet that her bedroom door creaking echoed alarmingly. She was relieved to see the light under Skye's door. The least she could do was make sure that everything was okay between them. It mattered—maybe more than anything else.

She tapped lightly.

"You can open it."

Andie pushed open the door gingerly. The lamp cast a glow over the room, Skye lying propped up on her pillows with a notebook and pen. She put them aside, resting them on the nightstand. She wore a white tank top, with the sheets pulled up to her waist. Andie leaned her head on the door frame, already weak at how lovely she was. "Sorry. I didn't mean to interrupt anything."

"That's okay."

"That your diary?" she asked, nodding toward it.

It was cute, and so were those glasses. Skye wore contacts most of the time. She'd noticed the lens solution on the sink in the bathroom. There were so many little details about Skye that made her curious.

"It's a journal."

"A journal, huh? Do I rate a mention?"

"Don't flatter yourself."

"If you were writing about how I was rude to walk off on you, I'd deserve it. I'm sorry. Can you come down so we can talk some more?"

"You take off, and now you want to drag me out of bed?"

"I know. I'm horrible. Please?"

"I'll talk to you, but I'm not getting out of bed. You can come in."

Andie hesitated, looking back over her shoulder even though she knew nobody was home. "I don't know."

"C'mon, what does it matter now? Cary's not here. Just come and sit. Please."

Even though they were alone, she closed the door behind her and sat at the end of the bed. "Thank you."

Skye took off her glasses and laid them on the nightstand atop her journal. "That's the second time you've done that to me. Walked off right in the middle of an important conversation."

"Yeah. I guess I do that. Sorry."

"Why do you do it? Is that how you always deal with a conversation you don't like?"

"Not usually. I've always been a fighter, but I have all this energy around you, and I don't know where to put it. So, I just have to leave. Talking to you always feels…intimate."

"Why does feeling intimate with me feel bad to you?"

"You know why. Because we agreed it can't go anywhere."

"Did we? Did we agree on that for forever?"

Andie swallowed hard. When they'd spoken in the production offices, she'd known it wasn't really over. How could it be when there was this much frisson between them? She knew she should say something, but she was saved from figuring out exactly what when Skye kept going.

"For right now, there are different ways to be close. I feel close to you when we're working. That's a kind of intimacy, right? And there's nothing wrong with it?"

Andie drew up her knee and rested her chin on it. Skye seemed to have no idea how hard it was to be close to her without taking things further. The creamy skin above her tank top, the firm roundness of her breasts underneath, those eyes. Sitting here and talking about it rationally didn't come naturally, but she was trying.

"There's nothing wrong with it, no. I like it too. But, sometimes, it feels like it's blurring into something else, and I can't deal with that. And downstairs, you weren't listening to me. I'm clear on what I want."

"That doesn't mean you get to decide for both of us."

"That's fair, I guess."

It was quiet for a moment. Andie closed her eyes. She was in Skye's room, on her bed, and their chemistry was electric.

Skye had been right before, because what did it matter now? Why was she trying so hard to do the right thing? She'd already blown it. She'd never been good at it.

"Hey, what is Andie short for, anyway?"

"My God, you're so strange sometimes," she said, laughing.

"What? I've been wondering."

"Andressa."

"That's beautiful."

"Only my mother calls me that. I've always just been Andie."

"C'mon, lie down. It might be our last night to talk," Skye said, holding back the sheet and quilt. Her voice was sensual, and Andie thrilled at it.

Andie crawled underneath the sheets, skin hypersensitive as they brushed across her. Skye rolled over and flicked off the lamp. She never thought they'd do something like this—lie beside one another talking in bed. She was careful to not get too close, staying over on her side of the mattress.

"I'm sorry that this will probably affect *Shelley*, too. I'm not going to be much help after all this. You could still talk to Dad, but it would be best to act like I hadn't even read the script."

"You don't know what's going to happen."

"I think we can assume that people will take my calls even less often than they did before."

"I'd still take your calls."

"Aww, thanks. You're too kind. Maybe we can shoot your movie on a video camera. In my house."

"I know you're kidding, but it'd still be better than what anyone else would do."

"You don't have to say that. But I appreciate it," she said, rolling onto her side and propping herself up on an elbow.

Skye's head was pillowed on her hands. Even in the half-dark, she was luminous. Andie would miss shooting that face so much, miss just looking at it.

Now that she might be leaving, she couldn't think of one good reason they shouldn't kiss.

"What are we going to do tomorrow? I want to respect your wishes, but I don't think I can," Skye said. "I want to speak with your father and Ben."

Andie tried to bring herself back to the conversation. Maybe Skye really did just mean for her to come in here and talk. It was hard to believe when she kept looking at her like that. "It's okay. I'm not going to tell you what to do. If you want to talk to them after we've had our meeting, I'm not going to hold you back."

"Does that mean I can rally the troops? Get Darryl in? And Cary, and I'm sure Sid would come? And some crew, too? There are so many people who'd want to support you. Let them."

"Let's just wait and see what happens before we call in the cavalry. I assume they'll call me into a meeting in the early evening, and then we'll talk about the next steps from there."

"You promise you'll let me know if there's anything at all I can do to help?"

Andie lay down, resting her hands on her stomach, trying to quell her nerves. She wasn't sure what scared her most. The prospect of this big meeting or making the wrong move with Skye. "I promise. Now that we have a deal, I should go back to bed."

It was a question, and she was flooded with relief when Skye told her not to.

"Stay and talk a while longer."

"All right. Which out-of-the-box question would you like to ask me, now?"

"Ha. I'm sure I can think of something."

"I look forward to it."

"It's not a question, but there is something I've been thinking. I don't know whether I should say it or not."

Without noticing it, Andie had moved closer to her on the mattress, realizing Skye had been doing the same thing. She could feel her so near, the heat from her body radiating.

"Whatever it is, maybe you should. Last chance, remember?"

"It's what you said, about how you have energy around me that you don't know what to do with. I feel the same way. It's not a familiar feeling, and it never goes away."

Andie exhaled slowly, inching closer still. Her leg came into contact with Skye's, and she realized with a jolt that she was only wearing underwear with her tank top.

The whole front of her body brushed against Andie's, sending an overpowering thrill through her. Her breasts were so soft and luscious, and she thought about that brief touch on the balcony that night.

They weren't touching with their hands, but they were touching everywhere else. Skye's breath was on her lips. "Can I kiss you?"

"I thought you'd never ask..."

CHAPTER THIRTY-SIX

Skye's every thought and sensation was filled by Andie. The soft hair brushing her cheek and the clean, lovely scent of soap and shampoo. Andie's hand on her shoulder, and more than anything, the divine taste of her lips. She lay on her back with Andie at her side, leaning over.

Whenever they had kissed it was awe inspiring. It was even better this time. They were all alone in the villa, so for once there was no fear of being caught. It made Skye's toes curl to think they had all night.

One hand was on the soft curve of Andie's hip. With the other, she ran a hand through her hair, then cradled her neck.

So many nights, she had lain in this bed dreaming of this. She'd been thinking of Andie right before she came in, wishing she'd come but never believing she would. If she hadn't stayed when she asked, Skye might have begged. "You smell so good," Skye said. It was crazy how much she wanted to drink her in.

"I love the way you smell."

It didn't take long for Skye to seek a deeper kiss, to have that electric feeling of their tongues sliding against one another's. Andie moved her leg on top of Skye's, the sensation of skin-on-skin delicious.

They kissed for a time that felt endless, Skye becoming lost in it, though a tiny part of her brain worried that Andie might want to stop like she had the last time. After a while, that fear dropped away. Skye might be the initiator, but Andie's lips and tongue were insistent. She was barely breaking for air, her fingertips dancing along Skye's arm or tracing her lip now and then.

Andie put a hand on her jaw, and Skye caught her fingers, noticing how they trembled. "Are you all right?"

"Yeah, just super nervous. Is that weird?"

Skye knew the feeling, but she wasn't nearly as nervous as she thought she'd be. Her hunger was too powerful to leave room for much else. "You're not weird. I just want you to be okay."

"It's just that it's been a while for me, and half the time I was drunk, before…" She broke off and buried her face in her shoulder. "Now I'm really embarrassed. I'm sorry. This must be such a turnoff."

Skye stroked Andie's hair, thinking it simply wasn't like that. Maybe some people thought you shouldn't be so vulnerable in these moments, but all those rules felt silly when they were together. She loved that Andie was confiding in her. "Don't say that. Not at all."

"I mean, I'm not assuming anything more will happen tonight. It's just that even kissing you feels like a big deal."

"It's a big deal to me, too," she said, not sure how to say that she was hoping for so much more. She felt ready for anything, whatever Andie was comfortable with.

They came back together, and soon there was a change in how Andie kissed her, as if she'd forgotten to be afraid. The shaking disappeared. She could only feel the urgency in how Andie moved against her.

Andie's fingers toyed with the hem of Skye's tank top. Her hand crept higher, Skye shivering when she felt it on her stomach.

"Is this okay?"

Skye whispered a yes, and Andie palmed her breast. She stroked softly while they kissed, rubbing her fingers gently over Skye's nipple.

"Andie?" she asked, her voice coming out like a stranger's. She hadn't known this could feel so amazing.

"Yeah?" Andie said, lightly scratching down Skye's belly and then back up again, rolling her nipple between her fingers.

"Do you mind if I take my tank top off?"

"You said you'd ask me some weird questions, and that has to be the weirdest. Of course, I want that."

"And you'll take yours off, too?"

"These questions are great. Keep them coming."

They laughed in unison. Skye sat up to pull her shirt over her head, watching eagerly while Andie did the same. She stared at Andie's slim waist, gaze drifting from her beautiful breasts to her stomach.

"You're so…" Skye said, breaking off, not knowing how to describe how it made her feel.

She cupped Andie's breasts, adoring how their weight felt in her hands. She drew her thumbs over the peaks until they stiffened.

Pushing Andie onto her back, she bent over her. When they kissed, their breasts brushed together in the most lovely, sensual way. Skye slid the flat of her palm across her chest, and Andie's breath came harder. It was wonderful how much Andie reacted to her, how overcome she seemed.

She wanted more of *that*, and she wanted Andie's skin under her lips. She bent down further, kissing a path to her nipple. She licked it, then pulled it into her mouth, grazing it with her teeth.

"Oh," Andie said breathlessly, putting a hand at the back of her head. "Do that again, please?"

Exploring Andie's body, Skye allowed herself to be tugged along by desire. She touched her everywhere—hip, stomach, neck. She licked and kissed her breasts for so long, feeling like she could never grow tired of it. Beyond Skye's wildest dreams, Andie moved under her mouth, asking her for more.

There was no conversation about what happened after that, no plan. It was a dance in which each movement flowed effortlessly into the following, and they didn't need words for it. A faint voice told her that there was so much they hadn't talked about. She hadn't even told Andie that this was her first time with a woman, but it felt so irrelevant at this moment. It would also mean stopping, which was the last thing she wanted to do.

She moved up to kiss her mouth, sliding her hand down Andie's belly to the waistband of her shorts. "I wanted this so badly, that day by the lagoon," she said, thinking how special it was that she could say anything to her.

"So did I. You were wearing that blue dress, and I thought you were the most gorgeous woman I'd ever seen," Andie replied, running her hands over Skye's back.

Skye's hand strayed downward and touched her over her underwear, hearing Andie's breath quicken. She felt hot and wet even through the fabric, and Skye's heart sped like a train. "You really did?" she said, teasing with two fingers.

"Walking away from you that day was so hard. You've been driving me crazy."

Andie's thighs were parted, and she raised herself up toward her hand, asking silently. Skye took in how her brows knitted together like she ached with desire. She did too.

They both sighed when Skye's fingers found her clit and stroked, Andie letting out a long moan that went right through her. Skye tore herself away for a moment to pull down her shorts and underwear, Andie helping her, kicking them to the floor. She took a beat to take in Andie's full nakedness, and she had no words for what she saw.

They arranged themselves on the bed again, Andie resting against the pillows while they kissed sweetly. After so much tension between them, they could finally relax. They knew what was going to happen next.

"Not too nervous? You're okay?" Skye asked, though she wondered whose heart was racing faster.

"Yeah," she replied, pushing a lock of hair behind Skye's ear then pulling her down for another kiss.

As their lips joined, Skye trailed her hand down between them. Andie was so slick under her touch. It was such a turn-on, as was the way she rocked against her hand. She bit her lip and closed her eyes, unable to believe that she was here, that she was touching Andie so intimately.

She was meant to do this. It was the easiest, most precious thing in the world to have Andie underneath her, looking up, her face full of need. She circled her clit slowly and firmly, unconsciously grinding herself on Andie's thigh.

They looked into one another's eyes. The warmest smile crossed Andie's face, and it shot through Skye. She stroked, and the smile was replaced by something hotter.

"Take those off," Andie said.

"I don't want to stop touching you."

"Just for a sec. Please. I want to feel you."

Skye paused, impatiently removing her underwear and then getting back on top. Andie pushed her thigh up between her legs, and she moaned.

"See, that's it," Andie said.

"Shhh," Skye said, laughing, but when she did it again a moment later, gasping. For a while, she'd forgotten about her own body—she was too focused on Andie. Now, her desire flooded in with full force.

It made her utterly disinhibited. She raised her hand to her lips, tasting what she'd been touching. The smell was intoxicating, and the taste even better. Andie's look said everything. She loved that she'd done that.

With wet fingers, Skye stroked again, keeping the same languorous pace. There was no need to rush, and she loved the sensuality of this, the scent of Andie as she grew more aroused.

Andie's breath picked up speed. Caught up in the pleasure of it, Skye moved her hand faster, at the same time grinding into Andie's thigh. She couldn't believe how much touching Andie stoked her own satisfaction, and she loved watching Andie's face, flushed, her mouth hanging open.

She sensed that Andie was close. She leaned down to kiss her, making sure she didn't slow down. "What do you need?"

"Harder," she said, moaning when Skye increased the pressure, drawing tight circles. She felt Andie shudder underneath her, and she slowed down, helping her ride it out for a moment before taking her hand away.

This time, when they kissed, it felt different. Andie clung to her, arms around her neck, her breathing settling. She couldn't believe she'd made Andie come. She wanted to do it again.

Her arousal skyrocketed during their long kisses, Andie trailing her hands over the sides of her breasts and then over her back. She sat up with Skye in her lap, pulling Skye's legs around her waist, digging her fingers into her thighs.

Looking down between them, she scanned Skye's body, staring down at her center so long that Skye nearly blushed. "You are too good to be true."

Andie kissed her again, first her lips and then her neck, fondling her breasts. She teased between her legs lightly until Skye was panting into her neck. The back of her legs tingled. Andie swirled her tongue around Skye's nipples, which were begging for her mouth.

At last, she slid her fingers firmly against Skye's clit, and she couldn't help but cry out.

"You feel amazing," Andie said, biting her lower lip gently, caressing her.

They stayed like that for a long time, Andie stroking and kissing, sometimes cradling her breasts or tonguing her neck. She felt unmoored by the touch—but like Andie would always catch her. She pressed her forehead to Andie's, feeling her fingers moving downward.

"Do you like this?"

Skye nodded into her forehead. She wanted to feel everything with her. Andie pushed inside gently with two fingers, going slowly until Skye nodded again. Soon, she was moving up and down, Andie driving up simultaneously. She put a hand on Skye's hip, guiding her forward, fucking her until she saw stars.

They looked into one another's eyes. Andie's expression was so intense, her eyes burning. This was the only thing in the world that mattered. Andie leaned forward and spoke close to her ear, making her shiver.

"I just want to do this all night. I love your body."

Skye wrapped her legs more tightly around her. The words made her almost as hot as Andie's fingers.

There was something else, though. Skye had thought Andie was going to continue by saying, "I love you." Even through the bliss of her touch, Skye understood clearly that if Andie had said that to her, she would've said it back. Maybe it was crazy to think it so soon, but she did love her. How could she have ever risked letting her go, by not making her a promise?

Andie's fingers made her lose herself again. When Andie used her thumb against her clit, her whole body drew tight.

When she'd barely recovered, she fell onto her back. Andie climbed on top, lightly stimulating the area worn sensitive by her touch.

Floating on a tide of pleasure, Skye wrapped her arms and legs around Andie, wanting to keep her close. Andie raised herself up enough to kiss her softly, and desire sparked a fire in her belly all over again.

She traced Skye's cheek and forehead with a finger, her look so adoring that it turned Skye's want into something softer and sweeter. This was everything she'd ever hoped for with Andie and so much more. How could she have ever thought that Andie wasn't right for her? There was nothing more right in the world.

"I feel so lucky right now," Andie said, echoing her thoughts perfectly.

"That was so good. You are so good."

"So are you," she said, resting her head on Skye's shoulder. The feeling of her soft hair on Skye's neck was thrilling. "We should get some sleep. It's such a big day tomorrow. I'm glad I could forget about it for a while."

"Just a little while longer," Skye said, shifting to the side, joining their lips, and sighing.

CHAPTER THIRTY-SEVEN

Skye awoke with Andie's arms wrapped around her from behind, one of her hands on her stomach. Andie stirred and arched against her like a cat.

"Mmm," said Andie, using her hands to ask Skye to turn. She rolled onto her back. Had she ever seen anything more gorgeous than Andie staring down at her, naked in the morning light? A single silver chain hung over firm breasts, those green eyes clear and calm. They grinned at one another.

"Your hair looks even wilder than usual."

"Well, what do you expect after the ravishing you gave me?" Andie replied, eyes dancing. She bent down and kissed her, making her stomach flip.

Skye spread her hands flat on her back while Andie lay between her hips, angling down and into her.

"You are so goddamn sexy," Skye said, tugging Andie closer.

"No regrets about last night, I take it? You're feeling okay? I know we didn't really plan it…" Andie said, her expression suddenly serious, a hand on the side of her face.

It hadn't occurred to Skye that there could be any problem. It was perfect, from start to finish. "Of course. Are you okay with it, too?"

"Yeah. Don't really think there was any stopping it, you know?"

Andie's soft lips were on Skye's neck, a hand sliding up her thigh. Her legs fell open. She was already so wet—or still wet—and eager to have Andie's fingers inside her.

The alarm rang shrilly, and it was like having a bucket of water thrown over her. They both groaned, and Andie smacked a hand onto the mattress, then flopped onto her back while Skye reached over to turn it off.

"Do you think we could stay in bed, even for ten minutes?" Skye asked.

"I'd love to, but I didn't realize the time. We should get up," Andie said, rising and stretching. Skye stared, and Andie threw a pillow at her. "Stop looking at me like that, or we'll never make it out the door."

She searched beside the bed for her clothes, not quite comfortable enough to get up naked like Andie had, though she was getting her shorts on now. Skye pulled her tank top over her head. "I'm glad we don't have anything too taxing to shoot today. I'm too nervous to concentrate much. You must be, too?"

"Terrified," Andie said, pulling her hair from the neckline of her shirt.

"I can understand why. Like I said last night, I'll help in whatever way I can."

Andie chewed on a thumbnail, frowning. "You know what? I'm going to take the bull by the horns. I'm going to ask Todd to back off because I want to tell them myself."

"That's not a bad idea. You can control the message, then."

"Exactly. We can ask for a meeting and present them with the ideas. Explain everything and show them footage from the death scene. They'll be furious, at least at first. But I think it'll make a difference if they hear it from us."

Warmth spread through Skye, like the sun. "Us? You want me to come with you when you tell them?"

Andie walked over, standing between Skye's legs while she sat on the bed. "Is that something you'd want?"

"I want. I absolutely want," she said, pulling Andie close by the shirt.

CHAPTER THIRTY-EIGHT

When Andie arrived on set, the sky was still pink, the sun just poking over the horizon. You really could get used to anything, and there were times during this shoot when she'd forgotten to appreciate the stunning beauty of this location. She turned around, breathing it in.

The calm before the storm.

Her eyes stung from lack of sleep, and she was terrified of everything she had to do today. Speaking with Todd was her top priority. And as soon as she could slip away for half an hour, she'd ask a driver to take her to the production offices to pin down her editor.

Walking around the set, she checked in with the crew to see how they were doing. Shooting on the beach could be a hassle with the wind and sand, not to mention the noise of the ocean. The sea was calm, and the air relatively still. The scene was part of a sequence where the characters set up camp near the trees.

The team had just finished unloading the fake lean-to, constructed with branches and palms. Andie checked it out, stepping back to take in the full picture.

"Looks great, guys. Thanks."

While she'd been walking around, Skye had arrived. She sat in her chair with her hair wrapped, reading a book. Even from this distance, the sight made Andie's breath catch in her throat. Last night, she acted like it simply wasn't an option for Andie not to finish this movie, which gave her courage. This movie was hers, and she had to fight hard for it.

They were fighting this together. It meant everything.

Her attention shifted to Todd, who stood not far from Skye, speaking into his walkie-talkie. She'd love to tell herself that he was the cause of all her problems, but she knew she was dealing with the consequences of her own choices. She had to own that.

He clipped the walkie-talkie to his belt. Then he lit a cigarette, walking over to her with a pissier expression than usual.

"Hey. You ready to meet?" said Todd. He flicked ash from his cigarette, barely meeting her eye. They caught up with some of the production heads every morning to go over the schedule. She respected that he wanted to stick to the routine. It was professional. Still, she wasn't going to act like nothing was happening.

"I'd like to meet with you for a few minutes alone first if that's okay."

"You're the boss."

They trudged along the beach. When they got far enough away from the set, he planted a boot on a rock and pinched out his cigarette. "I'm guessing you want to try and talk me out of going to the producers."

"No. I know there's no point in doing that."

"You going to tell me again how you haven't been doing what I know you're doing?"

"Nope, not that either. I'm sorry I wasn't honest with you last night. I should've been."

"Okay," he said, rubbing his chin uncertainly. She'd caught him off guard.

"I'd like the opportunity to go and talk to them myself before you do."

"Why, so you can feed them some line of bullshit and get me fired? I don't think so," he scoffed.

There was one objective for this conversation—convincing him to let her handle it. It wasn't the time to be a hothead. This was only the first step in the plan, so she kept herself calm. "I can understand why you'd be suspicious, but I just want them to hear it from me. I'll be coming clean. Completely. I'll show them footage. You have my word."

"Not sure your word is worth that much."

"Fair enough. I can't prove it, but we both know you have me over a barrel anyway. The evidence is right there on film, and it was always going to come out sooner or later."

He rubbed his chin again, studying her. "That's what I don't get. You've got to be the most self-destructive chick on the planet. You had to know that this was never going to work out, not really. It's not like you've got final cut. So, I gotta ask, why? Did you just want to get one over on your father or the studio?"

"It's simple. I just wanted to try and make a good movie. You know that sometimes, the best stuff happens in the cutting. I truly believe that maybe, if they see how good a different version of this movie could be, they'll change their minds."

"That's crazy. But I kind of believe you after seeing how you work. You're dedicated. I'll give you that."

"Thank you. Listen, you're a great first AD. Everything has been running like clockwork, thanks to you. I appreciate your work immensely. I'm sorry that I didn't tell you that."

He looked her in the eye for the first time since they'd started speaking and nodded. "Thanks."

"What's your goal? Career-wise, I mean?"

"I want to get into producing."

"Thought so. It'd be a good fit for you. When you get there, you're going to have to deal with people like me, fighting for their creative vision, and we'll drive you nuts. But isn't that what this is all about? Isn't that what we're all doing? It's just that sometimes those things clash. Nobody is ever really sure what's going to make a good movie."

"Yeah. I guess."

"Do we have a deal? Again, all I'm asking is for you to let me break the news. And if by some miracle they let me stay on, I promise I'll play it straight with you for the rest of the shoot. Okay?"

"All right," he said, offering his hand. They shook on it and then got to work.

For the next few hours, Andie focused intently on getting the day's scenes in the can. It soon felt like a regular day, rather than what might be her final one. There was little time for navel gazing, but in between takes, she had managed to get to the production offices to talk to Louise.

They broke for lunch, and she grabbed a turkey sandwich and an apple from craft services. She sat on the warm sand to eat by herself, trying to clear her head.

Cary sank down onto the sand next to her. "What's up?"

"How do you always know the absolute worst time to interrupt me?"

"You're not doing anything. Are you going to eat the other half of that sandwich?"

"Something wrong with your legs? Craft services is that way."

"Grouch."

Andie handed her the paper plate. It was a miracle she'd been able to get down as much of it as she had, anyway. Her stomach was a mess. "You're doing great today, by the way."

Cary smiled at her with a mouth full of bread. "Aw, shucks."

"No, you really are. Your timing is perfect. The humor is going to play super well. The movie needs you to break the tension."

The smile slipped until Cary looked back at her with narrowed eyes. "What gives? You seem all sentimental or something."

"I'm just telling you, you're doing a fantastic job."

"What's wrong? You look even more intense than usual."

"Nothing's wrong," she said, drawing her knees up to her chest. "If I look intense, it's just because I have a lot on my mind."

"Work problems or lady problems? It's got to be one or the other."

It was both, so she couldn't help but laugh. "It'll be okay. I don't want to go into detail right now, but I might have a problem brewing with Dad and Ben."

"That's not unexpected. You've been fighting with them since we got here. You seem to be doing okay with it."

"This is a little bigger than one of our creative differences."

"Oh, well. I'm sure it'll be okay. If there's anything I can do, let me know. I've got your back."

Andie bumped her with a shoulder. "Thanks. That means a lot."

"And is there anything else on your mind? I've barely been home to talk to you. How are things with you-know-who?"

She must've been quiet for a moment too long. Cary slapped her shoulder. "Did she change her mind? Are you two going to date now?"

Andie shook her head, stomach plunging. She felt like burrowing into her sister's shoulder like she had when she was a little kid. There was no time to wonder about a future with Skye or feel sorry for herself that she might not have one.

"No. She hasn't said that. It's nothing."

All night, she'd waited for Skye to say something—to tell her what this meant for her. It felt so magical between them, so beyond. There was a way that Skye looked at her that told her it couldn't be only in her mind.

They'd slipped into sleep at the same time, holding hands. It couldn't be only physical for Skye. It couldn't be that they were just friends and colleagues who happened to have good sexual chemistry.

They'd woken in the night, kissing and touching again. They whispered sweet words about what they were doing. She waited and waited for Skye to say more, but she was still waiting when the morning came.

So, that was it. It was nothing. Nothing at all.

CHAPTER THIRTY-NINE

Skye was reading a Stephen King novel twenty feet away on another patch of sand, but she couldn't stop watching Andie with her sister. They clowned around while they ate their lunch. She wished she were sitting with them. Andie might be sent packing, so every moment away from her felt like a waste.

She watched her get up and brush sand from the seat of her jeans. Knowing exactly what she looked like out of those jeans was enough to make Skye melt into a puddle.

One of the ADs came over as she got ready to head back. "Can you please go to the hair and makeup trailer? They need to make your hair look dirtier for continuity."

"Oh. Sure."

Skye sat in the chair with her book in her lap, not noticing Andie come in.

"When you're done, can I please have a moment to chat with Skye?"

The throaty voice made Skye's stomach tighten, with memories of how Andie whispered to her in the night. Their eyes met in the mirror, heat flashing between them. When they were alone, Skye spun in the chair to face her. "How's it all going?"

Andie looked over her shoulder, making sure everyone had cleared out. She leaned over, putting her hands on the arms of her chair. "I spoke to Todd. He's agreed to let me talk to them myself."

"That's great news. How did you do it?"

"It wasn't as hard as I thought. I just apologized and promised that I'll follow through on telling them everything."

"Good. I'm so happy he's giving you the opportunity to do that."

"Yep, me too. And I raced up to see Louise. She's got the footage from that scene ready for us."

"That's fantastic. Even with everything going on, I can't wait to see it."

"Me neither. You know, I'm starting to really believe that everything could be okay. Am I crazy?"

Skye moved forward in the chair and opened her legs so that Andie could step between her thighs. "Not at all. It has to be okay."

"I really wish I could kiss you without messing up all this work."

She put her hands on Andie's waist, her eyes closing. "I wish we could, too."

Andie took one of Skye's hands and kissed her knuckles, the tenderness making her stomach tighten again. She was like a dream.

"Thanks for being in my corner. It means the world to me. I hope you know that. It's so much easier, knowing you're behind me."

"I'd do anything for you," Skye said, words out of her mouth before she could think about it.

Andie kissed her fingers again, not breaking eye contact.

"Is it just me or was last night…" said Skye.

A knock on the door sounded. As Andie broke away and the assistant poked his head in, Skye finished the sentence in her head. Earth-shattering? One of the most special in her whole life? The best sex she'd ever had? All of them were true.

They were wrapping for the day when Skye saw Teri standing off to the side, watching the shoot. With a pang, she realized she couldn't recall the last time she'd spoken to her. She went over, Teri smiling uncertainly.

"Hey. Can we go for a little walk? I can go through all your messages and stuff with you," Teri said.

"Sure," she agreed, after figuring that Andie wouldn't be meeting with Ben and Doug for another hour or so. As far as she knew they hadn't arrived on the island yet.

Teri drew her small notebook from her shoulder bag, reading from it as they strode down to the beach. There were a few interview requests, and her agent had passed on a message that the Coen brothers were interested in her for their next film.

"That's weird. I wouldn't think I'd be on their radar," Skye said. She'd loved *Raising Arizona.*

"Do you want us to organize a call with them?"

"Absolutely. As soon as possible."

"Will do. Oh, and there was a call about a *Vanity Fair* cover."

"Maybe. I'm just still wondering why the Coen brothers would be interested in me. I thought I'd be too mainstream for their tastes."

"Probably word of mouth about this project. I keep hearing that everyone's buzzing about it back in LA. The talk is very positive, especially about your performance."

"Huh. I hope they'll keep buzzing for the right reasons."

"What do you mean? Is something wrong?" Teri asked, stuffing her notebook back in her bag.

Skye was kicking herself, but it was the force of habit. They really did talk about everything before. "Oh…no, sorry. I'm just being silly, don't worry about me."

They'd both stopped walking, and Teri shook her head, smiling kindly at her. "You're so self-deprecating. You're always so much better than you think you are."

"Thanks."

"Listen. I'm really sorry about how everything's gone down."

"Me too. I wish things were different."

"You've been a great employer over the last couple of years, but I don't see how things can go on as they are. You're uncomfortable around me now, and I don't blame you."

"Well, sure. A little. I hadn't made any decisions yet, just so you know. I would never take that lightly. I wanted to give it some time."

"I know. You're being very fair. But I've decided that resigning is the right thing to do. I've been asking around, putting the feelers out. Matthew knows Taylor Jackson, and he said she's looking."

"Oh, wow. A musician. That's different for you, isn't it?"

"It is. It'd be fun if I got it. I'd get to go out on tour."

"That sounds amazing. Well, I'm happy for you if you do get that."

"How would you feel about me staying on until we leave the island and you can find someone else?"

"Of course. I'd be more than happy with that. And I'll help in any way I can, with the new job. I can give you a great reference," Skye said, then hugged Teri. It didn't feel quite how it had in the past—it lacked some of that natural ease—but she'd miss her.

"Thanks. I don't know if I should ask this, but is everything okay with you? With Andie, I mean?"

"Still not ready to talk about that. But yes, I'm okay, thank you. You don't need to worry about me."

Last night, every lingering doubt she had about Andie had been swept away. Nobody had ever touched her with such tenderness. All she had to do was feel those touches and look into Andie's eyes to know this was right. Whatever mistakes Andie had made in the past were behind her now. That clarity she'd had about her feelings while they made love had survived into the daylight and only become stronger.

After all their troubles with the movie were over, she planned to tell her how she felt. The moment had to be right, but she wanted to tell Andie that it wasn't her that she hadn't trusted. It was her own judgment. If Andie would still have her, she wanted them to date as soon as she was comfortable.

They headed back up the beach. They made small talk, but Skye's mind was squarely on the evening ahead. Tonight, she would channel her inner Dr. Foster and go into battle for Andie.

There was nothing she wouldn't do, to protect her.

CHAPTER FORTY

"Are you sure they're coming?"

Andie broke off from staring at the open doorway and swiveled on her chair toward Skye.

"Sure as I can be. I know Carol passed on the message, and Cary said she saw them at the restaurant for dinner."

They'd taken their own meal in the villa, picking at their smoked meat and vegetables. They were supposed to be strategizing about what they would say to Ben and Doug. Instead, they spent the time joking around and making out. Andie wanted to make the most of every moment they had left. Too afraid of what the answer might be, she hadn't tried to ask Skye what might happen between them.

"I wish they'd hurry up and get here, then," Skye said.

"Are you all right? You look more nervous than me."

"I want this meeting to go well."

"It might not," she replied. She reached under the table, putting a hand on Skye's knee.

"Don't say that."

"I'm just trying to prepare you. You're going to see a side of my dad that you're not going to like. You might see a side of me that you don't like, too."

"Hey. Don't say that. I like all of you."

Even now, when the stakes couldn't be higher, that made Andie's heart sing. "It's true. I'm just saying. He brings out a side of me I'm not super proud of. I can be rude. It's that thing when you feel like a kid again. I act like one."

"I get it. I'm right here with you, okay?"

Skye's voice was warm, her eyes brimming with compassion. Everything about her said that she genuinely wanted to support her. It gave Andie a glimmer of hope about what might happen for them. She didn't have time to worry about whether it was misplaced.

They broke apart at the sound of voices in the hall, her father appearing in the doorway a moment later, with Ben right behind him. Andie sat back in her chair, crossing a leg over her knee. Doug looked at Skye and frowned, then raised his eyes quizzically at Andie.

"Hello," said Andie.

"Good evening, ladies," Ben said as he sat. "Carol told us we were wanted for a meeting, but I didn't realize you would be here too, Skye. I'm sorry it took us a while to get here. I needed to take a shower after dinner. You know how it is after you've been traveling. Now, to what do we owe this honor?"

"There's something important we wanted to talk to you about," Andie said. Her vision slipped out of focus, bright lights appearing. The idea that she might faint crossed her mind, and she wiped her hands on her jeans.

"Yes?"

"When you approached me at dinner a while ago, saying that you'd heard rumors about Darryl and Skye, I wasn't honest with you," she said, tipping her chin up. She put as much focus as she could on Skye sitting next to her. She couldn't project any weakness.

Predictably, her father pulled his cigarette packet from his pocket and put it on the table. Andie slid her water glass across to him, offering it as an ashtray.

"Okay, honey. You should've told us the truth, but we'll worry about that later," said Ben. "We can work together to get this straightened out. I'm glad you're here, Skye. It was brave of you to come and talk to us about this. We understand that things might be difficult with you and Darryl. It's not easy to work with an ex. You're doing a real terrific job under trying circumstances."

"Thank you, Mr. Haynes, but that's not really—I mean, I think we should let Andie explain the purpose of the meeting."

They all looked at Andie at the same time. Skye's presence grounded her, but perhaps she shouldn't have invited her to this meeting. It was challenging to steel herself and act like she didn't care what her dad thought. If her own father didn't respect her, how could she ask Skye to? But then she looked into her eyes for the briefest moment before she began to speak, drawing courage.

"I've been going off-book. As you know, I've never been happy with the script changes. I worked with Skye and Darryl on getting footage I might be able to put into an alternative cut of the film."

It was met with a long silence. Dad puffed blankly on his cigarette, and Ben's mouth hung open. Skye rushed in.

"It was actually my idea. I suggested it to Andie." She put a hand over Andie's on the table, then quickly pulled it away.

"Ultimately, it was my call. We all know that," said Andie.

"How could you do that to us? You've made us look like chumps. After we gave you this opportunity. We've given you the chance of a lifetime," Ben said, finally.

"I apologize for not being honest with you. I was doing what I had to do to make a better film."

"But that's just not right. The script, as it was, was never going to work. Skye's character was too unlikeable, and the movie would've played far too dark. How could you not understand that?"

"Unlikeable to whom?" Andie said stubbornly. They might be about to fire her, but she couldn't just roll over. She looked to her father, waiting for him to weigh in, wanting to get it over with. "Are you going to say anything, or will you just let Ben do all the dirty work, like always?"

"Did you do this just to screw us?"

"Why would I do that?"

"You tell me."

"The only reason I did this was because you guys wouldn't listen."

"Andie, Andie," Ben said, holding up his hands. "I can't believe what I'm hearing. We listened to your input, but then we explained clearly why these changes needed to be made. You went off and reworked the script until it was excellent. How could you undermine your own work like that?"

"What I'd like to know is exactly how much time and money have you wasted on this rebellious little act?" Doug asked, all cool fury.

"Nothing was wasted. We're still coming in on time and on budget. This was done with a lot of thought and care."

"That's what makes this so fucked up."

"If you could just see what we've done, I think you might change your mind," Skye said. The hope in her voice was heartbreaking.

"I have no interest in that. Unless it's to assess the damage. You understand?"

They could speak to her however they wanted, but Andie couldn't let them bully Skye. It made her forget how scared she was. "Watch your tone when you're talking to her."

"You're unbelievable," said Doug.

"I have never seen anything like this in my whole career," Ben weighed in, putting his head in his hands. "Such blatant disrespect. I think of you like a daughter. This breaks my heart. It really does."

"Again, I apologize for not telling you the truth. When you wouldn't listen, I felt like I had no choice but to be underhanded."

Doug's eyes were flinty, and as prepared as she was, Andie felt herself cower inside.

"Underhanded is way too mild for what you've done. Skye, I'd like you to leave us alone now."

Skye looked at her, and when Andie shook her head, she shook hers too. "No. I'm not leaving. Like I said, this was my idea. I support Andie in this, one hundred percent."

"You two are screwing, aren't you?" he snorted.

Andie cut her eyes toward Skye to check she was okay, wanting to reach over and slap him. Skye's face was impassive. She decided it was best to ignore it. "You can say whatever you were going to say in front of her."

"Fine. I didn't want to hire you. Ben thought it was a good idea. He should've listened to me."

Ben looked down at the table. He was embarrassed for her, and she didn't want it.

"You thought I would be easier to control than this, didn't you?"

Her father stared at her, twisting the knife. "Yes. Foolishly, Ben thought that you'd be so desperate for this and so indebted to us that it'd be like I was directing it myself. But of course, I'd still get to do my mob movie, which will be an important film. Better than this genre trash could ever be. I let him talk me into it."

"It wasn't just that. I knew you'd make a good picture, Andie. I really did see so much promise in your earlier movies, and I could see that you were on the straight and narrow. I begged Doug to have you do it because I believe in you."

Andie leaned back in her chair. Her father wanted her to be deeply offended, and Ben was trying to soothe her ego and manipulate her. Still, she could see everything with pristine clarity. She sat across from two scared, old men, made so distant from the world by their success that they no longer knew how to take a risk.

"I don't care why I'm here. I do care what happens next. All I want to know is if you're going to take me off the picture."

They stared at one another, silently communicating in the way only two people with their creative marriage could.

"It would ruin all your plans, wouldn't it?" Andie continued. "If you had to get someone else in, you couldn't sell this as some family-made movie. The bad publicity would hang over your gangster thing. You also couldn't trade on my little redemption arc."

Doug's chest moved up and down quickly, and he lit another cigarette. "You can't expect us to have decided anything yet. We don't even know what we're dealing with. I still don't even know how you thought this would work. You thought you would have enough footage for a totally different cut?"

"Yes. By the time we've finished the shoot, we'd have enough to fill out the storyline you wanted. But, we also could have done something special with the other takes. Even now, we'd have enough for a different cut."

"It's true. Andie was always so cautious," Skye added.

Doug held up his hand to shut her up. "You're right that replacing you now would fuck everything up for us. We'd have to halt production to find someone else, and the publicity would be a nightmare. I'd step in and finish it myself, but I don't care about this movie anymore. All I want is for it not to lose money. You'll finish the movie, and you'll release the version that we ask for. It's not a negotiation."

"Can you do that for us, Andie? If you care about your reputation or your career at all, you'll forget about this silly stunt and do what you were hired to do. There are so many people depending on you to deliver this picture. Don't make your father and me look foolish and don't throw all you have away. I've seen the dailies, and I know you have something here."

"Are we all clear?" Doug asked.

Andie pressed her leg against Skye's. Skye pressed back. She wasn't getting fired. She was going to get to stay here and finish the job. She blinked quickly, not wanting to cry in front of them. "We're clear. The film will be finished as you want it to be."

"Do I have your word?"

"Yes. Absolutely."

Ben sighed heavily. "I need a drink. I never saw this one coming."

Andie swallowed hard. Skye had been so hopeful, and she wanted to honor that. She had to at least try, even if it was crazy.

"There is one more thing. I'd like you to see the scene where Dr. Foster kills Adrian. Just take a look. That's all I ask."

Ben's eyes were like saucers. "How on earth did you shoot that scene on the sly?"

"We did it alongside the love scene."

Dropping his half-smoked cigarette into his water glass and pushing back from the table, Doug shook his head. "We're not watching that. Not interested."

Andie watched him snap his fingers toward Ben so that he'd follow. She suddenly felt desperate for him to see the scene and know how good it was. It depressed her that he'd lost the edge that had made him famous, that he'd rather go and make his safe gangster film and push her to make this a by-the-numbers action film.

What had happened to him?

"C'mon, Dad. I'd really like you to see it. Remember when you bungled that scene in *Second Prize* on purpose so that you could cut it? Because you knew the first act would drag if you left it in? Everyone thought you were wrong, but you did it, anyway. This is just like that."

He turned and glowered down at her. "Stop trying to change my mind. This is not even in the same ballpark as that. No. And don't ever waste the crew's time like that again."

When Doug had walked away, Ben stayed in the room, whispering loudly, "Kid, just fly right from now on, okay? I know your dad better than anyone. It's costing him a lot of pride to give you another chance, I know it. Will you promise me we're not going to have to sit in a meeting like this again?"

"I promise."

She held still until he was out of sight, then her shoulders dropped. "Jesus Christ."

Skye put an arm around her, their temples pressed together. "That was incredibly tense."

"Yeah. I'm sorry you had to hear all that."

"Your dad was so cold. Are you okay?"

"He's always like that. I was expecting much worse. But hey, it's going to be all right. I get to stay."

They stood up, putting their arms around one another. Andie held Skye tight, her eyes drifting shut. She wanted to fall into her and stay like this forever.

"I'm sorry," Skye said, kissing her cheek. It surprised Andie because the door was still wide open.

"What for?"

"That you had to deal with that, partly because of me."

"It was worth it. Sorry about what Dad said about us. It was crass. If it's any consolation, he probably doesn't really think that. He was just trying to embarrass us both. Me especially."

It was as though Skye was inside her head. She whispered softly to her. "If you're wondering, it's not going to scare me off. I want to get you back to the villa right now, so we can do it again."

"That sounds good to me," Andie said, trying to sound light when she was so awash with desire that it made her feel weak. Skye's body was deliciously close, hips melding into her own.

"I've been thinking about it all day. Have you?"

"What do you think?"

She pulled back enough that Skye could see her eyes, and they smiled at one another.

"What are we waiting for?"

"I have to go and talk to Louise. She was ready with the footage, and she will have had one of her assistants prepare the screening room."

Skye slipped her hands into Andie's back pockets. It felt so intimate—something a girlfriend would do. "I suppose I can wait a little longer, then."

"It makes it feel so anticlimactic. I was looking forward to seeing it."

"Let's watch it, then. It won't take long," Skye said, withdrawing her hands and stepping back.

"Yeah?"

"Yeah. C'mon," she said, taking Andie's hand.

They walked closely as they went down the hall to the room where they'd sometimes watched dailies together. A few rows of chairs were lined up neatly, Louise sitting in one of them, holding a glass of wine.

"Hey, Louise."

"Where are the guys?" she asked, looking past them toward the door.

Andie shook her head.

"Oh, shit. What happened?"

"It's okay. I'm not fired or anything. Thanks for all your work, but they don't want to see it."

Louise's nostrils flared, but she didn't say anything.

"We'd still like to see it, though. Would you mind if we just watched it, the two of us?"

"Of course. For what it's worth, I think it's dynamite," she said, heading toward the back of the room to cue up the projector. As she left, she closed the door behind her.

The light flickered over their faces as it began. Skye nestled into Andie's shoulder, and they locked hands.

It was achingly good. Of course, Andie knew every second of how it played out, but watching it like this was so different. The camera caught every nuance of Skye's breathtaking performance.

At the conclusion, she wiped a tear from her cheek. She clapped, the sound echoing in the empty room. Skye laughed joyously, grabbing her hand and squeezing it.

"That was incredible. Now, let's go home."

CHAPTER FORTY-ONE

They walked through the village, passing by the flames of tiki torches. Now that Andie was sure she would stay, the whole place felt even more magical than before. Even the air tasted crisper on her tongue.

Skye closed the sliding door after them then pulled down the shade.

Andie sat on the sofa and pulled off her shoes, then rested her elbows on her knees and her head in her hands. Skye's warm hand on her shoulder made her feel safe enough to let go. She cried tears of exhaustion and relief.

"Silly question, but are you okay?"

"Yeah," Andie said, wiping away a tear. "Sorry. I don't know what's wrong with me. I'm happy, just a little overwhelmed."

Skye bent to kiss the skin under Andie's eyes and sat down next to her on the sofa. She held her until some of the emotion was wrung out, their heads close together. Skye smoothed a hand over her hair.

"I really thought I was a goner."

"I know. I was so worried. I don't think I've ever been as nervous as I was during that meeting."

"Me too. Thanks for all your help. I literally couldn't have done it without you."

"I wasn't going to leave you to deal with it yourself. I kept telling you that."

"Thank you."

"I was proud of you, you know. You really kept your cool. You said that you were worried you would lose your temper or something, but it wasn't like that at all. Not that I'd have blamed you if you had."

"You don't think it was weak? The way I rolled over and agreed to what they wanted?"

"How can you say that? You handled them perfectly, and now you're staying. That's all that matters. I'm just sorry about the way they spoke to you. I'm sure your father didn't mean a lot of what he said."

"He meant it. But at least you were there to stand up for me."

"Then I'm sorry that they can't see in you what everyone else can see. They'd get such a better movie if they would only allow you to do what you know is right. You're so talented. You're amazing," she said, eyes on Andie's lips.

Skye looked like she wanted to be kissed, and Andie felt the same, a hunger so deep it couldn't be denied for another second. She framed that gorgeous face with her hands and pressed their lips together. Skye kissed back greedily, grabbing Andie by the wrists.

It felt like coming home. Even throughout this crazy day, Andie had thought about doing this a thousand times. Skye's lips were so sweet and soft against hers, and when their tongues joined, they both moaned. She lightly ran her fingers over Skye's breasts, and they lay down together on the sofa.

When Andie was on top of her, Skye pulled her down. She grabbed Andie's thighs and pulled them around her as though they couldn't get close enough. They kissed roughly, moving against one another. She loved knowing where this was leading, when she could only hope last night.

"I've been thinking about you all day. Last night..." Skye said.

Andie nodded eagerly. She'd never needed another person like this, and it should scare her, but all she could do was succumb. She couldn't help herself, even when she knew how dangerous it was to keep drawing nearer to someone who didn't feel the same way.

In the back of her mind, awareness grew that she was using their sexual connection to keep Skye close. But Skye was an adult, and she acted like she wanted this just as much.

She propped herself up on an arm to touch her face, fingers on those amazing lips. "What would you like me to do?" asked Andie.

"Whatever you want," Skye said, lips curving under her touch.

"Don't be shy, please, tell me. Whatever you want. I want to make you feel good."

"I don't know," she said, looking away from her with her hands still on Andie's shoulders.

Brushing hair away from Skye's face, she apologized. "I don't mean to embarrass you. It's only that I don't want to do anything you don't like."

"I like everything you do."

Andie smiled, but she was surprised. Skye had seemed so comfortable the night before that she hadn't expected this shyness. "I take it you don't like talking about this stuff? I'm sorry, I didn't know. If that's what it is, I'll stop."

Skye bit her lip, looking past her shoulder. "It's not that. I'd like to talk to you. I just don't know what to say."

"Oh. Well, that's okay. Just promise that you'll tell me if you don't like something?"

"Of course. It's...there are things I haven't tried yet. You're the first woman I've been with. But I want to do everything with you."

"Oh," Andie said, still stroking Skye's hair, trying to hide her surprise. Skye had always gone after her in a way that suggested more experience. She never would have guessed.

"Sorry I didn't tell you."

"That's okay. You never had to tell me anything if you didn't want to. We'll work it out together, then," she said, gathering her in to hold her.

"That sounds good to me. I'd love that."

They held one another close. It was quiet, and Andie hated to think that she'd made Skye feel awkward. It would be strange to dive right back into kissing her with the mood broken.

As the seconds ticked by, she realized something didn't feel right about all this. Why hadn't Skye told her this, anyway? If not last night, there were other times they could've talked about it. Before she knew it, doubt had put its hooks into her. She couldn't let it go. She was too afraid of what it could mean.

"Hey. I'm serious when I say you didn't have to tell me, but I can't help wondering why not. I bet Teri knew, didn't she? That you hadn't gone there yet." She didn't know why she brought Teri up. She was grasping to understand, and she was so jealous that Teri knew Skye better when she was starting to wonder if she knew her at all. She felt Skye stiffen in her arms, then get up. They sat next to one another, Skye looking down at her hands.

"Yes. Teri was aware. She's my friend. Do you have a problem with that?"

It was such a sensitive subject. Andie knew that, even if she was hurt. She didn't want to fuck this up. She tried to choose her words carefully. "Of course, it's not a problem. I guess what upsets me is that I told you how I was feeling last night. That I hadn't been with anyone for a while. You know so much about my past. More than I wish you knew, sometimes."

"I don't know that much. I haven't asked you many questions about it all because I don't care about that."

How could she say she didn't care? It was the reason Skye didn't trust her. Maybe she didn't care, period. Andie's chest ached. "You knew how nervous I was. You must have been nervous too, and we could've shared that."

"Actually, I wasn't nervous. Not really. I was just excited."

It made Andie feel worse. Maybe Skye wasn't nervous because her emotions weren't involved. Andie pushed her hair back, her face hot. "I didn't mean to assume. Either way, it's a little strange you couldn't talk to me about that."

"I wasn't a virgin. I just hadn't slept with a woman before," Skye said, frowning.

"I understand that. It's not, like, this is not some old-fashioned thing where I'm worried about your virginity or whatever. I just wish you'd felt comfortable enough to tell me."

"Why? Would you have stopped it if you'd known?"

Andie almost laughed. The only reason she'd have stopped would have been if Skye hadn't wanted it. Nothing else could have mattered. "No, of course not."

"So then, what difference does it make?" Skye asked, throwing up her hands.

Was she going crazy? Skye was acting like she was wrong to be upset, but it was obvious to her that it was worth mentioning. It wasn't fair that Andie's history was exposed, but Skye had guarded her own. It was yet another example of how Skye didn't trust her and didn't want to let her in. After everything they'd shared last night, she thought they were getting somewhere.

"I just think we should've talked about it. That's all."

"It was my business," Skye said, pointing to her chest.

"Of course, it's your business. I understand how private it might be for you. I thought we were getting close, though. I want you to be able to tell me things."

"Do you think it's been easy for me to have to hide who I am? Teri is literally the only person who knows."

"She can't be the only one. You told me you'd dated Dana Rivers," Andie shot back.

"I wasn't thinking about her because that was nothing. We met one time, and Teri set that up, anyway. Why are you making me feel bad about this?"

"I don't mean to make you feel bad. I'm only trying to understand."

Skye's face was stony, shuttered to Andie. It reminded her of how it'd been when they first met, and she'd known Skye didn't like her. Did she even like her now? The thought exploded in her mind like a bomb.

"You still don't trust me. I thought all this meant something, but I was wrong. You don't even like me. Not as anything more than a friend, anyway."

Skye's eyes flicked toward her. "That's not true."

"You've told me you don't trust me. You've said it, plain as day. And this just proves that there's nothing I can do about it."

Skye's eyes softened for the first time since they'd started talking. "Things change, Andie. I know you better now than I did when I said that."

Andie wanted to believe it, but her heart hurt. Jesus, all of this hurt. "I hope you enjoyed it, then," she said, getting up and walking away toward the kitchen.

"What does that mean?"

"That all you wanted out of me was a fuck, and now you've had it."

Skye stared back like she didn't recognize her. "That's not right."

Andie scrubbed a hand over her face, willing herself not to cry. This was the part of her she hadn't wanted Skye to see, the one she'd managed to cover up when they met with her dad. "I'm sorry. I'm not even angry with you. I'm angry with myself."

"Why?"

"Because you told me you didn't want this to go anywhere right from the start, and I kept hoping things would change. I kept thinking that you'd see if we spent enough time together. I shouldn't have done that. I should've kept my distance, but I just wanted to be close to you. I was stupid."

Skye got up, walking quickly over to her. She didn't look angry anymore, but Andie was so close to crying again that she barely registered it. She didn't want to fall apart in front of Skye. She should get upstairs before she made more of a fool of herself.

"Andie. Can't you see that things are different now? They have changed. Of course, they've changed," she said, standing right before her.

"They have?"

Skye took Andie's hands, cradling them in her own. "Yes. I've wanted to tell you today. I'm sorry that it took me so long. And I'm sorry that I made you feel like I only wanted that."

Andie was still trying to catch up when Skye leaned in, kissing her softly on the lips. "I trust you. I do like you, so much."

"How long have you been feeling that way?" Andie said breathlessly.

"It's hard to explain. But it started to click when all that stuff happened with Carol. I knew right away that nothing would have happened between you. It made me understand how much I believed you. How much I believe in you."

They kissed again and pressed their foreheads together.

"I don't want to pressure you, but what does this mean? You're open to dating?"

"Absolutely. I really, really want to be with you."

Andie picked her up and spun her around, Skye laughing as she was lifted off her feet, arms around Andie's neck. When she put her down, Andie held her tight, her pain receding like the tide. Finding out that she would get to finish the movie, and now this? It could be the best day of her life.

Skye's arms were still around Andie's neck, and she looked up at her. "I kept saying I didn't trust you, but the problem was that I didn't trust myself. Looking back, I think a part of me always knew it'd be okay. I just didn't know whether to believe it."

"You can believe it. I promise. I know myself. I know I'm not going to hurt you."

"I know that. I see who you are. What do our pasts matter? I haven't been with any women, but I don't think it'd make a difference if you were the first or the hundredth. I know what I feel."

They moved toward the sofa, Andie guiding her toward it and making her intentions clear. Skye lay with Andie on top of her.

"I take it this means we're on now, right? You're not going to suddenly decide you want to wait until we get back to LA for anything?"

"Doesn't seem that way, does it?" Andie said, kissing her neck.

"Thank God."

CHAPTER FORTY-TWO

As soon as they got home from work the next day, they fell on one another in the living room. They kissed hungrily, starved after a whole day of not being able to touch.

"Where's Cary? She didn't work today. You sure she's not upstairs?" Skye said, Andie pushing her into the back of the door.

"I bumped into her when we were packing up on the beach. She was going to Sid's before dinner."

"I'm so glad she hardly comes home anymore," Skye laughed, running her hands up and down Andie's arms. She loved how strong and soft she felt, and she couldn't wait to undress her. She'd been staring at her body all day while they worked, unable to believe that things were falling into place between them.

They were a couple, now, or at least on their way. She was desperate to tell somebody—to let them know that this amazing woman wanted to be with her. It wasn't the right time, but it would be soon.

"Me too."

Andie grabbed Skye's leg, digging her fingers into her thigh. There were so many things she wanted to do with her. Having sex against the door was tempting, mainly because it meant it would be right now. Still, it was too risky, something to be saved for another time.

"Let's go upstairs," Skye said, after moaning into Andie's mouth. Andie had reached under her top, fingers splayed over her breasts.

She turned, leading Skye up the stairs. "Your place or mine?"

"Mine. Come with me."

"Yes, ma'am."

They took one another's bras and shirts off in Skye's room, tossing them on the ground. She pushed Andie onto the bed and crawled up until she was straddling her, then laid a bruising kiss on her mouth.

"I love it when you take charge."

Skye held Andie's wrists over her head against the mattress. "Why, you tired of being the boss?"

"Never. You're just very good at it."

"There's something I've wanted to do all day," Skye said, biting her lip. She moved back and unbuttoned Andie's jeans, the zip loud in the quiet room. Andie lifted her hips so that Skye could pull her jeans and underwear down. When she kissed Andie's lips again, sliding a hand between their bodies and then between her legs, Andie gasped.

Slowly, she kissed her way down her neck and kept going. She lightly grasped her breasts and used her tongue on Andie's nipples.

It was like a dream, pressing her lips to the taut stomach she'd stared at every chance she got. Andie's hand was on the back of her head.

"Oh, that's what you meant," Andie said as Skye kissed further down her belly, voice raspy.

She looked up at her, and their eyes locked. "Yeah. Is that okay?" asked Skye.

"Of course. I'd love that."

Skye kept going. Andie's legs fell apart, her head falling back on the pillow. She tasted like nothing else, and Skye loved it. There wasn't any need to worry about whether she was good at it. Andie made her pleasure known, and it was beautiful.

It didn't take long for Andie to come. Leaning against her stomach, Skye smiled at how Andie was breathing so hard. "Wow. That was…"

She broke off because someone was banging on the door downstairs. Skye raised her head.

"Who the hell would that be? Maybe Cary forgot her key?"

Andie got up, grabbing her jeans. "I bet it's someone needing me for work. Jesus, lucky we didn't stay downstairs."

Andie ran down while Skye smoothed down her hair. As she walked along the hall toward the bathroom, she heard a male voice and Andie's agitated response.

"What's going on?" said Skye.

Andie stood by the door with her father and Ben. Her heart dropped to her feet when it occurred to her that they might have changed their minds.

"It's okay. They're just being dramatic. They want us to go with them while they burn the footage of the death scene."

"Hey, Skye. We hate to ask, but we think it's best to get rid of it. We'll take it down to the beach where they usually have the bonfires. Everyone's at the restaurant, so nobody will know what we're doing," Ben said.

What the hell? Skye shook her head. Burning the evidence was so dramatic. Her heart went out to Andie for having to deal with a father who could even think about doing such a thing.

She made eye contact with Andie and felt reassured. It was awful, but things were so different now that they really had one another.

They could get through anything together.

CHAPTER FORTY-THREE

The flames licked at the reel, sending up plumes of smoke. The film caught fire and burned quickly, destroying footage of the scene that meant so much to them.

Andie and Skye stood on one side of the bonfire while Ben and Doug were on the other. Skye didn't want to give them the satisfaction of reacting, so she kept her expression blank. Andie did the same, but her defiance was evident.

At this moment, all that mattered was supporting Andie. Skye didn't care what either of the men thought, so she put her arm around her. Andie answered with an arm around her waist. They held one another up.

After a few silent minutes, all of them staring at the fire, Andie called across to the men. "You've made your point. Are we all done here? I'd like to go and have dinner if you don't mind."

"Do whatever you want," Doug replied.

They set off toward the restaurant. Skye was still astonished by the needless cruelty of Doug making his own daughter watch as her hard work burned. "That was weird. Is that kind of thing normal for him?" Skye asked.

"Pretty much, I'm afraid to say."

"Are you all right?"

"I will be," she said, quickly putting an arm around Skye's shoulder. "Thank you for being here. It helps."

"Of course."

They moved apart before they went into the restaurant, heading toward a buffet of roast chicken, green beans, and mashed potatoes. They sat, Andie staring at the door when Doug and Ben came in.

"They'd better not try and sit with us. Acting like nothing happened is just the kind of thing he'd do, but I may stab him with my fork."

"I'd cover for you. In fact, I'll stab them myself."

"You're very cute when you're angry."

"Hey, ladies," Louise said, holding a plate with her half-eaten meal. "Saw you come in. Would you mind if I joined you?"

"Of course, sit down," Andie said, waiting until she was seated to lean forward. "I planned to find you later, after dinner. I know the producers came to see you about that footage. I'm sorry I didn't get the chance to warn you."

"That's okay, sweetheart," she said, patting her hand.

"I'm sure they were assholes about it. I hate that you got ambushed like that."

"You're sweet, but I'm far too old to be bothered about it. I do my work and ignore all the politics, and that's how I've lasted so long."

"Still, I'm really sorry that you were put in a difficult position because of me."

"Because of us," Skye added.

"Don't worry about it, seriously. I know how to deal with the money men. You take their notes and tell them what they want to hear, but you don't pay too much attention. They hired me, but you're the director."

"Thanks, Louise. It's just a shame they had to throw their weight around like that."

"They did come in swinging their dicks. What are they doing with that footage, anyway? They didn't tell me."

"Don't worry about it. It's gone, though."

Andie was being stoic, but Skye caught the slight downturn of her mouth. This was harder on her than she was letting on.

"You ever hear about the MGM fire in '65?" said Louise. "I don't know if you know this, but my great-uncle was an editor. Part of the inspiration for me going into this line. He cut a whole bunch of silent pictures. A lot of the only prints went up in flames in that fire. He talked about it, often."

"I hadn't heard about that one, no."

"Film is sacred. I always heard those stories from my uncle, so I'd never rely on just having one version of anything, even if I'm not sure it'll make it into the final cut. And if something is special, I make extra sure," she said, grinning as she bit into a juicy chicken leg.

"What are you saying?" Skye asked, because Andie looked too overcome to do so herself.

"Take it easy, girls. They're probably watching us talk. I switched out the labels before they got there, so they would think they had the masters. I know a top-secret operation when I see one, and I knew how to play it. Even the boys at the lab wouldn't have known what they were copying."

Skye started to smile but pulled back because Louise was right. She could feel the producers watching them from where they sat across the room.

"You're a genius, Louise."

"You really are. Where are you keeping the footage now?"

"In my hotel room, in the safe. That's for now, but it's mislabeled, and I'm the only person who knows what's what. I'll be mixing them in with the rest before they get transported back to the studio. At which time, I'll take them home, along with anything else you want to save. Sound good?"

Andie wiped a hand over her mouth, trying to keep a smile at bay. "Any time you want a job with me in the future, it's yours. I only want to work with you from now on."

"I'd be delighted. Now, I'm going to hang out by the pool. Have a lovely night."

Skye and Andie stared at each other across the table, lost for words. It meant everything that their work was being preserved. She hoped Andie understood how much respect, love, and admiration she'd earned from her team. They were willing to do anything for her because she'd led them so well.

"Shall we get back to the villa? I know just how I'd like to celebrate," Andie said.

Heat crept over Skye's skin as Andie looked at her, tongue stuck in the corner of her mouth.

"That makes two of us. Let's go."

CHAPTER FORTY-FOUR

A festive atmosphere had fallen over the village as they celebrated and mourned the end of the location shoot. Most of the cast and crew would reunite in LA to film on the soundstage, but they were saying goodbye to the few Fijian locals from the mainland, who'd maintained the village.

Darryl, Sid, and their friends had delivered on their promise to throw the party to end all parties. There wasn't a soul on the island who'd stayed home this afternoon.

Skye pulled herself away from Andie's side, knowing that many people wanted to talk to their director today. She sat with Darryl, Cary, and Sid, dangling their feet in the pool.

The cold water was heavenly on her legs, contrasting with the hot cement of the pool surrounds. Frankie, the camera guy, had jumped in fully dressed and floated on his back in front of them, his big belly pointed to the sky.

"Can I get you a drink while you're lying there, old man?" Sid asked.

Frankie lifted his head from the water. "You're older than me, buddy."

"But I'm young at heart. So, how about that drink?"

"Forget him. I'll take one," Cary said.

Cary leaned against Skye, pressing their shoulders together. Even if Cary didn't know it yet, she was so important to her. She wanted them to be friends, and she liked that they were on their way.

"This has been such an amazing shoot, hasn't it? I've had a ball," said Cary.

"It's been wonderful. I've loved working with you."

"Same. If I have my way, we'll be working together again. I hope I get to work with Andie again, too. Hey, she's been telling me about some mysterious project she's hoping you two will get off the ground. I've told her this already, but you can always keep me in mind."

Skye beamed. They hadn't discussed *Shelley* again over the last few weeks, so it was thrilling to hear that Andie might have changed her mind about directing it.

"It'd be so great to work with you again."

"Yeah. She keeps going on about how amazing the script is and how talented the writer is, but she dodges when I ask for details. I don't suppose you'd want to give me a few hints?"

"All in good time. You'll find out."

"All right, all right."

They watched as Darryl and Sid pushed off the edge into the water, carrying out a plan they'd made for dunking Frankie.

"I never would've imagined those two being friends, but sometimes I think I should step aside. They're having the true love affair," Cary said.

"Yep. How's that going, if you don't mind me asking? Do you think you'll keep seeing one another back in LA?"

"You know, I think we will. Plus, he said he wants me to meet his daughter, which surprised me."

"Hmm. I thought you said you weren't the serious relationship kind?"

"Still not, but we have fun together. I'll be happy to spend some more time with him and see where things go."

"Fair enough."

"What about you?"

"What about me?"

"You never answered me about being the serious relationship kind. That's how I had you pegged. Are you?"

Cary's eyes held a challenge. Skye had her own protective older siblings, so she understood. "I am."

"Good."

"I mean, not that I've got anything on the horizon," Skye said, knowing how serious Andie was about keeping things private until the shoot was over. If Cary had her suspicions, she couldn't do much about it, but she still had to be careful.

"Oh, please. I live beneath you. I might not have been staying at the villa all that much, but I've still heard your footsteps when you creep back and forth across the hall to one another's rooms."

"Shush," she said, eyeing the distance to the people in the pool.

"I know, I know. Don't worry, they can't hear."

"If you tell her I confirmed it, I'll have to kill you."

"Oh, like she'd even be mad at you. She thinks you hung the moon. I've never seen her this smitten."

"I don't know how much she's told you. I did take a little while to make up my mind, but you've got nothing to worry about, okay? I'll do right by her."

"I know. You're a good one. I can see that. You were probably smart to be cautious, but I know my sister. She's got her act together. So you don't have anything to worry about, either."

"I'm not worried. Not anymore," Skye said, spying Andie across the pool. She was laughing at something Louise had said to her. They locked eyes, holding for a long moment.

Cary sighed. "See? That look just about boiled the pool. You two are going to be great. I can't wait to host you for dinners and stuff."

"That sounds pretty good to me."

Cary nodded and jumped off, swimming over to the guys while Skye grinned. She looked around, and her eye fell on Teri, in a group with Carol and a bunch of the women from the makeup department.

It was hard to believe that their time together was ending, but it felt like the right thing. Teri had worked diligently over the last weeks, wrapping things up and making a list of potential replacements to meet when they got home.

"Hey, you."

"Hey. I'm going to miss this place," Teri said, gesturing around. They stepped away from the group to talk.

"I know what you mean. It's going to be hard to leave tomorrow. And I'll miss you too, you know."

They shared a quick hug.

"Thanks for being so cool about everything."

Skye shrugged. She'd never seen the point of holding a grudge, so she'd been polite and friendly toward Teri the last few weeks. "I know it sounds trite, but I really wish you all the best."

"Thanks. Same here."

Skye narrowed her eyes when she realized how closely Carol was watching them. It looked a little possessive.

"Have you started something up with her?"

"Her room's right across the hall from mine. We kept running into one another."

Skye chuckled. It was all so incestuous. "Okay, well, I hope you've been having a good time together."

"Thanks."

She patted Teri's arm and walked away, still shaking her head. She couldn't wait to tell Andie about this. When she found her in the crowd, she leaned against one of the palm trees on the party's edge.

"I was hoping you'd pick up on my signal and come over," said Andie.

"Of course. This has been fun, but all I want is to be alone with you."

"The feeling is mutual. I think I should put in one more hour of mingling, though."

"I'll come up half an hour later than that?"

"It's a date," Andie said, giving her one more smoldering look before walking back to the crowd.

There was nothing like the anticipation of walking up the stairs, knowing that Andie was waiting for her. Skye shed her clothes as she came into Andie's room.

"Sorry I'm a few minutes late. I got stuck talking to someone."

"That's okay. You're worth the wait," Andie said as she sat up, gaze trailing hotly over Skye's breasts.

Skye pulled back the sheet and got underneath, her naked skin meeting Andie's. "I'm glad you saved me the trouble of undressing you."

"Whatever I can do to help," Andie said, their lips joining, kissing hard. "Even if I do especially love that shirt you were wearing." Andie stroked Skye's breast and kissed the sensitive spot on her neck.

"I know. That's why I wore it."

"What can I say? I like how fitted it is."

Skye's legs fell open as Andie moved down her stomach, saying her name loudly when her sure hand slipped through wet heat.

"Wow. You like it a lot."

Skye gripped Andie's thigh then put her fingers between her legs. "You're the same."

They'd slow down later—they knew they'd do this again before the night was through. For now, they needed the speed of it, Andie kissing Skye fiercely and then biting her earlobe. She licked her neck, their breasts brushing together, the bedhead thumping against the wall as their movements intensified.

It burned so hotly between them, and it was always this good. Skye loved having her fingers inside Andie and loved the look Andie was giving her right now.

"That's so good, so good…"

They kept losing focus but were unwilling to stop, stroking until Skye came, Andie following moments later.

They lay on their sides, Andie spooning her from behind, kissing her shoulder.

"I can't believe we're leaving tomorrow."

"I know. And then only another couple of weeks of shooting. I'll be sad when it finishes, but it'll be nice not to have to sneak around anymore."

"You don't have to tell people if you're not ready yet. I'd understand. I'll wait as long as you need, " said Andie.

"You keep saying that, but you don't have to worry. It's not like I'm going to go running to *Entertainment Tonight* about it, but I want people in my life to know. I'm proud to be with you."

The kiss on her shoulder was so tender she closed her eyes. "I'm proud to be with you, too."

Andie's hand was drifting down again. Skye arched back into her, craving her so much it almost blotted everything else out. A moment later, she remembered that she'd wanted to ask her something.

"Wait," Skye said, gently pushing her hand away and rolling onto her back. They faced one another.

"What's up?"

"I was talking to Cary before, and it sounded like she was talking about *Shelley*. We're a little overdue for that conversation, don't you think?"

"Cary and her big mouth. I was just thinking out loud."

"Well, let's talk out loud about it."

"Funny. I just thought it might be a little premature. We're just figuring this all out."

"I know, but she made it sound like you were excited about it. Does this mean that you might be interested in directing it, even with us together?"

Andie pushed her hair back from her face, stalling, and Skye willed her to answer honestly. She wanted this. She couldn't think of anything better, in fact.

"I'm interested. I don't know if it's a good idea. This is all still so new between us. We don't know what's going to happen."

"Are you scared that we'll break up or something while we're working together?"

"Yeah. Or a million other different things. I think we should wait to make a decision like that, but I also really think you should try to get it made. I don't know. What do you think?"

"I think that it'll work. I love the idea of working with you again, but I couldn't give up any part of this to make it happen. Don't you trust that everything will be okay with us?"

Skye knew the irony of her being the one to ask for trust after the doubts she'd had about trusting Andie. Still, she just knew. Nothing could be more certain for her, that they would stay together. Working on another project would only bring them closer.

"I want to..."

Skye held Andie's face in her hands, looking deeply into her eyes. "If you want this, then trust."

"I want to, but how can you know?"

"I know. I know that I love you."

"I love you, too."

Andie's expression made Skye swell with still more love. It was vulnerable and happy and so, so beautiful. "Let's make another movie."

EPILOGUE

Film File Magazine Review
Creature Island: The Director's Cut

When *Creature Island* was released five years ago, I gave it a two-star rating. It was widely seen as a disappointment, but the film's lukewarm reviews didn't hurt the box office. For critics and book fans alike, *Creature* was a baffling smash hit.

The two-star rating nagged at me because I wished I could have awarded it more. Given its dazzling set pieces, stunning cinematography, and compelling performance from lead Skye Buckley, it was still worth watching. I saw *Creature* as one of those frustrating near misses. The kernel of a good movie was hidden under a schmaltzy romance and silly dialogue. The movie erased key plot points from Cynthia Quinn's brilliant cult novel, much to the disgust of its fans.

It turned out that I was right about the better movie underneath all that. Following *Shelley*'s commercial and critical success, Andie McKenzie has been given the rare opportunity to rerelease her film. The new version not only restores missing scenes, it's cut so that viewers will feel like they're watching a completely different film. McKenzie's recent *Creature* is darker, funnier, and superior to the theatrical cut in every way. If it had been released in its original form, it might not have made over a hundred million dollars. Instead, it might have been considered an instant classic.

Andie McKenzie has a reputation for a patchy resume, but this version more than lives up to the promise of her early work. When this version is evaluated alongside the highly acclaimed *Shelley*, any lingering doubts about her talent can be dismissed. This recut of *Creature* sees her stepping out from under her father's shadow forever. Under her skillful direction, the tone and look come together beautifully. It has the beating, bleeding heart missing from the original.

Darryl Edwards's performance has been reshaped into an interesting character turn. Still, there's no doubt that the movie belongs to Skye Buckley. It seems unjust that this DVD version of the film won't be eligible for awards. Suppose voters had seen this performance five years ago. In that case, Buckley might not have had to wait until *Shelley*'s release to secure her first Best Actress Academy Award nomination.

In interviews, McKenzie has been coy about why the 1994 release of *Creature Island* diverged so much from its source material. There were whispers of studio interference. If the rumors were true, at least the studio has come to its senses now.

A word of caution: the less you read about the Director's Cut before you see it, the better. I'll say that the book's fans will be delighted. So will lovers of smart, moving cinema. *Creature Island: The Director's Cut* redefines what genre movies can do.

Five stars.

Bella Books, Inc.
Women. Books. Even Better Together.
P.O. Box 10543
Tallahassee, FL 32302
Phone: (800) 729-4992
www.BellaBooks.com

More Titles from Bella Books

Mabel and Everything After – Hannah Safren
978-1-64247-390-2 | 274 pgs | paperback: $17.95 | eBook: $9.99
A law student and a wannabe brewery owner find that the path to a fairy tale happily-ever-after is often the long and scenic route.

To Be With You – TJ O'Shea
978-1-64247-419-0 | 348 pgs | paperback: $19.95 | eBook: $9.99
Sometimes the choice is between loving safely or loving bravely.

I Dare You to Love Me – Lori G. Matthews
978-1-64247-389-6 | 292 pgs | paperback: $18.95 | eBook: $9.99
An enemy-to-lovers romance about daring to follow your heart, even when it's the hardest thing to do.

The Lady Adventurers Club - Karen Frost
978-1-64247-414-5 | 300 pgs | paperback: $18.95 | eBook: $9.99
Four women. One undiscovered Egyptian tomb. One (maybe) angry Egyptian goddess. What could possibly go wrong?

Golden Hour - Kat Jackson
978-1-64247-397-1 | 250 pgs | paperback: $17.95 | eBook: $9.99
Life would be so much easier if Lina were afraid of something basic—like spiders—instead of something significant. Something like real, true, healthy love.

Schuss – E. J. Noyes
978-1-64247-430-5 | 276 pgs | paperback: $17.95 | eBook: $9.99
They're best friends who both want something more, but what if admitting it ruins the best friendship either of them have had?

CPSIA information can be obtained
at www.ICGtesting.com
Printed in the USA
JSHW010213290323
39626JS00002B/3

9 781642 474336